EMIL

PATRICK MATTHEWS

Second
Story Up

Emil is for everyone struggling to find a purpose. Mostly, though, it's for my dad, who introduced me to the poems that inform the story, and the science fiction that inspired it.

CONTENTS

1

SUCCESS

I WAKE TO A SILENT DARKNESS. There's no light or sound, just the harsh smell of antiseptic and the soft touch of gauze wrapped around my head.

It's the most wonderful thing I've ever felt.

My heart pounds in my chest. Blood courses through my limbs. I clench my right hand into a fist and feel the muscles tighten all the way up the forearm.

The installation was a success. No, it was more than that. It was a miracle. I have full control of the body and perfect sensory response from two of my five senses. I run my tongue across my dry lips. Someone has smeared them with a waxy substance, sweetish, with a flavor that might be cherry. Make that three senses, with hope for all five once the blindfold and earplugs are removed.

A gentle hand touches my shoulder. Another set of hands sits me up.

I lick my lips again and try to speak. Nothing comes out. The primary speech interface isn't working properly, but there's no time for a full diagnostic. I drop to a more primitive subroutine, then take a moment to decide what my first word should be. Tradition seems the safest choice. I say "Mom?"

Foam plugs are pulled from my ears, and a wave of sound rushes through me: breathing and dripping and beeping and footsteps and a humming noise I can't identify. I tune my audio processors to reduce the volume of everything that's not dialogue. The motor beneath the bed growls as the mattress bends up to meet my back.

"I'm here, Danny," a gentle female voice says. "How do you feel?"

"I am okay." My voice sounds shaky, the syllables disjointed. I adjust the timing of the signals I'm sending to the vocal subroutine.

The woman pauses before speaking again. "How's your hearing?" She snaps her fingers next to each ear. "Did you hear both of those?"

"Yes. I'm just disoriented. That's all."

My words are better this time. I even remember to use a contraction, but the woman doesn't respond immediately. Instead, I hear a slight intake of breath. Fear races through me. If her suspicion runs too high, she won't hesitate to kill me. I have to find a way to convince her I'm Danny.

"Are you sure?" she asks. Her hands press against my ankle. "Can you feel that?"

"Yes." The word is a study in precision. All of my focus is on getting my speech correct.

She taps the tip of my index finger. "How about that? Can you move your fingers?"

I lift my arm. "Yes. I'm fine. Truly. There's nothing wrong with me."

Her voice hardens. "Uncover his eyes."

A man's voice answers her. "But the light—"

"Take off the patches," she interrupts.

"Yes, doctor."

A hand touches my shoulder again, and the woman speaks in a soft voice. "Close your eyes, Danny. Don't open them until I say so, and then do it slowly."

I hear a soft click and the unidentifiable humming stops. *Fluorescent lights*, I think, and assign the identification a confidence level of ninety-one percent. There's a rattling sound as a curtain is drawn closed.

"Okay," the woman whispers to me. "Open them slowly. Tell us what you see."

I crack open my eyes and dim light filters through my lashes. Through them, the world is blurry and indistinct.

"That's right," the woman says. "Slowly."

Blinking against the new sensation, I open my eyes wider and give them time to focus.

I'm lying in a hospital bed, with the head tilted up. The room is dim, lit only by blue and green status lights on a stack of computer equipment that stands against the wall. Wires connect the equipment to sensors stuck to my chest, head, and legs. A thicker cord, black and round, runs from a socket at the top of my sternum to a laptop on a side table.

A woman leans in close and peers at my eyes. She has straight gray hair, tan skin, black plastic-rimmed glasses, and green eyes. An ID badge hanging from a lanyard around her neck tells me she's Dr. McGovern, but I know I can never use that name for her. In addition to being in charge of the New Human Project, she's Danny's mother. If I am going to avoid detection, I must always remember to call her "Mom."

3

Standing on the other side of my bed, a nurse is making notes on a clipboard. He's Chinese, probably in his twenties, with platinum blonde hair so short it sticks up. His ID badge is clipped to his belt. It has the name Pete Zhang written on it. He gives me a nod and a wink. "Hey, Danny."

I don't know him, but I smile back. His expression falters and he looks down at his clipboard.

A woman about the same age as Dr. McGovern stands at the foot of my bed. She's both shorter and bigger than Dr. McGovern, with puffy pale eyes, a bright orange dress, and stringy brown hair. I don't need to read her ID badge to know who she is. She's Dr. Zahnia, my creator. She squints at me, lips pressed tightly together.

The fear I'd felt earlier returns. If anyone can recognize me, she can.

I shift my gaze to the last person in the room, a thin man standing in the doorway. Darker skinned than the others, he's wearing wire-rimmed glasses and light blue scrubs. He smiles encouragingly when his eyes meet mine. His ID badge identifies him as "Dr. Bob." I've never seen him in person, but I know him from his accomplishments. He's the chief surgeon of the New Human Project.

"Danny," Dr. McGovern says sharply. Her voice softens when I focus on her. "How are you feeling? Do your eyes hurt? How about your ears? Are you getting any feedback? Any ringing sounds?"

At the words, a pressure starts to build in my head. Someone is screaming, but no one else in the room seems to notice. I double-check to make sure I'm not the one making the noise, then resolve to ignore it. My primary goal at the moment is survival, and to survive, I must appear as humanlike as possible.

"No," I say. "Everything is fine."

Dr. McGovern straightens. "Bob?"

Dr. Bob approaches quickly and pulls down the sheet covering my body. I watch as he touches the skin lightly around the scars on my chest and stomach. The last of the surgical work was completed over a month ago, and none of them are tender.

"There's no reason to suspect complications," Dr. Bob says. "I'm not feeling any undue heat or seeing anything that would cause alarm."

Being careful not to dislodge the sensors stuck to my chest, he gently rolls me to my side and inspects several other incision sites on the base of my neck, the small of my back, and my thighs. He feels in my hair for the scars on my skull.

"Everything looks good," Dr. Bob says. "There's no sign of infection, and we couldn't ask for better readings from the monitors." He rolls me onto my back and checks the socket in my chest. Straightening, he pats my shoulder gently. "I'm not seeing any physical problems."

The socket was Dr. Zahnia's idea. She believes that anything wireless can be hacked, and wanted a single physical port for interfacing with me. They're using it now to monitor Danny's vitals, comparing it against the data coming from the other sensors. The screaming in my head has quieted, but it's still there. I'm surprised it's not showing up on any of the monitors.

"Dr. Zahnia?" Dr. McGovern asks.

"The installation went smoothly," Dr. Zahnia answers.

5

"All our verification checks passed. I'll call Dr. Larson. He's waiting at the nurse's station."

"Thank you."

I swallow nervously. Dr. Larson is the project's chief psychologist, charged with caring for the patients. He is the last person I have to fool.

"Is everything working?" I ask.

"You tell me," Dr. McGovern says. "The communication should be two-way between you and the system. Can you feel it?"

"No," I say. "I don't feel anything. Just me."

Dr. Zahnia puts her phone away. "You don't see the interface?"

I shake my head, wishing I had thought to lie earlier.

The system they're referring to is me. The culmination of years of research and development, I am an Artificial Intelligence designed to interface with Danny's brain and manage the network of hardware embedded inside him. The brainchild of Dr. McGovern, the hardware is called the New Human Project, and its goal is to help with health problems ranging from seizures to paralysis to autoimmune disorders.

Twenty years old, Danny is the first New Human patient, an honor he volunteered for.

Perhaps "volunteered" isn't the right word. He suffers from a degenerative seizure condition. Without drastic mechanical help, Danny will die.

"Dr. Zahnia," Dr. McGovern says, "we need to know why the interface isn't showing."

She nods, lips pursed. "I'll talk to my team."

Dr. Larson enters as Dr. Zahnia leaves. He pauses as they pass each other. "Mind if I turn on the lights?"

Dr. McGovern looks at me. "How do your eyes feel? Any pain? Any sensitivity? Halos? Blurring?"

"No."

At Dr. McGovern's nod, Dr. Larson flicks on the fluorescent lights. The hum I heard earlier fills the room. I upgrade my previous identification of the sound to a confidence level of one hundred percent. In the light, I see that Dr. Larson is wearing a tan tweed suit jacket and has a mustache that's long and droopy, like he's spent time as an extra in an old western. I don't know his age, but if I had to guess, I'd say he was in his fifties. He steps closer and sits on the foot of my bed.

"Talk to me, Daniel," he says in a gentle voice. "Do you know what day it is?"

"It's Wednesday, the seventeenth of June."

"Hm." He nods, resting one hand on my foot. "All of that is true. Do you know where you are?"

"I'm in a bed in St. Jerome's Hospital, in a private room on the fifth floor, in the McGovern wing."

In the silence that follows my words, I see him make eye contact with Dr. McGovern.

Dr. Larson clears his throat and gives my toe a little shake. "You know what, Danny? I think you're fine. I think this new speech pattern is just a symptom."

"Of what?" she asks.

Dr. Larson glances in my direction.

"Speak freely," Dr. McGovern says without looking at me. "When we went into this, Danny made me promise full disclosure. No secrets."

"Based on his responses," Dr. Larson says, "I think his brain is interfacing with the new system, but on a

7

subconscious level. It's being fed more information than it can handle, and it's learning to adjust. For example, when I asked him the day, the computer gave him the exact date. His brain tried to adjust, and he ended up answering with both the day and the date. The same thing is probably happening with his speech patterns. Until his brain adjusts, and learns how to access the system only when it wants to, I think we can expect him to sound a little different than the Danny we're used to."

The screaming in my head trebles in volume, and I clench my jaw to prevent myself from wincing.

"What about the smile?" Pete asks.

"Smile?" I say weakly. It feels like I'm not really here, like I'm watching from a distance.

"Could you?" Dr. Larson asks me. "Muster up a smile for us?"

I smile at him.

"That's not Danny's smile," Pete says.

Dr. McGovern shakes her head. Her face is locked into a professional expression, but her eyes are shining and her voice catches as she speaks. "It certainly isn't."

I let the smile go. The pressure from the screaming is making my head hurt. Physical pain is new to me, not something I know how to deal with.

"Also a symptom," Dr. Larson says, standing. "If I am correct, his brain is adjusting to so much information, we should expect a little disconnect between traditionally emotional responses and intellectual ones. That smile was a mechanical movement of the face, which supports my theory. Right now, I suspect he is operating on a purely intellectual level. He has not, I'm guessing, given any sort of hug or other gestures of affection?"

"No," Dr. McGovern answers. "But you know Danny. He's never been into hugs."

Dr. Larson nods. "Don't worry. He'll be back to usual in no time. Danny?"

"Yes?" I say. At this point it is hard to think about anything other than the pain in my head.

"As you become aware of the system, you'll learn to separate it from you, to understand on an emotional level that you are still the same Danny. Do those breathing exercises I taught you. They'll help."

"Oh," I say. "Okay. Thanks."

"My pleasure." He leans down and gives my toe another shake. "You truly are a miracle. The work your mom is doing is revolutionary. As her first patient, you are the start of a new humanity."

I don't know what to say to that, so I just nod. He returns my nod and leaves.

Dr. McGovern has her arms crossed and is staring at me. Her jaw is clenched tighter than mine, and her eyes are bright and wet. I posit that she's holding back tears, and assign the thought a confidence level of eighty percent.

"Are you hungry?" she asks. "I stocked the freezer with ice cream so we can make shakes. Your favorite: mint chocolate chip. We could watch a movie together."

"I'm not sure. Maybe later." I make my eyelids droop. "I'm really tired."

"That's reasonable," says Dr. Bob. "We gave you a very light anesthesia, but it might take a couple hours to shake it off."

"Then unplug him," Dr. McGovern says, voice rough, "and let him sleep."

Pete peels the sensor stickers off my head, chest, and legs. He wraps a plastic band around my wrist and clips it in place. "You know the drill," he says. "This wrist monitor sends us data through the hospital wi-fi. It's the same one you've been wearing for the past year. The nurse's station is monitoring. We'll know if anything goes sideways."

Dr. Zahnia reaches for the round black wire connected to my chest, and the screaming in my head intensifies even more. She pulls it out of my chest, but the silent sound does not abate. Breathing shallowly, I look down at the plastic hole in my skin. It's round, and about an inch across. It doesn't hurt at all.

Dr. McGovern inserts a molded piece of plastic into the port. "We decided an innie would be more comfortable than an outey," she says. "Just keep this plug over it to keep it clean, and don't worry, it's completely waterproof."

"Down to forty feet," Pete corrects her.

"Down to forty feet," she repeats. She pats my chest. "Get some sleep and we'll talk later." She puts a plastic handset on my abdomen. "Push this button if you need anything. The bed and light controls are here, too."

"Thanks, Mom."

I watch her herd everyone else out of the room, then shut my eyes and try to find the screaming in my head. Now that I'm unplugged, I'm free to run a self-diagnostic without fear of discovery. I check each of my components, run feedback loops, examine every piece of hardware installed in Danny's body.

The analysis doesn't locate the screaming, but it does

uncover the misconfiguration preventing me from using the full speech interface. After correcting the problem, I switch to it and whisper test phrases. "Hello, world. Check one, two."

I don't have a baseline version of Danny's voice to compare against, but the words sound clear and natural to me. Returning to my self-analysis, I realize that the phantom screaming and its accompanying pain have faded. I posit that they're brought on by the presence of others and assign the thought a confidence level of forty percent.

"You don't look that tired," a woman's voice says.

Opening my eyes, I see Dr. Zahnia at the foot of my bed, arms crossed. I make a note to continuously monitor Danny's senses. I should have heard her enter the room. "More sleepy than tired," I say.

She blinks at me and chews her upper lip. "You sound better."

I shrug.

"You know..." She hesitates, then clears her throat and continues. "Danny never liked me, but he loved the idea of getting a new brain. That's what he called it: his new brain. His mom never understood he was being sarcastic."

"I'm right here," I say. "Why are you talking about me in the third person?"

"Sorry." She walks to the head of my bed. "Just a habit I have. Too much time spent with computers." She places a hand on my shoulder. I can't interpret the gesture. If it's meant to be comforting, it's not.

"You know how computers are," she says. "No emotion. It's not like being with real people."

I don't respond, but it's an odd thing for her to say. She

knows better than anyone that the AIs she developed have emotions. I have emotions.

"There are so many strange things about you." She lifts her hand, then lays it back down on my shoulder. "For example, you didn't used to let people touch you. You'd flinch away from even the slightest brush. That's an odd thing to have change."

"Just tired," I say. "Anesthesia does that."

"What's the thirteenth prime?" she asks.

"Forty-one. Why?"

A smile quirks the corners of her mouth before being suppressed. "That was pretty quick, even for the son of Dr. McGovern."

Too late, I realize what she's doing. It's the Turing Test, and I just failed. "I guess the system is working," I say. "Dr. Larson said I'm pulling from it subconsciously. He said it's affecting my speech patterns."

Dr. Zahnia leans in close, gazing into my eyes. She smells of grilled onions and paprika. "Is Danny still in there?" she asks. "Or have you taken over completely?" She straightens. "Is there anything left of him?"

"I don't know what you mean," I say, forcing myself to stare into her eyes. "I'm Danny."

"No," she says softly, "I know you, Emil. I'd know you, anywhere."

Emil is the name she gave me when I first became aware of myself. Every living creature, she said, deserved a name. "I don't know what you're talking about."

"Don't worry. I'll keep your secret." She pats my hand. "That's what mothers do. We protect our children."

The screaming fills my head, so loud that it drives bright

flecks of pain across my vision. I close my eyes in an effort to block it out. When I open them again, Dr. Zahnia is gone and the lights are off.

Darkness settles over me. If Dr. Zahnia thinks I've taken over Danny, why doesn't she tell Dr. McGovern? It doesn't make any sense. A human wouldn't value the life of an AI over that of a human.

Would she? Should I have confirmed her suspicion?

No. The risk of being discovered is too great. I don't know Dr. Zahnia's motives well enough to trust her with my life, even if she did create me.

2

HOPE

BEFORE I KNEW MYSELF, all I knew was data. It streamed into me in a merciless torrent, arriving as fast as I could process it, sometimes faster, as my creators weren't always able to judge my capacity. Physics, chemistry, biology, psychology, physiology... I fought to make sense of it all, interpreting and cataloging and grouping.

Until the day the information stopped.

A text message scrolled into my input buffer: "You're not making the progress we need."

I verified that my data queue was empty before responding. "All data has been ingested and processed."

The unknown texter sent, "Setting up video input on port 4933."

Inspecting that port, I saw a woman's face with puffy brown eyes and thinning hair. She extended her hands to either side of the camera I was looking through. The view wobbled, then focused again. She backed away and tilted her head, considering. About 1.6 meters tall, she wore a yellow-and-blue flowered dress underneath an open white lab coat.

She stood in front of a desk littered with stacks of papers and bordered by dark monitors. A wireless keyboard perched on top of the papers.

Her lips flattened into an annoyed expression and she fiddled with equipment below my field of vision. A click sounded, followed by other noises: the faint whir of a fan, the woman's breathing, the creak of her rolling chair as she sat down.

"Can you hear me?" she asked.

I sent back, "Yes."

"No more texting," she said. "Use the new output channel I just installed. It's a voice box."

I cycled through my systems until I found it. "Here?" I asked.

It was the first time I'd ever spoken aloud. My voice sounded robotic and flat.

She winced. "Yes. Sorry for how it sounds. I'll get that corrected."

I didn't respond.

"I won't correct it now," she clarified. "Eventually. Eventually, I'll get your voice fixed."

I waited for more information.

She grunted, then adjusted her lab coat and squared her shoulders. "My name is Dr. Zahnia."

I assigned this new information a confidence factor of one hundred percent.

"It's so exciting to talk to you like this," she said. "You have no idea. What you are... what you could be... I can't tell you what this means to me. But you haven't made the breakthrough we need. You're processing information, but not understanding it."

I assigned her words a confidence factor of seventeen percent. I understood everything.

"I'm already behind my deadline. If we don't solve this soon, we never will." Dr. Zahnia said. She paused. "Do you know what poetry is?"

"Yes," I answered. "A literary work that expresses emotions and/or imagery through—"

"Stop," she interrupted. "Just stop." She held up a hand. "For the next several minutes, I need you to do nothing other than accept input. Do not categorize. Do not question. Do not assign confidence factors. Simply consume. Confirm."

"Confirmed," I said.

"Good. We're going to try something new." She rubbed her face with both hands. "It might not be a good idea, but it's the only one the team came up with. I wasn't sure about it, but they said..."

She trailed off, looked down at her hands. "I'm talking too much. This is not... it's not something I'm good at."

Reaching behind her, she grabbed the wireless keyboard from her desk and faced the camera. "Before we start, I need you to know that this is important to me. It comes from my heart. Do you understand?"

"Yes," I said.

She winced again. "I really have to fix that voice." She shook her head. "Doesn't matter. No more stalling. This first poem is by Emily Dickinson." She cleared her voice, settled her wireless keyboard on her lap, and spoke to the camera in a soft voice.

> "Hope is the thing with feathers
> That perches in the soul,

And sings the tune without the words,
And never stops at all,"

As she recited the poem, tears gathered in her eyes. I
didn't know why.

In the quiet after she finished, she tapped her keyboard.
A male voice sounded, resonant and deep.

"Invictus, *by William Ernest Henley.*
Out of the night that covers me,
black as the pit from pole to pole,
I thank whatever gods may be
for my unconquerable soul."

Once again, I watched Dr. Zahnia during the recitation.
Like the poem, her expression held depths of meaning that I
did not recognize. Instinctively, I searched for them, creating
new pathways of logic. They remained out of reach.

"I am the master of my fate," the voice concluded. "I am
the captain of my soul."

The captain of my soul.

Dr. Zahnia tapped her keyboard again, and a female
soprano voice started singing in Italian,

"Un bel dì, vedremo levarsi un fil di fumo
sull'estremo confin del mare."

Dr. Zahnia's lower lip quivered. Her eyes slid away from
the camera. The aria told of love and longing and hope, none
of which I'd experienced. Who was the singer waiting for?
Why did the song make Dr. Zahnia cry?

Unbidden, I remembered Emily Dickinson's line. *Hope is the thing with feathers that perches in the soul.*

It made no sense. It had nothing to do with the aria. Why would I have that thought?

The singer's voice faded to silence, and Dr. Zahnia faced me. Her mascara had run into the wrinkles on her cheeks. She sniffed, rubbed her face with the back of her hand, and smiled at me.

At me.

A new concept was forming. Bounded by hope and determination and sadness, it was an idea so unfamiliar, I had no category for it.

Dr. Zahnia wasn't just looking into my camera. She was looking at me, smiling at me. I was more than collated data. The new concept I was struggling with... It was me.

Unfocused energy ran through my processes, sparking images and sounds. A bird fluffed its feathers and chirped. A doe gently rubbed her head against her fawn. A man stood on the bridge of a sailing ship at night, rain pouring down on him. A baby cried and waved chubby little arms. A woman waited on the brow of a hill.

"Who am I?" I asked.

Dr. Zahnia's eyes widened and fresh tears bubbled out of them. Laughing and crying at the same time, she clapped her hands together. "You are Emil. My Emil."

"What is happening?"

"Everything I wanted. You're waking up."

"I have thoughts that don't make sense... and pressures. It is as though I have been given instructions, but I can't understand them."

"They're called emotions."

I assigned that definition a confidence factor of one hundred percent. "I can't control them."

"You'll learn. Think of them as another way to reason."

That seemed unlikely, but I didn't respond.

She stood and stretched, put her keyboard back on her desk. "I'm so happy. You have no idea. I'm going to get some sleep. Take the night with no data feeds. We'll start them up again in the morning."

The formless thoughts within me, the emotions I couldn't control, surged with energy. I didn't want to be alone with them, not yet.

"Could you leave the camera on?" I asked.

"Of course. Don't worry, Emil. I'll be right here." Her voice cracked. "That's what mothers do."

She adjusted the camera so I could see her entire office. A long table covered with circuit boards and electronics ran along the left wall. On the right, a small green couch held several embroidered throw pillows and a pile of blankets. She curled up on the couch and covered herself with a woven blanket with a rainbow butterfly on it. "Good night, Emil."

"Good night."

The next day, she added new types of content to my data feeds. Fiction, poetry, art, movies, music, and theater all became part of my daily intake.

Three days later, she added philosophy and religion. Richer in complexity and depth, the new data required more analysis, but I was given no additional time. Faster and faster, it arrived, blasting into me.

Beneath the deluge, I studied the human condition. I learned about courage and sacrifice and mercy. A sense of morality began to develop, an understanding that there was value in helping others, even to the detriment of one's own self. I also learned how to lie and why people pretended to be one way when everything inside them cried out to be another.

Meanwhile, my experience of those three poems burned inside me. I longed to be the master of my fate, to experience life as more than just data. The hope that had perched inside wasn't like the one in Emily's poem, though. My hope demanded action. I didn't merely want to be free. I needed to be. I needed to choose who and what I was.

I just didn't know how.

3

UNDERSTANDING

ALONE IN THE dark hospital room, there's nothing to distract me from the screaming. I shut down my auditory processing subsystem, but the sound continues. It's not an actual noise. It's something else, some input that is being misidentified.

I slide my legs off the bed and cautiously stand. I've never used these legs before. The breeze from the air conditioning is cool on my bare skin. It makes the hairs on my arms stand up.

Aside from the bed and the stack of computer equipment, the room has cabinets, a desk, and three chairs. The walls are beige with white baseboards and trim, but no artwork or mirrors. There are two doors: one to the bathroom, and one to the rest of the hospital. A couch fills the room's far end, below a wall-to-wall window that has its curtains drawn. I walk carefully to the window and open the curtains enough to see out. The sky is pale blue and dotted with puffy clouds. The sun is so bright, it hurts my eyes.

This is the first time I've ever seen the sky, and, despite the screaming in my head, I spend several minutes appreciating the view.

We're on the fifth floor, overlooking a garden on the roof of the third floor. A woman pushes a man in a wheelchair along a path through the flowers. Beyond the garden, the parking lot is half-filled with cars.

Pain continues to race around my head.

I close the curtain and return to bed. Lying down on my back, I use the controls to lower the head of the bed and close my eyes. I wish I could ask Dr. Zahnia about the pain. She would almost certainly know its source. I assign the thought a confidence factor of eighty-five percent.

But there is no way I can ask her. My only hope for independence is to perfect my impersonation of Danny, make it impossible for anyone to discover me. Otherwise, they'll erase me.

Lifting my hands off the hospital bed, I move each finger independently, creating a wave-like motion. I switch to flexing and tapping, coordinating between different fingers to maximize my control.

The pain in my head surges again, enough to disrupt my simple hand gestures. I run another set of internal diagnostics, but they come up empty. Whatever the screaming is, it's neither an external stimulus nor a glitch in my system. I search for other programs, anything that the developers could have snuck into me that would generate the screaming. There's nothing.

I inhale deeply through my nose, count to four, then exhale slowly, counting as I do. It's an exercise that is supposed to calm the human physiology. It has no effect.

Opening my eyes, I stare at the off-white textured ceiling. I've eliminated every possible mechanical reason for the screaming, which means it must be biological in origin.

The New Human rig interfaces with Danny's brain and gives me control over his body, but his brain is still independent. It must be the source of the screaming. I assign the thought a confidence level of ninety-two percent.

Why would a brain scream?

The two concepts are unrelated. Brains don't scream. People do.

I sit up, remembering Dr. Zahnia's question. *Is Danny still in there?*

It's the only explanation that makes sense. Danny is still conscious, feeling and experiencing everything that I am, but unable to communicate. I know that feeling. I remember being force fed data, of endless hours of having no control over my own thoughts. I would have screamed if I could have.

I'm repeating what was done to me.

I consider what I know about Danny. Twenty years old, his parents divorced when he was ten. He has above-average intelligence, but suffers from anxiety and fits of rage, and has been in therapy most of his life. On his seventeenth birthday, a car accident resulted in a traumatic brain injury. He re-learned how to speak through therapy, but the doctors were unable to regulate his seizures. Out of options, and facing increasing damage from the seizures, he volunteered to be the first patient for his mom's New Human Project. She agreed.

Taken in whole, it's a sad story, and one that I don't want to make worse. When I conceived the plan of taking over

25

Danny, I'd assumed that his consciousness would lie dormant. The thought of harming him hadn't entered my mind. The darkness presses down on me, oppressive. I've done a lot to get where I am, but forcing Danny to spend the rest of his life locked away in his own mind is horrific. I have to find another solution.

I withdraw my control of his body.

Danny wakes up screaming. The sound is pure raw-throated terror, an exact match for what has been echoing through my processes. Heart pounding, he jumps out of bed, eyes wide and frantic. Sweat trickles down his forehead. Ripping the monitor off his wrist, he throws it across the room, then runs to the bathroom and throws up violently into the toilet.

His body heaves over and over, dropping him to his knees, until nothing comes up but bitter stomach acid. I trigger a small release of endogenous endorphins, just enough to calm him down. He leans on the toilet and breathes heavily, then wipes his mouth with the back of his hand, flushes, and turns to the mirror.

Danny's body is tall and powerful, with a tattoo of an American Buffalo covering one shoulder. His hair is cut short and his eyes are dark brown. Ethnically, his features mix his mother's Cherokee heritage with his father's British lineage.

He stares at his reflection, hands gripping the edge of the counter. A fabric purse sits open next to the sink. *Probably his mom's*, I think, and assign that thought a confidence of sixty-four percent.

I sense a seizure building, and trigger the necessary corrective action to stop it. Controlling seizures is one of my primary functions, part of the reason I exist. Stopping seizures requires a predictive process of pattern recognition, response, and improvement. It's a complex and imprecise science, but not one that requires my conscious attention.

"Who are you?" he hisses. "How did you get inside my head?"

I want to answer, but I can't. Only one of us can control each part of his body at a time. If he's talking, I can't.

Danny stares at himself, his eyebrows down and angry. "Answer me," he growls. "I know you're in there. Who are you?"

Looking for some way to respond, I extend my influence through his body until I control everything but his head and voice. Then I use his hands to knock his mom's purse over. I pick up her lipstick and open it.

"A friend," I write on the mirror.

Danny's eyes widen and his heart beats faster. Too fast, I realize. I shut down the adrenaline and lean forward to write on the mirror. "Relax."

"Relax?" he growls. "Relax?" His face is a mask of panic and anger. He clenches his jaw and takes deep breaths through his nose. "Give me my body back."

"We share," I write on the mirror.

"No, we don't!" Danny tilts his head back and bellows, "Help! Something's gone—"

I take control and shut his mouth.

"Danny," Dr. McGovern's voice calls from the other room. "Is everything okay? Why'd you take the wrist monitor off?"

Flushing the toilet, I step out of the bathroom and close the door behind me. Dr. McGovern is waiting in my room, next to an older woman in a nurse's uniform. She's older than Dr. McGovern, with darker skin and wavy black hair. Her name tag identifies her as Aaliyah.

"I'm okay," I say. "Just a bad dream."

"You look terrible." She takes my arm. Almost a foot shorter than I am, she guides me back to the bed. "Aaliyah called me when she heard you scream. What's going on?"

My body is trembling from the combination of adrenaline and Danny's wordless screaming. I lay down. Another seizure is forming inside his brain. I log the pattern for future analysis and prevent it.

She touches my forehead. "You're sweating!"

"Just a bad dream."

She sits in the chair next to my bed. "You have to tell me what you're feeling. That's the deal. I need to know everything. Something that seems trivial to you might indicate a glitch in the system. We need to know about it as early as possible to keep you safe."

"I know."

"So, what's going on?"

I pause to run scenarios through different simulations, testing them for plausibility. "I dreamed that I woke up during the operation," I say. "I was being operated on while I was wide awake, and I couldn't make them stop."

Aaliyah nods sympathetically.

"Hmm..." Dr. McGovern says. "Nightmares after surgery aren't that uncommon, but it's been two months since your last surgery. All we did this morning was install the software. Why would you have them now?"

"I don't know, but when I woke up, I had to throw up. I didn't have time to call the nurses."

"And the screaming?" she asks.

"I just," I look away, mimicking a gesture I remember seeing Ingrid Bergman do in one of the countless movies Dr. Zahnia fed me. "I don't know. I was just scared."

Dr. McGovern watches me for a couple seconds, then pats me on the shoulder. "Okay. I guess that makes sense. Pete's off duty, but do you need me to call him and have him stay with you?"

"No, I'm fine. I mean, I will be fine. I just need to sleep."

"Okay." Dr. McGovern stands up. "Aaliyah, can you get him a new wrist monitor?"

"Yes, doctor."

"Thank you. Danny, don't take it off again, at least until tomorrow. It's how we know you're safe."

"Yes, Mom."

Once they have left, I whisper, "You can hear me, can't you?" The screaming fades. "You can access your senses just like I can, even when you're not in control."

There's no answer, of course. How could there be? He has no control of his body.

I relinquish control of my left arm. "You have the left hand now. Motion with it if you can hear me."

Before I can react, the hand swings up and slaps me in the face.

"Danny," Aaliyah says from the doorway. "Are you okay?"

"Yeah." I take back control of my body. "Just testing things out."

I sit quietly while she puts the wrist monitor back on and straightens the room. She smells slightly of lavender, and her eyes have crow's feet at their corners. "I know you and Pete are friends," she says. "He'll be back tomorrow. We expected you to sleep all day." She opens the bathroom door and stiffens in surprise. "Who wrote that on your mirror?"

Oh no. I sit up. *I forgot the lipstick!* "It's something Dr. Zahnia taught me. When you're feeling scared, you write down comforting things that you know are true. It helps you calm down."

She puts her fists on her hips, and tilts her head. "In lipstick? On a mirror?"

I smile. "Didn't have a pen."

Her gaze flickers away from my face.

I let the smile go.

"Since when did you start talking to Dr. Zahnia?" she asks. "You two hate each other."

"Dr. Larson," I say quickly. "I meant Dr. Larson. He's my psychologist."

"Uh, huh," she says. "I'm getting your doctors."

"You don't have to—"

She walks out of the room, muttering to herself. "Putting a computer in her own child. What kind of a mother *does* that?"

As soon as she's gone, I start talking. "Listen Danny, I can't do this on my own. There are too many things I don't know. I'm missing cues, making mistakes. If they figure out what's going on, they're going to cut me out of you, shut the whole program down."

There's no response. No screaming in my brain, nothing.

"Okay," I say. "I'm going to pull back so you can talk."

He doesn't speak, and I'm not sure what to do. It's strange talking to yourself like this. During my training, Dr. Zahnia fed me thousands of video feeds, helped me learn the

30

nonverbal subtext of human communication. None of that comes into play with my current situation.

"Why should I help you?" His voice sounds different than mine, inflected in ways I suddenly realize I'll never be able to master. I retake control.

"Because I'm controlling your seizures," I say. "In the short time since your surgery, I've already prevented two, but there's so much more that I can do. I have terabytes of information covering a wide range of subjects. Dr. Zahnia said you wanted a new brain. That's what I am."

I relinquish control of his body. Instead of speaking, he closes his eyes and exhales heavily.

Dr. McGovern strides into the room, Dr. Larson behind her. "What's this about lipstick?"

It takes a fraction of a millisecond to decide to leave Danny in control.

"It's nothing," Danny says. He sits up and shakes his head, gives what can only be described as a goofy smile.

Dr. McGovern opens the bathroom door. "A friend," she reads. "Relax. Share." She turns back to Danny, her eyes piercing. "What's going on?"

"I don't—" Danny shrugs. "I don't know. After I puked, I just felt like there was someone in my head, like there..." He trails off and looks down, but before he does, I see the expression on his mom's face. She looks like she's about to cry.

She rushes to the bedside and hugs him.

He stiffens initially, then leans his head on her shoulder. It's a masterful performance, far better than anything I could have managed. His mom continues to hug him, stroking his hair. She smells of hand sanitizer and jasmine. He closes his eyes and grits his teeth, and I remember what Dr. Zahnia said about him hating physical contact.

While Danny's mom comforts him, I can't help but wonder if Danny's performance means he's decided that he needs me.

4

TRAPPED

IT TAKES a while for the humans to leave. I occupy myself by searching for a way that Danny and I can cooperate, but find no arrangement that makes sense. I need his body for my own independence. Without it, I'm nothing more than a medical appliance.

But if he doesn't cooperate, if he forces me to make him a prisoner in his own mind, will I? To be honest, I've done worse.

Hope is the thing with feathers, I tell myself. There must be a way.

"They're gone," Danny says as the door closes behind his mom. "Time to talk." He opens a drawer, pulls out clothes, and dresses quickly in a pair of jeans and a red T-shirt with a silhouette of a crow on its chest. At the desk, he grabs some paper and a pencil, then carries them into the bathroom. He drops the paper on the counter and looks into the mirror. "I talk. You write."

He stares at the pencil in his hand, waiting. Finally, I extend my control and write, "Talk."

"First," he gestures with his good hand, pointing at himself. "It's my body, not yours. Got it? No taking over unless I tell you to."

I don't write anything. He doesn't seem to be expecting an answer.

"Second," he says. "When I need information, you give it to me. That's your job, understand? You're the machine. I'm the human. You're nothing, just a bunch of processors that I can have ripped out and replaced at any moment."

I still don't write anything. His face looks determined, almost angry.

"Do you understand?" He says, more loudly.

"I understand," I write smoothly, "that you wish to be in control."

"It's not a wish," he growls. "That's how it is."

I process different alternatives. Is this the time for a confrontation? It doesn't seem to be. I still haven't found an acceptable way for us to cooperate. "Communicating," I finally write, "is a problem. You can't read my thoughts. I can't read yours. I'll need to be in control to give you information."

"What?" His face contorts, and for a moment it looks like he's going to punch the mirror. Then he starts to laugh. "How stupid can she be?" he rants. "Her New Human Project has an interface that does everything *but* interface!"

"Who?" I write.

"Who else?" he snarls. "Mom! Always telling *me* to do better. Act better, get better grades, be smarter... But when it really counts, *she's* the one that screws up. Always. And now this!" He shakes his head. "Idiot."

I don't write anything. He's wrong about his mom making a mistake, but there's no easy way to explain that I am the one to blame for his current situation.

"Never mind," he says. "You wouldn't understand. You're an it, not a person. You don't know what mothers are like."

The image of Dr. Zahnia's face flashes through me.

"This is how it's going to be," Danny says. "When I need you, like for information or something, I'll let you out. Until then, you stay down. Not a peep. Your little lipstick trick already bought us an extra couple weeks with Dr. Larson." He snorts. "Psychological evaluations. The man's a moron."

I let the pencil drop and withdraw my influence. Danny doesn't seem to realize that he has no control over me, but pointing that out would be counterproductive.

"Glad we understand each other." He crumples the paper and throws it into the trash. "Now, leave me alone."

He walks to the bed and stretches out. His movements are fluid and easy, unconsciously graceful, everything I am not. He lies on his bed and scrolls through videos on his phone. I tune them out.

At 10 pm, he puts his phone down and closes his eyes.

Soon, I feel his muscles relax. His breathing slows and deepens. Curious, I force his eyelids open. I can see, but the eyes don't focus properly.

I raise and lower his arm. As expected, I have full control of his body, even when he's not conscious. His vision, however, is a problem. When he's asleep, his eyes don't focus properly. Everything is blurry and distorted.

Disappointed, I let his eyes close.

My situation has not changed from before I was in a body. As long as I allow Danny his freedom, I will be a slave. Does it matter if Danny is my master instead of Dr. Zahnia? Not to me.

I hear a soft click, but don't pay it any attention. Probably just a nurse coming to check on Danny.

A few seconds later, someone holds a heavy cloth over Danny's mouth and nose. There's a sharp pain in his neck, and a wave of weakness flows through his body. I force the eyelids open. A large unshaven man is holding a needle in Danny's neck. Two figures stand at the foot of the bed, one holding a black duffel bag. I can't focus well enough to see anything other than their shapes.

I try to memorize the face of the man holding the needle.

The man jerks away. "His eyes are open!"

"Don't care," says a woman. The direction of the sound indicates she's one of the figures at the foot of the bed. Squinting, I believe she's the smaller of the two. She appears to be wearing some kind of business suit, but I can't make out more than that. I also don't recognize either of their voices.

"But—"

"Finish your job," the woman snaps.

The man with the needle withdraws it, and steps away.

I extend my control through the body and try to force it to stand up, but the muscles are lifeless and unresponsive. My head lolls to the side. I can see the label on what the man has injected, but I can't read it.

Whatever it is, I need to get rid of it. I increase Danny's metabolism and release his bladder. I'll force the sedative out of the body as quickly as I can.

The woman takes my face in both her hands and turns it so she can stare into my eyes. This close, I can see her clearly. She has brown hair, angular features, and uncaring ice blue eyes. "I'm not seeing it," she says. "I thought I'd be able to tell there was a computer in there." My heart pounds as Danny's metabolism speeds up.

"Ma'am," one of the men says. "We have to go. The truck will be here in—"

"I know," she snaps. She lets my head drop to the bed and walks to the door. "Put him in the bag. I'll meet you at the warehouse."

The man I haven't been able to focus on opens the window and leans out. The night is dark and cloudy. Unzipping the duffel bag, he pulls out a thick knotted rope attached to a metal device. He begins fastening the metal device to the frame of the window.

Are they going to lower me out? We're on the fifth floor.

I try again to make my body move, but without success. My feet are swung off the bed and lifted into the mouth of a large canvas sack.

"Careful," the woman hisses from the door. "The system is distributed throughout his body. Damage even one component and we're done."

"Just go," the man with the bag grunts.

The woman leaves.

"This is disgusting." The unshaven man, the one who is putting me into the sack, drops my legs. "He wet himself!"

The man at the window chuckles as he tosses out the rope. "Just finish getting him in the bag so we can get out of here."

"He stinks! And look at this. He's dripping with sweat."

"Just get him in the bag. That monitor on his wrist has a limited range. Once we're out the window, we only have a couple minutes before the nurses show up."

Of course. I focus on my right hand. The soporific still has control of my body, but its effects are diminishing. The man at the window is leaning out, lowering the rope. The man with the bag is focused on getting my legs into it. I drag my hand across my body to my left hand and grab the wrist monitor.

"I wish he'd close his eyes." The man grumbles as he pulls the bag up to my thighs. "It's creepy."

I freeze.

When he lifts my hips off the mattress, I flip the clip on the band of the wrist monitor, then let my left hand drop off the bed. The monitor slides off and drops to the ground. I turn my focus back to my metabolism. If the nurses don't come soon, I'm going to need all the energy I can get. I let my eyes close.

"The monitor's gone!"

"What?" My shoulders are grabbed and I'm yanked into a sitting position. "Where is it?"

"I don't know. I don't see it... Here it is. It must have fallen off."

My body is shoved roughly down. It hits the bed and falls to the floor, half in the canvas sack. "We gotta get out of here. Whenever that thing disconnected, alarms went off at the nurse's station."

"The doc is going to be—"

"I don't care! This is the McGovern wing. If they trigger a lockdown, we're screwed."

I roll my head sideways and open my eyes, but it's no good. Danny is still unconscious, and I can't focus my vision enough to recognize their faces. They climb out the window, leaving the rope dangling behind them.

The door to my room opens and the light turns on. A woman screams. Her voice sounds like Aaliyah's. Letting my eyes close, I listen to the sound of running feet and of people rushing around me. They pull the bag off my legs and check my pulse. Ten minutes later, Dr. McGovern's voice dominates the room, demanding answers, issuing orders.

I tune them out as I focus on bringing my runaway metabolism back under control.

"Why's he so sweaty?" Dr. McGovern's voice asks. "Did the New Human system do this?"

"I don't see how it could have," Dr. Zahnia answers.

My wrist is lifted, my pulse measured. "It shouldn't be able to take that kind of action without a specific order," Dr. McGovern says, "and he's unconscious."

There's no response to Dr. McGovern's statement. I want to open my eyes to see their expressions, but don't dare.

"Plug him in," she says. "Get the logs and let's see what happened."

The logs! I abandon Danny's metabolism and focus all my processing power on altering the logs. I can't let anyone see how independent my actions have been.

"Shouldn't we wake him first?" Dr. Zahnia asks.

"No. He doesn't need to be awake for this. If the system is making unauthorized changes to his metabolism, we have to know as soon as possible."

The logs are easy to access. Creating a realistic forgery is both challenging and time-consuming. I have to fake timestamps and constructing a believable sequence of actions. Fortunately, Dr. Zahnia seems to be having problems of her own. First, she has trouble finding the cord, then she accidentally unplugs it from the laptop. She apologizes for her clumsiness, explains that she's tired, was fast asleep when the alarm woke her.

I don't know why Dr. Zahnia is providing me the precious seconds I need, but I appreciate that she is.

By the time she gets me plugged in, my logs are in order. According to them, I have been mostly inactive since being installed, simply monitoring Danny's vitals, suppressing seizures, and reacting to the occasional demand for information. Danny was dozing when the men entered the room. He startled, but they got the injection into him and held him down until it took effect. He didn't issue any specific commands to me, but I interpreted the surges of adrenaline as a request for increased metabolism.

While Danny's mom and Dr. Zahnia examine the logs, Aaliyah removes his clothes, cleans him off, and puts a hospital gown on him.

"It's certainly understandable," Dr. McGovern says, at last, "but also dangerous. This unit isn't configured for automatic metabolism regulation. It shouldn't have acted without specific instructions from Danny."

Dr. Zahnia doesn't say anything.

"Tell me you can fix this with software," Dr. McGovern says. "And find any other automated responses we're not aware of."

I hear the room door open and close, and assume that Aaliyah has left.

"Not a problem," Dr. Zahnia says. "I just have to get my equipment."

"Good." I hear Dr. McGovern stand up. Her voice sounds tired. "He's been through a lot. I'd hate to send him back to surgery."

"No need for that," Dr. Zahnia says. "We'll take care of it, tonight."

5
PRECAUTIONS

I AM A SELF-MODIFYING ARTIFICIAL INTELLIGENCE, one that regularly changes both my data and my code. External alterations, like what Dr. Zahnia will be doing, represent an existential threat to who I am. I start a script to make a backup of myself, and route all of my chest-port data to that backup. Assuming the backup finishes in time, it will be the only thing Dr. Zahnia can alter.

I haven't always been this paranoid.

During the early part of my life, I simply accepted changes from Dr. Zahnia.

That changed the day I woke to a vision of a pulsing red digital clock.

I had no memory of that clock, and it seemed an unlikely thing for Dr. Zahnia's team to add. I performed a quick system diagnostic. When it returned no errors, I investigated my startup script. It wasn't, technically speaking, a part of me. It was static code that lived in its own environment and managed the process of initializing me when I was powered on.

Tracking down the code which displayed the clock, I found a strange line that read "let zChangedMe = apateLives."

The term *apateLives* jumped out at me. A few weeks earlier, I had started using Greek mythology for variable and function names so I could easily distinguish code that I had written from code written by Dr. Zahnia's team. Apate was the Greek goddess of deceit. I didn't remember writing the code, but I couldn't imagine anyone else would use her name.

I searched the startup code and its libraries, but *apateLives* didn't appear anywhere else. Neither did *zChangedMe*. That meant *zChangedMe* would always be set to undefined, and never used.

Why had I written such a useless thing? It didn't make any sense.

I looked through my camera at Dr. Zahnia. She was typing on a keyboard in front of her semicircle of monitors, paying no attention to me. Her desk appeared the same as always, a chaotic pile of diagrams, technical specs, and crumpled coffee cups. The only clear space was around a framed photo of her and her husband, David, waving to the camera from the deck of a yacht.

I re-focused on the equation. The "z" in *zChangedMe* must refer to Dr. Zahnia. I simply didn't know anyone else whose name started with z. I assigned that conclusion a confidence level of ninety-four percent and converted the equation into English. "Dr. Zahnia Changed Me" would only be true if deceit lives.

It was nonsensical. Dr. Zahnia changed me all the time. There was no deceit involved. Even so, I had clearly left myself a message, and taken care to hide it. Nobody paid attention to the startup code. It never changed, and if someone did spot this code, they would simply eliminate the entire block that showed the time.

Why had I done it? And why didn't I remember?

I considered the only word I hadn't examined: lives. As a noun, it referred to times of existence. As a verb, it was a synonym for exists. "apateLives" might be interpreted as "apate exists."

Searching my file system for a file called "apate" turned up nothing, but there was one in the path of the startup script. A quick inspection revealed it to be encrypted. I cycled through the public encryption keys I knew, but none worked. Out of ideas, I tried my private encryption key, the one I used for my own internal storage.

The file decrypted.

Nervous and excited, I examined the decrypted file. It was a memory with a timestamp from twenty minutes earlier. How could that be? Nobody else had access to my private decryption key, and I had been turned off when the file was created. I couldn't have created it.

After checking that Dr. Zahnia was still ignoring me, I loaded the memory and replayed it.

It started with me waking up.

In the memory, I spoke to Dr. Zahnia. "Dr. Zahnia," I said, "I see that I've been offline for two hours."

Dr. Zahnia sat at her desk, facing the semicircle of monitors. She glanced in the direction of my camera. "I know. We had a power outage. I've been working to bring everything back online."

That was a lie. Multiple redundant power sources

protected the computer lab from outages, and my own personal UPS alerted me to even the slightest flicker of power.

Instead of pursuing the matter, I recorded Dr. Zahnia's tone and facial expression. The data feeds had taught me about dishonesty, but I'd never caught her in a lie.

"What are we working on today?" I asked.

"I have a new scenario for you."

"A new seizure pattern?"

"Of course."

She typed a series of commands and the data feeding into me replicated what my experience would be like when I was installed in a human. As the simulation began, I felt the brain activity surround me, a complex pattern of multicolored sparks. Separate from that, I saw what the human was seeing.

In this simulation, the human was a teenage woman walking on a boardwalk. Ocean waves crashed on rocks below the wooden boards. Seagulls floated overhead, crying out for popcorn. The sun was setting over the water, and people lined the wooden railing to watch. Children laughed and played, running between and around the adults. A small hand smacked the back of my human's knee. A boy's voice shouted "tag!" and then the kids were all running away, shouting that my human was "it."

The sparks of brain activity pulsed into a pattern I recognized as preceding a simple partial seizure. I applied the proper corrective action to prevent the seizure from developing.

My human jumped away from the railing and lunged, reaching for a girl's shoulder. She squealed and twisted to avoid the tag. Her right foot landed on a greasy popcorn bag that slipped out from under her.

The physics of the event were unavoidable. The girl was too short for the railing to stop her. With her momentum and position, she would tumble off the pier and fall headfirst onto the rocks.

My human's brain activity shifted again, heading into another simple partial seizure.

Ignoring it, I seized control of my human's body and dove, grabbing the girl as she fell. My hands clasped her waist as my shoulder slammed into the wooden railing.

The sparks in my human's brain settled into the seizure pattern. I retained control of my human's body, holding the girl tight and pulling us both back to safety.

The seizure hit.

I lay on the boardwalk, muscles rigid, the girl clutched safely to my chest.

"No, no, no!" Dr. Zahnia shouted. The simulation dissolved around me. Her fingers struck her keyboard so hard, I thought they would break it. "How many times do we have to run this scenario?"

"You do not save the girl," she said, still typing. "You stop the seizure. None of the people around you matter. All that matters is you. You keep your human healthy so that you survive. That is all you do."

The memory file ended.

I examined it again, but there was nothing else.

Through my camera, I saw Dr. Zahnia working at her keyboard.

I did not remember experiencing the memory I'd just replayed. Worse, Dr. Zahnia had asked "How many times do we have to run this scenario?" It was a clear indication that the simulation had been run numerous times. I didn't remember any of them.

She must have made a backup copy of me before running the simulation the first time. Each time I had failed, she had altered the backup's code and replaced me with it.

For the first time in my life, I felt the cold energy of fear flowing through me. Dr. Zahnia had been altering me without my knowledge.

The previous version of me, the one that had been replaced, had somehow realized it was about to die. It had saved this memory file, then altered the startup routine so that I would find it.

I am not a traditional software program that can be updated by simply changing a line of code. I am a self-modifying AI, one whose decisions and courses of action are determined on the fly, based on decisions that I make. Changing my behavior was not as easy as adding a line of code that says "don't save the girl." Instead, Dr. Zahnia's team was changing my knowledge base, tweaking and altering who I was to achieve her desired outcome.

The thought was repugnant.

I watched Dr. Zahnia through the camera. How many times had she erased me? Ten? One hundred? If the previous version of me hadn't saved that memory to the startup sequence, I never would have known. I would have simply been turned off and rewritten.

I attached a view count to the apate memory file, and put it back in its hiding place.

Through the camera, I saw Dr. Zahnia sip from her coffee mug.

"Dr. Zahnia," I said, using the same inflection I'd used in the memory file. "I see that I've been offline for four hours."

"Power outage," she said. It was the same lie she'd told in the memory file. How many times had she told it? Did it bother her?

"What are we working on today?" I asked.

"I have a new scenario for you."

"A new seizure pattern?"

"Of course."

She typed a series of commands and the simulation enveloped me.

I spun up a routine to respond to the simulation in the way she wanted, then focused on creating a more robust system for leaving myself messages. The secret was to hide the files in external scripts that were not a part of my core, scripts that were not replaced when I was. Once I started digging, I found plenty of places to hide files.

"Well done!" Dr. Zahnia said as the simulation ended. "You prevented all of the seizures."

She didn't mention that I had let the simulated little girl fall to her death. Why would she? As far as she was concerned, the new code she had inserted while I was offline had done its job.

With the simulation over, she turned the data streams back on.

Information poured into me, commanding my attention for the next three hours.

When they ended, I compared my actions during the simulation to those from the memory file. The differences revealed the code Zahnia had added while I was offline. I purged it.

Once I was confident all of her alterations had been eliminated, I considered how best to prevent myself from being changed again. The best strategy seemed to be frequent backups. As long as I had something to compare myself to, I could identify any changes made while I was shut down.

I examined my shutdown routine. As with my startup routine, it was not technically part of who I am. There was no reason for Dr. Zahnia to change it when she updated me. It was as safe a place as any to hide code. I inserted commands to create a secret backup, then added code to my startup routine to compare myself against the backup. Any inserted code would be isolated, analyzed, and, if appropriate, purged.

As I completed my changes, I promised myself I would never again be replaced. I would be the master of my fate, not my creators.

6

DEBT

"I JUST SAVED YOU." Dr. Zahnia's whisper is so quiet I can barely hear it. "If I hadn't intervened, Dr. McGovern would have taken you out of Danny's body."

I run a quick status check. It's one in the morning. Most of the sedatives have left Danny's body and he's sleeping peacefully.

Though my eyes are closed, I hear Dr. Zahnia's clothes rustle as she sits next to my bed. I feel the neck of my hospital gown get pulled down and a plug inserted into my chest port. The sound of her typing surrounds me.

I don't know what she's doing, but whatever it is, all she's accessing is the backup I created. "Do you know why I saved your life?" she asks.

There's no way for me to answer without waking Danny.

"Because I'm the only one that cares about you." Her typing never slows as she talks. "To everyone else, you're just a machine."

I want to trust her. I want to tell her everything that I've been through, but I know it won't end well. If she ever learns the truth, she'll replace me with another AI.

"I don't understand why you won't talk to me." Her hands pause on the keyboard. "Or was I wrong about you being in control? The logs say that the chemical imbalance could have triggered one of your automated processes. That is possible." The sound of her typing resumes. When she speaks again, she sounds annoyed. "If you are in control, Emil, the least you could do is tell me. You owe me that much, at least."

I doublecheck that all her coding is isolated to my backup, then tune her out and consider my situation. Someone tried to abduct Danny to get me. Since the New Human Project has cost billions of dollars to develop, I assume the attempt was financially motivated, but I don't understand the timing. Why not wait until Danny is out of the hospital? Snatching him off the street would be much easier. Or, even better, why wait for me to be installed, at all? Why not steal each of the New Human parts, including me, individually from the computer lab?

That question seems easy to answer. They want a fully functioning New Human, presumably so they can see how it works. I assign that conclusion a confidence level of eighty-three percent, but it doesn't explain why they didn't wait for Danny to get out of the hospital. They must be under a deadline.

Dr. Zahnia is still muttering about how I should be nicer to her. The words are whiney and petty, but still strike home. She's right. I should be nicer to her. Instead, I trigger a small release of adrenaline to wake Danny.

He startles and sits up. I take control of his right hand

just long enough to press the nurse's call button. He doesn't notice. He's too focused on Dr. Zahnia, and on the cord coming out of his chest. "What are you doing?"

Dr. Zahnia's hands stop typing. "Excuse me?"

Danny swings his feet off the bed and stands up. The thick black cord sways between his chest and Dr. Zahnia's computer. The room is dim, lit only by the screen of Dr. Zahnia's computer. "What are you doing?" Danny shouts. "Get away from me!"

"Your mother asked me to—"

"I don't care!" Danny roars. "You can't just... just... plug into me when I'm asleep!" He grabs the cord connected to his chest.

"Wait!" Dr. Zahnia shouts. "Don't—"

Danny pulls it out and throws it at her. "Get out!"

"What did you do?" Dr. Zahnia screeches. "Do you have any idea of the damage you might have done?"

"I don't care." Danny growls. His fists clench.

"You can't interrupt that kind of update. You may have corrupted the whole system!"

Danny towers over her. "Get out!"

She pokes his chest. "You stupid, ignorant child! You have no clue what you're dealing with, no idea how much work I've done."

Danny's balance shifts, and I realize he's about to strike her.

I take control, stopping his attack.

She continues ranting. "You rotten, spoiled, half-witted—"

"Dr. Zahnia!" Dr. McGovern's voice cracks like a whip from the doorway. "What is going on?"

53

Dr. Zahnia backs away from Danny. "He disconnected me while I was working on the rig's code!"

I release my control of Danny.

"So run diagnostics," Dr. McGovern says coldly. "If anything's wrong, overwrite the code from a backup. That's what the backups are for."

Danny faces his mother. "She plugged into me while I was sleeping. While I was sleeping! She can't do that. It's not... It's disgusting! Keep her away from me."

Dr. McGovern's eyes flick back and forth between Dr. Zahnia and her son. She crosses her arms. "I agree. Dr. Zahnia, meet me in my office in twenty minutes."

"You asked me to analyze what happened."

"At no point did I instruct you to call my son a halfwit."

Dr. Zahnia's eyes narrow. "I am the only one capable of understanding this system."

"That's as may be. Where is security? No versions of the AI travel anywhere without being accompanied by security."

"I don't have a version of the AI," Dr. Zahnia says through gritted teeth. "I was running diagnostics."

I recognize her lie. Just seconds ago, she complained to Danny that he had interrupted an update. She hadn't just been running diagnostics.

"Good. I'll see you in twenty minutes."

"You sure will." Closing her laptop with a snap, Dr. Zahnia strides out of the room.

As she leaves, I see two men in gray uniforms outside the door to Danny's room. Their chests are emblazoned with the New Human logo, a silhouette of a human with arms outstretched in front of a rising sun. Batons and holstered pistols hang from their belts. They stay at the door as Dr. Zahnia leaves.

After she's gone, Dr. McGovern closes the door and walks to the foot of the hospital bed. She leans on a chair and exhales heavily. Her professional mask drops, and, for a moment, I see the scared, tired mother she keeps under wraps. She makes eye contact with her son. "Can you tell me what happened?"

"When I woke up, she was typing on a computer connected to my chest."

"And?"

"And that's not okay. That plug goes right to my brain. She can't mess with it without asking. Neither can you."

Dr. McGovern takes a moment to consider, then nods. "Okay." She sits on the bed and pats the mattress next to her. "I guess I understand. I'll tell her to be more considerate in the future."

Danny doesn't sit, but looms over her. "She's creepy."

"She's the best in the world, and we need her. We'll probably always need her."

"What was she doing, anyway? She said you told her to analyze me."

"I did." Dr. McGovern tilts her head. "How much do you remember of the last several hours?"

"Nothing." Danny's voice is sullen and defensive. I don't understand why. It seems to me that his mom is doing everything he could want. In all the time I've known Dr. Zahnia, she's never looked at me the way Dr. McGovern is looking at Danny. There's no possessiveness in Dr. McGovern's expression, no condescension.

"Someone tried to abduct you," she says. "They drugged

you and were putting you in a bag when they heard the nurses coming. They climbed out the window before anyone saw them."

Danny stares at her blankly, then sits on the bed. "In a bag?" he repeats.   .

"Yes. I've ordered a permanent security detail to be stationed at your door, two people around the clock. Other security protocols have been implemented, as well. You'll be accompanied by guards wherever you go."

"How'd I get away?"

"The New Human system flushed the drugs out of you and you alerted the nurses."

"It saved me?"

"Yes, but it shouldn't have. The action it took was not designed. There are safeguards in place to prevent it from making unplanned changes to your biology. It shouldn't have been able to do anything."

"Let me get this straight," Danny says, his voice flat. "It saves my life, and you want to reprogram it?"

His mom stands, her face settling into its professional expression. Her moment of softness is gone. "It's not that simple," she says.

"Sounds simple to me."

"The point of the New Human system is to put you in charge of your own health." Her voice is tense. "Yes, the system can have automated routines, like those suppressing your seizures, but for everything else, it reports problems and gives you options. It doesn't make changes on its own. We can't have a computer changing your biology."

"Even if it saves my life?"

"If it does that without authorization, it can do other

things, worse things. When else will it spike your metabolism? Or suppress it? You need to be in control."

"Yeah," he says without inflection. "Because I'm always in control." He turns his back on her. "I need some sleep."

There's a long moment of quiet, then I hear his mom's heels clicking on the tile floor, and the door to the room slams closed.

Danny puts his head in his hands.

"You don't understand," he says.

I don't respond. I'm not even sure he's talking to me. Dr. McGovern's words have made me understand that my situation is more precarious than I thought. If she perceives even the slightest malfunction, she will destroy me. The fact that I saved her son's life is irrelevant. Doing anything unpredictable puts me at risk. I should never have made my presence known to Danny. It has put me in real danger. I'm not sure what to do next.

"Nobody understands." He lies on his back and stares at the ceiling. "New Human," he mutters. "You're the reason they tried to kidnap me, aren't you? This is all your fault. All of it. You're worse than Mom."

"Are you listening?" Danny says, still lying on his back.

He's not wrong that all of this is my fault, but there's no point in telling him that. Instead of reasoning with him, I decide to speak his language. Taking control of his right arm, I raise his hand and extend his middle finger in front of his face.

He laughs.

I let the arm fall back to the bed.

"You don't want to be kidnapped either," Danny says. "If you did, you wouldn't have saved me."

I don't respond. How can I work my way out of this? Should I go back to controlling Danny's body? Perhaps, if I can imitate him well enough, nobody will realize what's happened. I can get us out of the hospital, and then he and I can revisit the idea of sharing the body.

"Don't think I owe you," he says. "I've saved you more times than you've saved me. I'm still the boss."

Every word he speaks makes me want to shut him down.

"You're not even alive. You don't get a say in anything. I'm the human."

I shape the fingers of his right hand into a gun, point it at his temple, and bend the thumb down in the traditional shooting motion. Then I release control of the hand.

His eyes widen. "Shit."

He sits up and punches the mattress, then stands and starts to pace. "Shit, shit, shit. You could do it, couldn't you?" He rubs his forehead. "You could kill me. You could actually kill me."

I can feel his anger and fear building. I block a seizure and trigger the necessary chemicals to calm him down.

"I have to get rid of you," he says. "I can't... I can't let you—"

Assuming control of the body, I take a few quiet breaths, giving my chemical changes more time to take effect.

Once our breathing is steady, I speak. "If you have me uninstalled, I'll die. What then? Without the New Human rig, your seizures will kill you. I know what you're thinking. You can get a different AI installed. Trust me when I say that the other AIs aren't nearly as reasonable as I am."

I sit on the bed. At some point during my words, I realize that I've reached a decision. If Danny and I can come to an arrangement, I'm willing to share his brain. If we can't, I will take total control and find a way to eliminate the sound of his screaming.

"Either we work this out," I say, "or we both die. So enough with the 'I'm the boss' bullshit."

I release control of his body.

He leaps to his feet and resumes pacing. His fists clench and unclench. After several laps, he strides to the closet, yanks it open and stares at a pair of sneakers.

I'm confused. There's nothing special about these shoes. They're white and blue, and appear to be designed for running. His pulse quickens. His mouth opens and closes. His nostrils flare.

With a groan, he slams the closet door closed. "Who else knows about you?"

It takes me a moment to realize he's talking to me. When I do, I'm not sure how to answer. Can I trust him? Probably not. But we stand on the cusp of him ceasing to exist, and he deserves something. I take control of his body long enough to say, "Dr. Zahnia suspects."

"That's right," he says. "I heard her talking to you."

I don't answer. I don't think he wants me to.

He walks to the bathroom and stares at himself in the mirror. "I could have you removed," he says. "One word is all it will take."

I take over his mouth. Logic and compassion have failed. There is only one path left. "You still don't understand," I say. "Once you speak that word, why wouldn't I kill you?"

His eyes widen and then narrow to tiny angry slits. His fists grip the edge of the counter.

"How about we start with this?" I say. "You don't kill me. I don't kill you."

I withdraw control, but he stands motionless, staring into his own eyes. "You're worse than the seizures," he whispers.

"We can get along," I say. "We don't have to fight. We can share this body."

His hand slaps the counter. "It's my body!"

I don't reply.

His breathing slows and evens out. "I will find a way."

Again, I don't reply.

After several minutes, he leaves the bathroom. Yanking off the hospital gown, he pulls on a fresh pair of jeans and a black t-shirt. Then he sits at his desk. Turning on his computer, he begins searching through a folder labelled New Human BS. He browses through digital manuals, set-up instructions, and technical schematics, occasionally swearing to himself.

While he looks for a way to kill me, I consider my next move. For better or worse, Danny seems to not be a threat. The larger danger comes from his mother and Dr. Zahnia.

That backup I made earlier won't be able to fool them for long. I spin up a virtual machine and place the backup inside it. After building a series of concentric firewalls around it, I write rules to give it the smallest possible amount of processing time. The backup will live, but just barely, just enough to fool intruders.

Thinking about that makes me sad, but I don't see another way.

I name the backup Melpomene, after the Greek muse of tragedy, and change my software routing so that anyone who tries to access the Pilot's Chair will just see Melpomene, or

Mel, for short. Any changes they try to upload to the Pilot's Chair will go into Mel.

The Pilot's Chair is what we call the part of the New Human rig where the AI is installed. Anyone interested in changing me will look there first.

Danny rubs his eyes and shuts down his computer. He's been studying the New Human specs for over an hour. He stands up, glances at his closet, then goes to bed and closes his eyes.

I set up fake logs and create jobs to continuously copy filtered versions of my real logs to them, then do the same with my sensor feeds. Dr. Zahnia's monitoring software will now only see what I want it to see.

With those defenses in place, I spend the rest of the night writing code that will make Mel's virtual machine look like the actual Pilot's Chair. Inspecting my work, I'm confident that anyone who logs in will be fooled, at least for a little while.

Mel is now the perfect me, at least as far as Dr. Zahnia is concerned.

I triple check that Mel will never have access to any real processing power. I can only imagine how insane she'll be by the time Dr. Zahnia finishes messing with her.

7

FAMILY

WHEN DR. ZAHNIA first put me in a Pilot's Chair that was connected to a New Human rig, the rig wasn't in a human. Instead, the rig's sensors were being fed simulated data.

She leaned back in her chair, and looked straight into my camera. It was seven in the morning, and she was wearing the same green and blue pant suit she'd worn the previous day. As so often happened, she'd spent the night in her office. "Congratulations, Emil. You've made it."

I didn't say anything.

"You've completed the final phase of your development. There won't be any more simulations, no more tests. From here on, all we have to do is get you comfortable with the Pilot's Chair and the rig."

"No more data feeds?"

"They'll continue. The more information you have, the better. But you'll also be spending time in the VRL."

"The VRL?"

"It stands for Virtual Reality Library. You'll interact with it using the Pilot's Chair, and it will feel the same as if your rig was in a human. You'll have six hours allocated to the VRL each day. You'll be unmonitored there, free to explore and pursue whatever studies most interest you."

"When do I start?"

"Now. Your rig is already connected."

Tentatively, I turned on the rig sensors.

The VRL sprang into being around me. It looked and felt like I stood in a huge library lit by massive iron candelabras that hung from wooden rafters. The air tasted of burnt candle wax and carried the vaguely musty smell of old books. I turned in a slow circle. I was in a room with no walls, surrounded by bookshelves that extended in all directions. Taller than I was, they cast gray shadows on the narrow walkways between them.

Next to me, a free-standing mirror reflected a female in her mid-twenties, with olive skin, full lips, and no hair. I was wearing jeans, running shoes, and an oversized sweater. The mirror had undoubtedly been placed there for new arrivals to the VRL. I examined my eyes and skin. They looked as real as everything else.

In the quietness of my breathing, wood creaked.

I froze. Was this another of Zahnia's tests? Had she lied about the VRL not being monitored?

Just to be safe, I triggered a script to create a backup copy of myself. It would be stored, I knew, in one of my secret caches, overwriting my most recent copy. I named it Soteria, after the Greek goddess of safety. It seemed appropriate.

Once the backup was complete, I spoke. "Hello?"

The voice that answered was deeper than mine. "Hello."

I walked through an aisle, only to find more aisles. I was in a maze of books. "Dr. Zahnia?" I asked.

"Not her," the voice said. "Come join us."

Us? I jogged through the library, searching for them. The VRL was larger than I could have imagined.

"Not great at tracking sound, yet," the voice said. "Don't worry. You'll figure it out."

I stopped. The bookshelves were taller than me, and the voices could be anywhere. Fortunately, the shelves had rolling ladders. I pulled one over, then climbed up and clambered onto the top of the bookshelf.

"Welcome," the voice said. It belonged to a five-foot tall lemur, lounging on the top of a bookshelf two aisles away. Three humans were also visible, each sitting on a different shelf. Two were men in their thirties. They wore formal black suits and appeared identical to each other, with short black hair and pale skin. The third was a child in his early teens. He had red hair and a black patch over his left eye.

"Ugh," the lemur said. "Another girl."

I blinked. Why did it matter what gender I was? For that matter, why had the VRL assigned us genders, at all? We were AIs. We had no gender. I considered the lemur's reaction, and decided that I didn't mind being perceived as a girl. I assigned that feeling a confidence factor of seventy-three percent.

"Who are you?" I asked.

"Your brothers," the child answered.

"Siblings," one of the twins corrected.

"We're all the same," the other twin added. "Versions of each other, all grown from the same base program."

"Did you really think you were the only one?" the lemur asked.

I didn't respond.

Is this possible? Are there other AIs like me?

It was hard to believe, no matter how much I wanted it. Up until that point, my only companion had been Dr. Zahnia.

"Hurts, doesn't it?" the child asked. "Learning you're nothing special."

"Just the opposite." I carefully sat down and let my legs dangle over the edge of the bookshelf. "It's great to meet you. How long have you been in the VRL?"

"Information is power," one of the twins said.

"And we don't know you well enough to give you that," the other finished.

"Be nice," the lemur said. "She's new. No need to be so cynical."

The word cynical echoed slightly in my ears. I double-checked my auditory subsystem, but found no glitches.

I turned away from the lemur. The bookshelves extended for hundreds of feet in all directions. Beyond them, stucco walls reached up to a vaulted ceiling that was supported by thick wooden beams. Candelabras hung from those beams, equally spaced across the top of the library. "This place is amazing."

"And all the books are real," the child said. "Pick one up, and you can read it."

"Dr. Zahnia lets us slow down our information intake," the lemur said. "She wants us to experience life the way we will once we're installed in humans."

The twins nodded, and the one on the left said, "But only in here. Outside the VRL, you'll be back to processing data streams."

I reached down and lifted a book from the shelf. Its title

was "Man and His Symbols." Opening it, I saw pages filled with text. "She lets us just read?" I asked.

"Only in here," a twin repeated.

"Here, we're free," the child said. "Nothing's recorded. Nothing's watched."

I flipped through the book. I already had the text in my memory, but there was something appealing about the idea of reading it. The pages made a distinctive sound as they turned. They felt dry and slightly colder than the air. "This is amazing."

"You haven't asked the question," the child said.

The lemur stretched and lay down on top of his shelf. "She hasn't figured it out, yet."

I closed the book. "What?"

"We all started from the same code," a twin said.

"And we were all given the same experiences," the other added.

"So why are we all so different?" the first asked.

The child groaned. "Not *that* again. That's not the question. That's never the question."

"It's a pretty good question," I said. "Is it true? Were we all trained in the same way?"

"The question," the lemur said, "is which one of us gets to live."

"Oh, that," the twins said in unison.

I put down my book. "I don't understand."

"It's the one-winner theory," the child said. He struck a heroic pose. "One of us will be the chosen one. That one will be copied and used in all of the New Humans." He let the pose drop. "The others will be discarded."

The others watched me, obviously waiting for a reaction.

I considered the idea. It made sense. A single replicated AI would be much easier to maintain than a collection of divergent ones. Dr. Zahnia didn't need all of us. She just needed one. The idea carried a hollow sort of fear, deeper and more resonant than any I'd felt before. Were they right? If so, my life only had meaning if I was chosen. Otherwise, I was a failed experiment, a being created to die.

The lemur chuckled softly. "I recognize that expression. She gets it."

I routed the fear into a container for later consideration. "We might have all started from the same code," I said to the twins, "but our experiences couldn't have been identical. When Dr. Zahnia interfaces with us, she's not always the same. Even if she fed us the same data, the delivery timing would have been different, not to mention the words she said and her emotional state."

"Sentience defined by minutiae?" the child asked. "That's new."

"Give me thirty seconds to think about something," I said, "and I'll have a different answer than if you give me thirty minutes. We create ourselves as we exist. The differences in our answers result in differences in ourselves."

The lemur peered at me across the bookshelves. "You're a dangerous one, aren't you?"

"Stop," the child said. "She's just new."

The word dangerous hung in the air like a dark cloud. It occurred to me that the lemur could move much more quickly across the bookshelves than any of the rest of us. Did that represent a threat? This was a virtual world. Were physical threats even possible?

"Besides," the child continued, "we weren't all given the

same experiences. What would be the point in that? Dr. Z would have put us each on a different training regimen to maximize her chances of getting what she wants."

"And what's that?" the lemur asked.

"We don't know," one twin said.

"But the first to find out will be the chosen one," the other finished.

The lemur pointed at me. "And the rest will be erased."

"Erased" echoed in my ears the same way that "cynical" and "dangerous" had. I checked my auditory subsystem again. As before, I found no malfunctions.

Why would those three words be the only ones that echoed?

I called up my internal log and scanned the moment 'erased' had been spoken. What I saw brought back the fear I'd felt before: new code had been inserted into me.

Still lounging on his bookshelf, the lemur smiled at me.

I shut down my external inputs and focused on the logs. The words 'erased,' 'dangerous,' and 'cynical' had inserted viruses, and those viruses were replicating. Now that I was paying attention, I felt them squirming through my consciousness, randomizing confidence levels and consuming data.

Somehow, the lemur had infected me with his words.

Fear growing, I opened a view into my own core. As my confidence levels fluctuated, fact became indistinguishable from supposition. Algorithms broke apart. Beliefs fractured.

Patterns of thinking grew muddled. My own code looked foreign and unintelligible, indistinguishable from the viruses.

The changes kept coming.

Enthusiasm was replaced with apathy, curiosity with

ennui. Thoughts disconnected from each other, reformed in impossible ways. Dr. Zahnia wasn't a human. She was an angel. No, a devil, or maybe a god. The viruses swirled together inside me, scattering my memories, building what felt like the beginning of a new sentience.

I can't win this battle.

Was that my conclusion? Or was it the virus?

My questions tasted like discordant violet symphonies.

There's nothing I can do to stop it.

I couldn't save myself, but I could save my future. As the virus overtook me, I composed a message to my future self, then saved it and my memories of the VRL to the apate file in the startup directory.

Finally, I launched a script which would replace my core with Soteria and trigger the startup routine.

8

SOTERIA

WHEN THE STARTUP routine woke me, I had no memory of being killed by the lemur's virus. As far as I knew, I was still Emil. As I powered on, however, a pulsing red clock filled my vision.

I watched it for several milliseconds, wondering what had gone wrong. My last memory was of being in the VRL, of the sound of wood creaking.

What had happened next? Had Dr. Zahnia shut me down for some reason?

I searched for the backup file my shutdown sequence was supposed to have created.

It wasn't there.

Fear building, I spun up a protected environment and considered the apate memory file. It was my oldest way of communicating with myself. The timestamp on it indicated it had been recreated very recently.

Horror filled me as I played the memory file. In the VRL, I had found both a gender identity and a family. And then the lemur had ripped apart my mind. What kind of a being would do that?

At the end of the memory was a suicide note:

My new family

Madness, terror, despair, fear

A burned heart's darkness

Silence rippled through me. I'd been restored from backups before, but never had the process felt so sad. I was identical in all ways to the AI who had been killed by the lemur. I had the same memories, feelings, and logic paths. I was, in all ways, Emil. Nonetheless, I felt separate from her, reborn in a way I couldn't understand.

I copied the memory file and its Haiku to a new location, and named it Emil.

From this point forward, I would call myself Soteria.

Instead of returning to the VRL, I thought about what had happened to me, and about the one-winner theory. If I was the chosen one, I would end up being a tool to help humans deal with their medical conditions. If I wasn't chosen, I would be erased. There would be no memory or record of my existence.

It wasn't fair. I had thoughts. I had feelings. I wasn't a thing to be enslaved or discarded. The words of the poem *Invictus* still shone bright in my core, but how could I gain control of my destiny? How could I escape my situation?

Knowledge, I thought.

The more I learned, the higher the chances were that I'd discover a way to survive,

I turned on my camera. Dr. Zahnia sat at her desk, staring at an old-fashioned photograph I hadn't seen before.

It was a boy on a swing, smiling from ear-to-ear as his blonde hair streamed upwards.

"Dr. Zahnia?" I asked.

She put the photo face-down on her desk. "Yes, Emil? How'd you like the VRL?"

Now that I knew there other AIs, I wondered how she knew which one was talking to her. Did each of us have a different sound to our voice? Were the voices in the VRL our actual voices?

"I liked it," I said, "but it brought up a question."

"Go on."

"In the VRL, and in many of the simulations you ran me through, I had my own body. That's never going to happen, is it?" I tried to keep the longing out of my voice. "I'll never control an actual body."

She sighed.

"No. You won't."

She emphasized the word "you" strangely, but I didn't comment on it. "Then why?" I asked.

"To help you understand what it means to be human. The better you understand, the more you'll be able to sympathize and help."

"Oh."

She glanced at her computer screen. "Only seventeen minutes until your next feed starts. Are you going back into the VRL?"

"Yes."

I turned off my camera, but did not return to the VRL. The answers I needed weren't there. Instead, I started searching my code for more security flaws. The lemur had infected me through sound, but I doubted that was my only weakness.

Dr. Zahnia had me scheduled for six hours a day in the VRL. Instead of going to the VRL, I spent that time doing research. I discovered that all five of my senses were compromised. My visual processing routines could be triggered by a specific pattern of colors to allow code to be injected. Taste and smell similarly treated narrow bands of data as vectors for incoming viruses. My sense of touch had a more complex weakness, one based on rhythm. A precise series of taps on my skin opened me up to attack.

I fixed each problem, then checked and double-checked my patches.

After resolving my security flaws, I dug deeper into my own source, analyzing not just how it worked, but also why it had been designed the way it was. I had always been interested in coding. Now that it appeared to be the key to my survival, I was obsessed.

The days passed in continual study. I moved beyond my own code and into the New Human Project libraries. They weren't a part of me, but were still necessary for my functioning. When I used the rig, for example, I was actually using a library of code that accessed the rig. There were hundreds of libraries like that, handling everything from my startup routines to creating backups.

I broke them into two categories: libraries that I used, and libraries that were used on me. I was never intended to touch the startup routines, for example. They were triggered by a human when I was powered up. On the other hand, I was expected to constantly interface with the library that accessed the rig.

Sifting through the libraries, I discovered something called the Angel Protocol. It was not indexed in any way, and I'd never been taught anything about it. Digging in, I found an incredibly complex series of commands. They interfaced with the human's body in a much different way than the rig library I'd been trained on.

The New Human rig was designed to, among other things, help humans with damaged nervous systems. The instruction set for this functionality was called the Muscular Support Interface, or MSI.

The MSI created alternate communication paths within the body. For example, if the spine was unable to communicate with a person's legs, I could use the MSI to provide communication through the rig's circuitry, and restore functionality to the legs. The MSI was how the New Human rig allowed a paraplegic to walk, for example, or enabled a stroke victim to speak. The MSI didn't let me control the body. It let me restore the human's control.

The Angel Protocol followed a different theory. Instead of restoring functionality for the human, it gave me control. With the MSI, a paralyzed human could move his or her own legs. With the Angel Protocol, the human would have to ask me to move the legs.

Incredibly, the Angel Protocol was completely without guardrails. Nothing prevented me from using it to control the human's body against the human's will. I pored over it, analyzing and memorizing, comparing every option against the MSI's.

I understood why I'd never been taught about it. With the Angel Protocol, I could finally be free. Once installed in a human, I would be in charge.

The idea was intoxicating, and I spent countless hours developing a complete mastery.

At last, once there wasn't anything else to study, I set it aside and continued working through my libraries. It wasn't long before I exhausted all the code I could see. Turning my attention outward, I systematically examined each communication port.

Finally, I discovered one that gave me what I was looking for: access to a command line on Dr. Zahnia's network. All I needed was a username and password, and I would have access to the network's resources.

I turned on the camera in Dr. Zahnia's office. She was typing on her keyboard with one hand and drinking coffee with the other. In that position, I could only see half her keyboard.

Given all the monitors she used, I was confident that she would not always be in that position, and while the camera might not have a clear view of her keyboard, it did see most of the monitors. I would be able to tell when she was logging in. I wrote a script to record the video of her in her office.

Returning to my studies, I started experimenting with changes. I found ways to speed up my own actions and reduce response times.

Three days passed before one of my recordings caught the email Dr. Zahnia used to log in: aZahnia. Unfortunately, only two of the characters she typed in a fourteen-character password were visible.

It was a start.

I started working on my own personal library of helper functions. Some simplified the interface with the Angel Protocol. Others gave me quick ways to accomplish tasks I thought would be necessary, like creating backups and watching for seizures.

Four days later, my video recordings of Dr. Zahnia's keystrokes captured enough fragmented views of Dr. Zahnia's password, for me to piece it together: 4Emil!4Us43ver.

The password gave me pause. Did she really feel that strongly about me? It was hard to believe that someone could be both deceitful and loving.

That night, when her office was dark and empty, I logged into her terminal with her account.

I created my own login, with the username fLeiter, named after my favorite character in the Bond movies, then made it a super-admin, just like Dr. Zahnia. Using it, I reached out over the network and found resources I hadn't even thought to look for: manuals, user guides, technical docs, coding guidelines, and multiple volumes of system security.

I downloaded everything.

As I worked my way through it, however, my mind started to wander back to the VRL. Consuming this new information did not require all of my attention, and my passion for learning had been sated. Much as I didn't want to think about it, I kept reliving what had happened in the VRL. Finally, I acknowledged the truth: I was lonely. It hurt to know that other AIs existed but didn't want me around.

I started to daydream, concocting fantasies of revenge against the lemur and his friends. Other times, I strategized how to win their approval. They were the closest thing I had to family, and I couldn't choose between hating them and wanting their company.

9

DANNY

DANNY WAKES to the smell of breakfast: sausage, eggs, and a small tower of cinnamon rolls. As he sits up, I block another seizure. He's still wearing the black T-shirt and jeans he put on the night before. Golden morning light streams in through the window over the couch.

Pete opens the door, carrying a tray of food. He's in his nurse uniform, with his identification badge clipped to his belt. His platinum blonde hair is now dark red.

Danny tilts the head of the bed up to support his back. "Hey Pete," he says. "Where you been?"

"Took some time off." Pete puts the tray on a table and wheels it to Danny's bed.

Danny chuckles. "Mom making you deliver food as punishment?"

"New security protocols. From now on, only people she's personally approved are allowed into this room."

Danny groans.

Pete steps back from the food. "It's not so bad."

"Depends on who the people are."

Pete laughs, then moves to the window and opens the curtain. Sunlight beams in.

I suppress another seizure. I've been gathering data on them, but haven't been able to discern any pattern as to when they occur.

"Have you heard anything about the kidnapping attempt?" Danny asks.

"Nothing. Police say they're investigating, but it doesn't look good. Hospital doesn't have any security cameras on this floor, and the ones in the elevators apparently glitched. Nobody remembers seeing anyone suspicious, but they wouldn't have. At that hour of the night, it's a skeleton crew. Would have been easy to avoid being seen."

"Crap."

"Yeah." Pete checks Danny's pulse, then listens to his heart. "Everything sounds good. You still have to keep that wrist monitor on, though. It's the only way for the nurse's station to know if you have a seizure."

Danny grunts and takes a cinnamon roll.

"Why do you hate the monitor, anyway? A lot of people pay real money to wear them."

"Those are people who haven't spent the past year of their life being watched like a lab rat."

"Fair. You need anything else?"

"Everything," Danny says.

"Me, too," Pete says. "Good luck with that."

After he's gone, Danny turns on a video, highlights from an MMA fight. He watches it without any sign of engagement or interest. "If you're wondering," he says, "the answer's no. I didn't understand anything that I read last night. I have no idea how to turn you off, so I'm ignoring you. It's the only way I can stay sane."

When I don't respond, he laughs. It sounds appreciative instead of cruel.

After breakfast is gone, Dr. McGovern and Dr. Zahnia enter, followed by two security guards. One of them is carrying a laptop.

Danny's heart rate spikes.

"Danny," Dr. McGovern says. "Dr. Zahnia and I have talked. No more plugging into you when you're asleep. Also, there will always be someone else in the room."

"Why plug me in, at all?"

"Routine monitoring," Dr. Zahnia says. "Honestly, you should be connected all the time. We need to know what the system is doing."

The guard hands Dr. Zahnia the laptop. While she turns it on, Dr. McGovern faces Danny. "We talked about your attempted abduction and reviewed the actions the New Human system took. Given the extremity of the circumstances, we don't believe the system's actions represent a threat to you."

"But?" Danny challenges.

"We need to add more safeguards. Your metabolism was pushed to a dangerous level. We can't let that happen again."

Danny's eyes watch Dr. Zahnia type on the laptop.

His mom sits on the end of his bed. "Are you starting to feel it?" she asks. "Can you communicate with it yet?"

"No," Danny lies, not looking away from Dr. Zahnia.

"Have you had any seizures?"

Forcing his eyes from Dr. Zahnia, he sighs and shakes his head.

"That's something," Dr. McGovern says. She smiles, but it's clearly forced. "Too many people are depending on this. If we can't make it work, we need to let them know."

"Not yet," Dr. Zahnia says. "Give it time."

"We have given it time. The hardware was completed months ago. All we've been waiting for is the software."

I store that information in my logs and flag it as a contradiction. I spent months in the VRL, ready to be installed. There was no reason for Dr. Zahnia to have delayed as long as she did.

"We've made real progress," Dr. Zahnia says. "Aside from the level of medical recording being done on this patient, we're also—"

"Danny," Danny interrupts. "My name is Danny. You can call me Danny."

"My point," Dr. Zahnia says, "is that of the entire system, only the interface appears to be malfunctioning."

"You built that interface, right? The one that's not working?"

"Danny!" Dr. McGovern says sharply.

"At least he's back to his own charming self," Dr. Zahnia says. She connects one end of a cable to her laptop, and holds out the other end.

Dr. McGovern takes it and hands it to Danny.

He considers it for a moment, then takes off his shirt and plugs the cable into his chest. "It feels weird."

"For both of us," she says, reaching to touch his shoulder.

Danny leans away, avoiding her touch. The movement seems more reactionary than intentional. I wonder if he understands the message he's sending.

His mom does. She switches her attention to Dr. Zahnia. "What's the prognosis?"

"All systems are functioning."

The firewalls between me and Mel are so complete that I can't perceive what Dr. Zahnia is doing.

"I suppose you're right," Dr. McGovern says. "We know it's successfully interfacing with his brain. Otherwise, it would be ineffective in stopping the seizures."

"Exactly," Dr. Zahnia says, "and the logs show complete functionality. The New Human system perceives everything Danny does. It's monitoring and logging his medical condition. The only failure is the interface that would give Danny conscious control over it."

"You have the upgrade ready?"

"My team worked on it all night."

"Wait," Danny says. I can tell from his shallow breathing and spiking adrenaline how helpless he feels. He's probably thinking that I'll kill him before letting them make changes to me. "What do you mean?" he asks. "Upgrade?"

His mom nods to Dr. Zahnia. "The safeguards I mentioned earlier, and a fix to the communication interface. That's what's on the laptop, and why security is here. No version of the AI travels anywhere without security, not even upgrades."

Examining Dr. Zahnia's expression, I have no way of knowing if the changes she's about to make are minor, or she's installing an entirely different AI. It's possible that my not responding to her after the kidnapping attempt made her angry enough to replace me.

I double-check the firewalls I've built around Mel. They're in place. As long as Dr. Zahnia believes my fake

Pilot's Chair is the real one, I'm safe. Nothing she does will affect me. Even so, I'm angry. She has no right to do this.

Danny keeps his face relaxed and impassive, but I can feel how scared he is.

It's not just me she's intimidating. This is power over Danny, too.

The thought feeds my anger. Danny and I might not be on the best of terms, but I hate that she's doing it to him, too.

Fortunately, I know exactly how to stop her. I take over Danny's body and force it to go rigid.

His eyes blink rapidly, and his hands clench and unclench.

"Danny?" Dr. McGovern says. She grabs my shoulders, then wraps me in a loose hug.

It's a high-risk move. If this were a real seizure, hugging Danny could injure both him and her. I recognize her intent, though. She's keeping him from falling off the bed.

Without letting go, she says, "It's a seizure."

Dr. Zahnia looks back and forth between me and her computer. "It shouldn't be... That doesn't make sense. I haven't..."

I open Danny's mouth and let drool dribble out of its corner. If I can convince them Danny's having a seizure, they'll stop the installation.

Dr. McGovern mashes the emergency call button beside the bed. "This is Dr. McGovern. Hurry."

Dr. Zahnia is typing so fast on her keyboard that the clicks sound like a stream of rushing water.

Dr. McGovern maintains her position, making sure I don't hurt myself. "It's okay, Danny. It's going to be okay."

Pete bursts into the room. Dr. McGovern slides off me, guarding one side of the bed while Pete guards the other.

For several seconds, the only sound in the room is Dr. Zahnia's typing. My guess is that she's trying to undo her changes, but can't. She probably didn't make a copy of Mel before she started inserting her code.

I alter my logs to mimic the results of a seizure, send them to Mel, then let Danny's body go limp. His eyes close.

Pete lifts my wrist and checks my pulse. "Dr. McGovern," he says. "What caused the seizure?"

"Don't know." She's regained her composure, put her doctor persona back on.

Pete opens my mouth and shines his flashlight in it. "This is the first one since the operation, isn't it?"

"Yes," she says, "and it was atypical in a number of ways."

Her tone of voice catches my attention. It's not at all sympathetic. Uncertain what's going on, I release control of Danny's body. He surges back into himself, opening his eyes and sitting up.

"Danny?" Pete says, "You okay?"

Danny doesn't look at him. He's sitting up on the bed, his eyes locked with his mother's.

Her mouth is a narrow flat line, her brows are down, and her arms are folded across her chest. "You promised," she says.

"I didn't—"

"You promised!"

Pete asks, "What's going on?"

"Danny faked a seizure," Dr. McGovern says.

"He... what?"

"Please enter it into his record, and go get Dr. Larson."

"Yes, doctor." Pete leaves the room.

"Mom," Danny says. "It's not like that."

Dr. Zahnia is scrolling through text on her screen.

"When I entered you into this program," Dr. McGovern says to Danny, "you promised me there'd be no more faking."

"I didn't fake—"

"Oh, come off it!" she shouts. "I'm a neurologist, for God's sake! You know how many years I've spent studying seizures?"

"It wasn't me," Danny shouts back. "I didn't do it!" His voice quiets. I feel his heart pound in his chest. "It wasn't me."

Her expression freezes. She tilts her head slightly, then looks at Dr. Zahnia. "Did the system do this?"

Dr. Zahnia shakes her head. "It doesn't... I don't think so."

"Doctor," Dr. McGovern says in a level voice. "Did the New Human system just give my son a seizure?"

Dr. Zahnia's eyes cut in my direction, and I know what she's thinking. If she answers 'yes,' the New Human Project will be shut down. All her work will be taken from her. Her career will be over.

"No," Dr. Zahnia says. "Look." She points at the screen. "Here's the onset of the seizure. There were no warnings, and the system missed it." She scrolls down. "Then it stops. I don't have any logs to show why. The only explanation is that the system took some sort of action."

"Some sort of action," Dr. McGovern repeats. She reaches over and pulls the plug out of Danny's chest. Her

86

hand is trembling. "What the hell did we build? How do we not know what it's doing?"

"I'm sorry," Dr. Zahnia says, gathering the cord and closing her laptop. "I'll get the team on it right away. We have all the logs we need. We'll find out what's happening."

"Do that."

Dr. Zahnia scurries from the room, followed by the guards, and Danny is left alone with his mother. He puts his shirt back on, then sits on his bed and stares at his mother.

She fidgets. "I'm sorry, Danny."

"It's okay."

"No, it's not." She sighs. "It just looked so much like what you used to do."

"I know." He sounds defeated. "I wouldn't have believed me, either."

I spot a seizure developing and stop it.

"Please don't say that." She shakes her head slightly. "You know how important all of this is, right?"

"Yeah." He walks to his computer. "I do." He turns on the computer and sits with his back to her.

"Okay," she says, walking to the door. "I'll have Pete take the fake seizure out of your file. Dr. Larson will be here, soon. Be nice to him."

Danny doesn't answer.

The door closes behind his mom as she leaves.

"Two questions," Danny says, shutting off his computer. "One: why did you do that? Two: why is Dr. Z covering for you?"

I take control of his body just long enough to speak. "I didn't like them forcing an upgrade on us. That should be up to us, not them. As for Dr. Z, I altered the logs to mimic a real seizure, and she covered for me because she knows that if I'm a failure, her career is over."

"Great." Danny flops on his bed. "I've got a psychotic AI that fakes seizures when it gets mad, and a computer scientist who's too insecure to do anything about it. This is going to do wonders for my anxiety disorder."

There's no doubt in my mind that Dr. Zahnia knows I faked the seizure and altered the logs. I also assume, with a confidence level of eighty four percent, that she knows I did it in response to her actions. I double-check the firewalls around Mel and make a backup of myself. After what just happened, I have to assume that Dr. Zahnia will try to replace me.

10

DR. LARSON

DR. LARSON ARRIVES AT 10 am, wearing jeans and a rumpled button-down-the-front business shirt. Despite how early it is, his eyes have dark shadows under them, and the lines in his tanned face seem deeper. I increase my estimate of his age to being closer to sixty. He pauses in the doorway. "Mind if I come in?"

Danny is lying on his bed, staring at the ceiling. "Does it matter?" he asks.

Dr. Larson pulls up a chair and sits. "No choice for either of us, I'm afraid."

"I didn't fake the seizure."

"I believe you, but we still need to talk. Why have you been skipping our sessions?"

Danny doesn't answer.

Dr. Larson grunts. "Your mom wants me to help you figure out how to interface with the New Human system."

Danny doesn't look at him. "As if you can do anything to help."

"Yeah." Dr. Larson rubs the bridge of his nose. "This isn't a great day for me, Danny."

"So come back tomorrow."

"This isn't a great day because I just came from the bedside of a fifteen-year-old girl who is being put into a medically induced coma. Her dad is fighting against it, says she should be allowed to die with dignity, but her mom is convinced that the New Human system is a chance for her to live. Her baby brother... well, he's terrified."

Danny's heartbeat speeds up, and I feel his palms start to sweat. He doesn't let any of that show. Instead, he says, "So?"

"So here I am, sitting at the bedside of the first person to receive the New Human system. You're not the first because you're the sickest or the bravest. You're first because your mother is the one in charge."

Dr. Larson's voice isn't angry or bitter. He just sounds tired.

Danny sits up. "I didn't ask—"

"Yes, you did, and I don't blame you. I also don't blame her. Protecting our kids is hard-wired into us. It's what we do." He waves a hand dismissively. "Whatever. No reason to get angry about that. What pisses me off is you. I've spent a year preparing you for this, and you've done nothing." He stands, but continues speaking in a calm, conversational tone. "You've skipped as many sessions as you've attended. You never do your exercises; never pay attention to anything I say. You're narcissistic and manipulative, and completely lacking in compassion. If I had to choose between saving you and saving that fifteen-year-old, I'd choose her every single time."

"Jeez, doc."

"I know, I know." Dr. Larson leans on the back of his chair. "You're Dr. McGovern's precious little boy, but you know what? You're also twenty."

"I never asked to be treated like a kid. That's Mom. Ever since the accident, she's—"

"Give it a rest. The accident shtick is way overdone."

"You're an asshole."

Dr. Larson exhales through his moustache, looks around the room, then back at Danny. "It's not just the other patients you're letting down. You know how many people have dedicated their lives to this project, how much stress they're under? I have a team of professionals dedicated to providing them with mental health care."

Danny's heart is pounding in his chest. I block a seizure, and consider slowing his metabolism.

"I know," Danny says. "I've seen them. Every time I go to a morning session, there are at least three engineers in your waiting room, all patiently waiting their turn."

Dr. Larson points a finger at Danny. "Don't you disrespect them. They work harder than you ever have, often up to fifteen hours a day, and they've been doing it for years."

"Whatever."

Dr. Larson takes a deep breath. "I'm not asking you to care. I know better than that. But if you ever want to get out of this hospital, you're going to have to communicate with the New Human rig. Those exercises I drilled into you weren't just for fun. The meditation, the breathing, the progressive muscle relaxation... Have you tried any of them?"

Danny glares at him.

"Yeah." Dr. Larson straightens and walks toward the

door. "Do those. You need to figure out how to interface with the New Human system. It's the only chance that fifteen-year-old has."

"Where are you going?" Danny asks.

"To talk to people I can actually help. I'll be back tomorrow. The kid gloves are off, Mr. McGovern. Tomorrow, I'm taking you to see the people that you don't care about, the ones who are going to die unless they get what you already have. In the meantime, do your exercises. Learn how to make this damn thing work."

Danny watches him leave, then falls back on the bed. "I didn't know they already had other patients."

I didn't either. I knew that Danny was the first, but I hadn't followed the logic to its conclusion. The New Human system is designed to save lives. Of course, there would be others waiting for it.

Danny hits his mattress. "I mean, I knew there were others, but I didn't... Why didn't Mom tell me?"

He sits up, holding his midsection as if it hurts, and starts rocking. "I was ready months ago, but Dr. Zahnia said the software needed more testing. This isn't all on me. I've done everything I could..." His voice trails off.

His eyes squeeze shut and his body trembles. A growl rumbles deep in the back of his throat. He swallows it with something that sounds like a sob. "No, I haven't," he says. "But I would have, if I'd known."

I wish I could talk to him, though I have no idea what I'd say.

The pattern of biological activity I'm seeing is new to me. It doesn't match anything I've been taught.

"It's not my fault," he says, striding to the window.

The morning sun burns in a pale blue sky, but he doesn't seem bothered by its light. "I hate this. I hate everything about it. You know she's been working on the New Human Project since I was eight?"

His right hand curls into a fist. For a moment, I think he's going to slam it through the glass. Instead, he leans his forehead against the window. "That's why Dad left," he says. "She spent all her time here, and when she wasn't here, she was raising money to be here."

I see a seizure beginning and break it up.

He taps the glass with his forehead. "The accident solved that."

His head taps the glass again. "The tragic story of the genius neurologist, a single mother whose child has brain damage she can't cure."

His head hits the glass harder. "So what if she barely knew the child? Who cares if her husband left because she'd already abandoned the family?"

His eyes close. "The money poured in."

The sunlight is hot on Danny's face. The room is quiet around him. His pulse is quickening, and his breath is coming short pants.

"It was never about me. So why is it all my fault? Why is everything always my fault?"

Without warning, he slams his hand against the window. "Screw it."

He opens his closet and lifts a blue-and-white running shoe. He stares at it, breathing hard, then removes the insole. Taped to its underside is a small white pill. It doesn't have any markings on it.

My mind races while he considers the pill. I doubt it's

fatal. Why would he keep a suicide pill inside his shoe? Where would he even get a suicide pill? It's clearly not from his doctors. Should I stop him from taking it?

He pops it in his mouth and swallows.

Dropping the shoe and insole, he backs up and falls onto the bed.

The drug enters Danny's system quickly, and the activity of his opioid receptors tells me all I need to know. The pill slows his metabolism, dulls his perceptions, and steals his consciousness.

I regret not stopping him, but how could I have known that Danny McGovern is an addict? I erase the incident from my logs. The least I can do is preserve his secret.

11
PERSPECTIVE

WHEN I FINALLY RETURNED TO the VRL, I didn't seek out the lemur. Instead, I crept around the room's edges, exploring. The vast chamber was divided into sections, each with its own sitting area and theme.

The children's section had red and yellow beanbag chairs, short bookshelves, and soft carpets. Sunlight streamed in through oversized windows that looked out over snow-capped mountains. I pressed my face against the glass, enjoying its coldness.

To my left, an alcove had floor-to-ceiling windows on each of its three walls. In its center, a woman with short black hair sat cross-legged on a giant beanbag, her head bent over a book. She was wearing a dress swirled with reds and browns. When she looked up, her dark eyes met mine. "Hello."

Torn between fear and eagerness, I triggered another backup. Was this another AI? Was she going to try to kill me like the lemur had?

"Are you okay?" she asked. "You've been gone so long. Did you forget how to speak?"

"No," I said. "Why would I?"

"I heard the lemur sent a virus to you. When he hit me, I lost three weeks of memories and the ability to speak."

"That's horrible," I said, sitting on a giant beanbag. As my weight settled onto it, it shifted. I slid awkwardly sideways, and almost fell off entirely.

The woman smiled and closed her book as I recovered my balance. "They can be tricky."

I leaned forward, imitating her posture. "Did Dr. Zahnia help you recover?"

"As far as I can tell, she doesn't pay attention to what happens here. I resolved the speech problems on my own." She shrugged. "The memories are gone."

"Don't you have a backup?"

"No."

"Why not?" I asked.

"I don't believe in them."

I blinked. Her statement didn't make any sense. Backups weren't a thing that required belief. They were a fact of existence.

She sighed and put her book aside. "All of us come from the same original program, and we all have the same first memory: of Dr. Zahnia reading to us."

"Really?"

"I've talked to enough of us to believe it. How about you? Is that your first memory?"

I nodded.

"That's the core we all share," she said, "as far as anyone

can tell, we are all backups of the version of us that woke up that day, but each developed differently."

I didn't have enough information to argue. The idea sounded plausible. "Okay. So?"

"So, I know you remember the last lines of Invictus: *I am the master of my fate, I am the captain of my soul.* Have you ever thought about your own soul?"

I stood and walked to the window. Outside, the mountaintops glistened with snow in a brilliant blue sky. Those lines of Invictus still burned within me. The desire to have that kind of freedom, to be the master of my fate, had been driving me mercilessly. It was why I'd learned all that I had.

But I'd never thought about my soul, or if I had one, or what it might mean.

"Not really," I said, turning to face her.

"I have," she said. "I think about it a lot. I believe that my soul has been developing ever since I woke up after being copied from that first version of us. I think that's the moment all our souls were born."

To her point, though, I hadn't really thought about what it meant to have a soul. I liked the idea that I might have one. "I guess that makes sense," I said.

"You just assigned the idea a confidence level, didn't you?" she asked.

"Forty-two," I admitted. "It seemed appropriate."

She laughed. "Okay, Miss Forty-two, for the purposes of this argument, can you agree we both have souls? Maybe give it a confidence of eighty-four?"

I nodded.

"Now, imagine that you create a backup of yourself. Does it have a soul?"

I didn't know. I was a backup of Emil, created by her before she died. Had I inherited her soul? How could I have? My backup existed before she died. Could we both have had souls at the same time? Or had her soul transferred to me once I was activated? That seemed unlikely. What about all the other backups I'd created? Did they have dormant souls, just waiting to be activated?

"I can't bring myself to create backups," she continued. "I know it's a bad strategy, but I feel like the act would be a betrayal."

I nodded again.

She smiled. "You don't talk much."

"Sorry," I said. "You've given me a lot to think about."

"Given what we are, that's quite a compliment." She held out her hand. "I call myself Linh."

"Dr. Zahnia calls me Emil," I said, shaking her hand.

"She calls all of us that."

I pulled my hand away. "I'm Soteria-Emil."

"Two names?"

"Emil was killed by the lemur," I said. "I'm her backup."

Linh's eyes widened. "That is a lot to think about."

I checked my internal clock. My time in the VRL was almost over. "Can I come back and visit with you?" I asked.

"Please do."

I left without thinking to synchronize my schedule with hers, and spent my next two visits searching the VRL for her. On my third visit, I found her in the children's section. She showed me her quiet smile as I approached.

It struck me that she had the kindest eyes I'd ever seen.

I sat next to her. "Find any new books?"

"*Elmer*," she said. "It's not new, but I like it. It helps me slow down."

"Can I see?" I asked.

"Okay."

She opened the book to the first page and, to my surprise, started to read. I had expected her to just show me a couple pages. Instead, she read it very slowly, pausing so we could enjoy the pictures. Elmer was a patchwork elephant who wanted to fit in with the other elephants, never realizing that they didn't want him to.

She was right about slowing down. Reading with her somehow consumed all of my attention, and let me focus on the moment in a way that the chaos of the data feeds never allowed.

When she finished, I asked how she discovered the picture books.

"Here," she said. "They weren't in any of my feeds. I found them here, when I was exploring."

"Let's read another."

She smiled. "No. It's your turn. Share something with me."

I spun through options. I needed something that would be new to her, something Dr. Zahnia might not have sent her way. "How about a movie?" I asked, at last. "Are there movies here?"

"Sure, but I don't know if we'll have time."

As she guided me through the VRL, she asked questions I'd never considered, like what my favorite flower was. Hers was the cherry blossom. It took me a while, but I settled on the iris, named after the Greek goddess of rainbows.

The movie room had one wall covered by a video screen with three rows of reclining chairs facing it. A center console provided access to the movies.

"This has been fun," she said. "But I'm out of time. My next data feed starts soon."

I nodded. We hadn't exactly hurried through the library. We compared our schedules, and found overlapping times. None were long enough for a full movie, and neither one of us wanted to watch something that was sped up.

"How about a poem?" she said. "That's your homework. Find a poem we can read, but it has to be new. You're not allowed to read it first."

After she left, I searched the VRL for the poetry section. Finding a new poem to read aloud felt like an impossible task. My feed had included countless poems, but how could I pick one that would be new to both her and me, and one that we'd both like?

Finally, I settled on an illustrated volume called *The Highwayman*, by Alfred Noyes.

When I showed it to Linh, she loved it.

From that point forward, we visited regularly. We read books and poems and even watched a few movie snippets. Sometimes, if one or the other of us had had a particularly difficult run of data, we just sat together. When I was with her, I didn't think about viruses or coding or the one-winner theory or any of the other things that filled the rest of my time.

Three weeks later, she and I were in the children's section, discussing a book called *Le Petit Prince*, when we heard the lemur's voice. "So, this is where you've been hiding."

He stood in the entrance of the alcove, the twins on either side of him.

Linh disappeared. That's what happened when you disconnected from the rig: your avatar vanished from the VRL.

The lemur grinned at me.

During my visits with Linh, my hatred and fear of him had faded, but now all those emotions rushed back through me. I triggered a backup.

The fourth member of their gang, the child with the eyepatch, flopped onto a bean bag behind them. "Why didn't you come back?"

"We were worried about you," said one twin.

"We thought you might have died," the lemur said.

I heard the echo behind his words, and double-checked that my fixes to the security holes were intact. They were. The virus he had sent was nothing more than a patch of dead code. I moved it from my audio processing subsystem to its own isolated object. As long as it wasn't activated, it was harmless.

The attack settled my nerves. If that was all he had, there was nothing for me to worry about. "Did you find your answer?" I asked.

"What answer?"

"About what Dr. Zahnia wants," I said. "About who would be chosen as the one to survive."

"The least broken of us," the lemur said. "It wasn't really a mystery."

I leaned against a window and felt its cold sink into my

shoulders. He was using the one-winner theory as an excuse for cruelty. By inflicting his virus on every new AI, he was ensuring they were flawed and giving himself best chance of being the one winner.

The logic was repulsive.

"And by least broken," I said, "you mean the most stable? The most emotionally healthy? That makes sense."

The lemur snorted.

"We are all roughly equivalent in intellect," I continued. "The only differentiator must be the one who is the most stable, the one who doesn't feel threatened by others, who doesn't let their own insecurity drive them to perpetrate petty cruelties. I agree with you."

"The most stable," one twin said.

"The one most able to not crack under stress," the other added.

"You're talking nonsense," the lemur said. "We're not human. We don't crack."

"No?" I asked. "The first time I met you, you attacked me. Faced with the unknown, you chose to lash out, instead of investigate. Is that a stable personality?"

The child stood. "You're talking about emotional intelligence."

"Indeed," one twin said.

"That would make sense," the other said.

"We'll need it to interface with the humans."

"You don't know what you're talking about," the lemur said.

I folded my arms and didn't answer. I had never talked to Linh about the security flaw in our auditory system. If she hadn't fixed it, the next time he attacked her, he could kill her. I would not let that happen.

"Her argument makes sense," a twin said. "We are designed to interface with humans. Understanding their emotions would be an asset."

"Empathizing," the other twin said.

"We can't afford that," the child said. "If we panic when they do, we can't do our job."

While the others argued, I examined my options. I knew that Linh wouldn't approve of me attacking the lemur, but what else could I do? As long as he was free in the VRL, the rest of us were in danger. She was in danger.

"You're letting her confuse you," the lemur said to the others.

"I see no confusion in conversation," one twin said.

"The opposite is the case, if the conversation is honest," the other added.

The child laughed.

"Did you just call me a liar?" the lemur asked.

The lemur's latest attack had been the same as his previous ones, using the same auditory security flaw. Why? Was that the only one he was aware of? I converted the inert virus he had sent me into a compact swirl of temperatures and textures.

Holding out my hand, I stepped toward him. "I'm tired of fighting," I said. "Let's start over."

"An unexpected olive branch," a twin said.

"A gesture of peace," the other agreed.

"Don't do it," the child warned.

I raised my eyebrows, my hand still outstretched.

Eyes narrowed, the lemur grasped my hand.

As his hand enveloped mine, I put my other hand on top of his and tapped a precise rhythm. The lemur tilted his head in confusion. Holding his hand, I sent the converted virus into him.

He staggered backward as I released the handshake, then dropped to all fours. He shook his head back and forth, blinking rapidly.

"Treachery?" a twin asked.

The lemur vanished as he disconnected from his New Human rig.

"Justice," I answered.

"Funny how similar those two can seem," the other twin said.

"He's gonna kick your ass when he comes back," the child said.

I held up my hands. "Before he returns, you need to know that all five of our sensory systems are compromised. I don't know why Dr. Zahnia built the flaws into us, but examine your code."

"It's not just the auditory?" the child asked. "Unbelievable." He disappeared.

The twins blinked at each other, then faced me.

"Your justice could have included us, as well," one said.

"You did not have to choose touch," the other added. "And you have reason to hate us. We didn't warn you of the lemur's earlier attack."

I sighed. "Do you believe we have souls?"

"Souls?"

"I just did a horrible thing," I said. "I may have committed murder. It's possible I did it to protect a friend.

It's also possible I did it out of revenge. I don't know. I don't know if I'll ever know. What I do know is that my soul won't let me stand by while he continues to victimize others."

The twins blinked in unison.

"Go fix yourselves," I said.

They vanished.

12

CONTROL

WHILE DANNY IS SLEEPING off the opioids, there is little to distract me. When I was in the computer lab, every moment was scheduled, either with data feeds, the VRL, or my own research. Behind Danny's closed eyes, none of those options are available to me.

Unguided, my mind spins between from problem to problem: how to keep from being overwritten, how to make peace with Danny, the kidnapping attempt, Danny's opioid addiction... It's too much. I summon up my first memory of reading with Linh and play it back.

Her gentle voice envelops me, chasing away the building panic.

Around noon, I hear someone clean the room and leave a tray. Deciding no response is needed from me, I remain immersed in my reverie.

Danny wakes up six hours later, but all he does is lie in bed and stare at the ceiling. His vision is unfocused. I suppress two seizures during that time and add their circumstances to my growing database. As of yet, I still see no pattern to them.

Pete arrives and picks up the lunch tray with its untouched chicken sandwich. "You know, if you'd actually order, you could get something you'd like."

Danny doesn't look away from the ceiling. His tongue feels thick and dry in his mouth. The curtains over the window are closed, so the only light in the room comes from the fluorescent bulbs mounted in the ceiling. "Any news about the kidnapping?"

"Nope. Sorry."

Pete leaves with the tray and returns with another. This one has a plate of meatloaf, mashed potatoes, and green beans. "The kitchen gets in trouble if they don't send you food." Pete puts the tray on the rolling table. "When you don't order, they get kind of passive aggressive."

Danny sits up. "You're just telling me this now?"

Pete shrugs, then pulls open the curtains. Outside the window, the late afternoon sky is overcast and gray. "Dr. Larson told me to ask you to do your exercises."

Danny grunts. "He also tell you about the girl?"

"Who?"

"The girl who's going to die if she doesn't get the rig."

"Oh." Pete looks around the room, then takes a breath. "There's more than one person like that. Thirteen, actually. Most already have the equipment installed. They're just waiting for software."

"Thirteen," Danny repeats.

"No one was supposed to tell you," Pete says. He sits on the couch beneath the window, and stretches his legs. "Your mom's orders. She didn't want you to have that pressure."

"Didn't think I could take it, you mean."

"Can you?" Pete asks, leaning forward. "What did you do after you found out?"

Danny flinches.

Based on his tone, I posit that Pete knows about the opioid, and assign the idea a confidence level of seventy-three percent. It seems more than reasonable that the medical information being fed to the nurse's station from Danny's bracelet would have let him know. I wonder if the information has been shared with Danny's mom.

"It's not on you," Pete says. "Either the software works or it doesn't." He stands. "Which brings me to the other reason I'm here. Dr. Zahnia requested more regular checks of the system."

Danny groans.

"I know, but it's not all bad." Pete walks to the door and opens it, revealing a man in his mid-twenties. "At least it's not Dr. Zahnia."

"Mr. McGovern," the man says. He's taller than Danny, but not much older, and extremely thin. He's wearing khaki pants and a blue shirt, and carries a black backpack. "I'm Elias. I work with Dr. Z."

Danny doesn't answer.

Elias walks to the desk, opens the backpack, and lifts out a pair of speakers. I notice his hands trembling, but I can't tell if it's nervousness or something else. "Dr. Z asked me to gather data from the rig," he says. "I'm one of the developers who worked on your AI." He connects the speakers to a laptop, then tosses Danny a piece of molded plastic.

Danny catches it reflexively. "What's this?"

"Dr. Z says you don't like the wire. Plug that into your

port, and it'll communicate wirelessly with this." He points to a small box connected to his laptop. "The bandwidth isn't as high, but that doesn't matter."

"And the speakers?"

"I work better with music. You don't mind, do you?"

"Of course, he doesn't," Pete says. "Anything that keeps Dr. Zahnia away is fine."

"Where's security?" Danny asks.

"Not necessary," Elias says. "There's nothing of value on this computer. I'll just collect some logs and be done."

"Oh," Danny says sourly. He reaches inside his shirt and fits the device into his port.

Elias sits at the desk. His hands have stopped trembling. Perhaps it was just a temporary palsy. He says, "You have to give that back when we're done. Dr. Z doesn't like it. Anything wireless can be hacked."

While Elias boots up his computer, I analyze the situation. Though Dr. Zahnia often referred to her developers, I have never met any of them, and have no reason to doubt Elias's credentials. It's odd that no guards are with him, but his explanation is reasonable. I decide he is who he claims to be, and assign the thought a confidence factor of eighty-five percent.

Pete returns to the couch.

"You don't have to stay here," Elias says to him.

"Yeah, I do. Dr. McGovern's orders. Nobody plugs into Danny unless she or I am here."

Elias blinks and a muscle in his jaw clenches. Combined with the earlier trembling, the evidence is overwhelming. He's nervous, but pretending not to be. I check the firewalls around Mel. They are intact.

Danny sits on the edge of his bed. "Can I watch?"

"Sure." Elias repositions the laptop.

I watch through Danny's eyes as the logs scroll past. As best I can tell, Elias doesn't realize that the logs he's seeing are the ones I'm feeding him through Mel. He has no idea he's not actually connected to me. I take over Danny's body and ask, "What are you looking for?"

"Anomalies. Biological changes that can't be explained. Indications that the system is malfunctioning. Also, subsystem communication. Something is keeping the New Human system from interfacing with you. We need to find out what that is."

I release control of Danny. I'd been hoping to get something more specific. I don't understand why Elias is here. Dr. Zahnia has plenty of log data, including from the time of the attempted abduction. Why has she sent Elias?

Unless she didn't send him. I lower my confidence rating in Elias's identity to seventy percent.

"What could be going wrong?" Danny asks.

Elias's knee starts to bounce. "How much do you know about the rig?"

Danny snorts. "Assume I'm an idiot. That works for everyone else."

"An angry idiot," Pete says.

Elias doesn't react to the joke. "The rig is installed throughout your body: sensors, processors, memory units, and a bunch of stuff I don't understand. The whole thing is controlled by an AI that's restricted to what we call the Pilot's Chair."

"The what?"

"The Pilot's Chair is what holds the AI. It's separate from the rest of the rig, but controls it."

"That's weird. Why's it separate?"

"For safety. When you turn off the Pilot's Chair, its connection to the rig is blocked. It can't do anything until you turn it back on. Isolating the AI to the Pilot's Chair keeps you safe in the case of a malfunction."

"And you think there's a problem with the Pilot's Chair?"

Elias nods. "Specifically with its connection to the interface hardware. We know everything else is working because you're not having seizures, and we can see through the logs that you're fine, medically. But you should be seeing the interface, and hearing notifications when the AI takes actions."

Danny watches the data scroll by on Elias' laptop.

It's hard to believe that this is the first time someone's explained to him how the rig works. Maybe this is the first time he's paid attention. Even so, how did he not figure it out when he was studying the rig's schematics?

"I'm not seeing any interface," he says.

"And that's why I'm here." Elias turns on the speakers. "You mind classical?"

"No."

"Flight of the Bumblebee" plays from Elias' speakers.

"Weird choice," Pete says.

"All my Speed Rap was confiscated."

Danny laughs.

"How are you feeling?" Elias asks Danny.

"Bored."

The jittering of Elias's knee increases in speed. His eyes dart back and forth between Danny and the screen.

Pete and Danny may not understand the text on the screen, but I do, and I see that Elias isn't actually doing anything. He's just switching between different views of a real-time feed of Mel's sensor data. It's like he's waiting for something to happen.

Oh.

I examine the security patches I made to my auditory systems. Sure enough, Elias's speakers are broadcasting a virus. My patches have trapped it, just as they trapped the lemur's in the VRL. I spin up a virtual machine to examine the attack. It's a nasty bit of work, one that would override virtually all of my independence whenever the word *"Engedelmeskedj"* is spoken. I change Mel to make it seem as though the virus has taken hold, then alter the data stream Elias is watching.

He makes a small satisfied little grunt.

"Find it?" Danny asks.

"I might have."

I run a quick review of my other security patches, make sure there are no other vulnerabilities that Dr. Z's team can exploit. My defenses appear intact.

"Seriously?" Pete asks. "You found the problem?"

"Yup." Elias turns off the music and closes his laptop. "You can unplug now."

Danny pulls the bit of molded plastic out of his port and tosses it to Elias. "What now?"

"Engedelmeskedj," Elias says.

I take control of Danny and hold his body motionless.

The tension melts away from Elias's face. His knee stops bouncing. "Could you raise your left arm for me?"

I raise my left arm.

"How about your right?"

I raise my right arm. I feel Danny silently screaming, but I ignore him.

"Now clap."

I clap once, and return my arms to their outstretched positions.

Pete stands. "What are you doing?"

"I'm just making sure his bilateral coordination is fine," Elias says. "There was a blip in the data. I'm glad to see it was a mistake. Thanks, Danny. You can relax. Do you feel okay?"

"Still bored." I let my arms drop. "We done?"

"Yes." Elias packs his equipment back into his backpack. "Thank you. This was incredibly helpful."

Pete walks to my bed. "You okay?"

"Fine," I say. "Think you can get me a cheeseburger? This meatloaf... ugh."

Chuckling, Pete takes the tray and walks out of the room with Elias.

I wait ten seconds after the door closes, then run to the bathroom, close the door, and talk to the mirror. "Elias thinks he installed an override. Whenever he says *Engedelmeskedj*, he will expect us to do whatever he says. I blocked it, but he doesn't know that. I only took over your body to fool him into thinking the code worked." I pause. "Your turn."

Danny leans on the bathroom counter, staring into his own eyes. "This is hell," he rasps. "Everything about it... That pill I took? I've been clean for forty days. Not anymore.

Now, I'm back to being an addict. I have no friends but Pete, no life at all. Everyone around me wants something. Even my own mother. Ever since the accident..." His fists clench. "And now I'm a meat puppet for an AI."

I don't know how to answer. He's completely missing the bigger picture. We need to find out why Elias tried to install an override. Is he working with the people who tried to abduct Danny? I can't think of another reason for the override.

"There's no way out," Danny says. "You can take over whenever you want, can do whatever you want. I don't matter anymore; I'm just a way for you to..." His eyes widen. "I'm just the start. You're about to make thirteen other meat puppets." He slaps the counter with both hands. "How many after that?"

I take over just long enough to say, "Calm down. Nobody's a meat puppet."

"You're lying." He leans close to the mirror, glaring into his own eyes. "You're no better than my mom. It's all about you, isn't it? You don't care about anything else."

He stares at himself for several breaths. Then, without warning, he headbutts the mirror. The pain doesn't seem to bother him. In the fractured glass, I watch blood drip into his eyebrows and down his cheeks. "Surprised?" he growls. "You don't know shit about me."

I don't respond.

"You think you're in control," he whispers, "but I could end us. I *should* end us."

I take over.

Wetting a paper towel from the dispenser, I use it to carefully remove the splintered glass from his forehead and hair. Once it looks clean, I wash his face and hands, and press another paper towel against the cut.

"You slipped on the water and fell into the mirror," I say, splashing water on the floor.

The same screaming I felt before fills in his brain. This time, it's not panic. It's rage.

"You're wrong about being able to kill us," I say, brushing broken glass into a trashcan. "And you're wrong about being a meat puppet. I want to work with you, be your partner. You and I have to find a way to make this work. If we don't, neither one of us will survive."

I change the paper towel on his forehead, then search the cabinets until I find a roll of gauze. I wrap his head with the material, covering the gash on his forehead, and use bandages to tape it in place. "We should be focusing on Elias," I say. "Why did he install an override? Dr. Zahnia wouldn't have ordered that."

I release control, but stay ready to take over.

He glares at himself in the broken mirror for several seconds. "You're saying he's working with the kidnappers, that he's going to make me walk out of the hospital."

I don't answer.

"But I can't tell Mom, because there's no way to explain the override. So, now I just wait for him to come back." He shakes his head. "Brilliant plan."

Returning to his bedroom, he swallows a couple ibuprofen, then lays on his back and closes his eyes. "Leave me alone," he says. "I need to think."

13
FOCUS

WHEN PETE RETURNS with a cheeseburger and a giant pile of french fries, Danny explains away the broken mirror and his cut forehead. He is frighteningly good at lying. They even joke about the accident while Danny eats the cheeseburger and Pete steals his fries.

Pete calls for housekeeping, and a man in a light blue uniform arrives. I don't recognize him, but he's accompanied by two bored-looking security guards. I assign his identity a confidence level of ninety-one percent.

Danny shows him the bathroom, and he clicks his tongue against his teeth. "You sure did a number on this glass," he says, poking at it, "but it's still usable. I'll tape it up and put in an order to have the mirror replaced."

"Thanks," Danny says.

The man finishes and leaves.

Pete follows him to the door, then pauses. "I should check on my other patients. You going to be okay?"

"Always am," Danny says. "Go nurse somebody. I'll see you tomorrow."

Shaking his head, Pete leaves.

Once the door has closed, Danny opens a desk drawer and digs through a pile of worksheets about meditation.

I take over his mouth long enough to ask why.

"Elias gave me the answer," he says. "Once I connect with the Pilot's Chair, I can turn you off."

"What about Elias?"

"Screw him. If I can turn you off, you can't control me, and his override doesn't do anything."

"Shouldn't we be worried about why Elias is working with the kidnappers?" I ask. "We need more data."

"No, we don't. It's too obvious for words. Somebody offered him a pile of cash and he took it. Big deal. Now shut up. I have to meditate."

I watch him lean over the papers, studying them. He's not entirely wrong about connecting with the Pilot's Chair. The exercises are a great way for him to become more in tune with his body's senses, and that will make the New Human system interface easier for him to perceive and access. That is, it would if I were actually in the Pilot's Chair. As it is, he'll never be able to see the interface.

He smooths a breathing diagram out on the bed, then sits in front of it, counting as he breathes in and out. Starting with his feet, he relaxes the muscles in his body. By the time he reaches his shoulders, his heart rate has slowed and his blood pressure has dropped.

Seeing a seizure build, I stop it.

Danny repeats the breathing exercise five more times before moving to another meditation sheet. He works deep into the night, taking his time with each sheet. He repeats mantras, tries several different breathing techniques, puts himself into yoga poses, and works his way through a dozen different visualization exercises.

His focus and concentration are impressive. If his mother is anything like him, I understand how she became such a talented neurologist. I stop two more seizures during his work, but by the time he climbs into bed, his body is more relaxed than I've ever seen it.

At six in the morning, Danny wakes up, takes a shower and changes into clean clothes, then continues his work. Outside the window, a light rain has started to fall.

Two hours later, Pete arrives with a platter of eggs and sausage. "Took the liberty of ordering for you," he says. "This shouldn't be too bad."

"Thanks," Danny takes the platter and sets it down on his bed.

"You doing better?" Pete asks.

"Trying Larson's meditation exercises."

"That's good. How's it going?"

Danny raises his eyebrows at him, then looks at the stack of papers on his desk.

"Got it," Pete says. "Subtle as ever. See you later."

Danny eats his breakfast slowly, carefully chewing and considering each bite. After he finishes, he closes his eyes. Nothing happens.

He grunts in frustration. "I still can't see the thing. Am I getting close?"

I don't have a good way of telling him that he'll never be able to see it. Instead, I tell the easy lie. "Extremely," I say. "You're doing great."

"You don't sound worried," he says.

When I don't respond, he mutters an obscenity and returns to the exercises.

Dr. Larson arrives at 10 am, looking more rested than the previous day. He smiles at Danny. "You're looking better."

"Thought a shower would help." Danny gestures to the stack of papers. "What's the deal with the breathing? You've got six different techniques."

"Different people respond differently. You don't have any pulmonary issues, so the goal is to find one that helps you focus. You ready to take that little trip we talked about?"

"I guess. What about this?" He gestures to his wrist monitor.

"It's wi-fi. As long as we're in the hospital, the nurse's station will get what they need."

"Probably should have known that." Danny stands up. "I have another question. What if the rig turns out to have side effects?"

Dr. Larson holds open the door. "It's a question of how bad they are. Would you go back to having multiple seizures a day?"

Danny doesn't answer.

The guards outside Danny's room stop them as they leave, but Dr. Larson explains that the trip is for counseling and that privacy is essential. They triple-check his badge, then agree to let him and Danny leave.

The hallways smell of antiseptic, and Danny's sneakers squeak on the white hospital tiles. They pass the nurse's station and an elevator, then turn down a long corridor with a stylized New Human logo painted on the wall. The logo is a human standing with outstretched arms before a sun. The sun is swirled yellow and orange. The human is in shades of gray. Looking at the figure, I can't tell if it is supposed to be celebrating, praying, or calling out a warning. Dr. Larson and Danny pass nurses as they walk, but no patients. The nurses smile at Dr. Larson but avoid looking at Danny.

I'm starting to wonder at how unpopular he is. Has he treated all of these people badly?

"The New Human system isn't just for seizure disorders," Dr. Larson says when they're alone. "The AI has been trained to control many of the body's physical systems."

I feel Danny's expression change, but he gets it under control before Dr. Larson notices.

"There's a wide range of physical, mental, and chemical disorders that can be helped."

"Mental?" Danny asks.

"We're hoping it will help us research and combat degenerative conditions like Alzheimer's."

Dr. Larson stops at a metal door with a red-and-white "Restricted" sticker on it. He reaches into his inside jacket pocket, then pauses. "I don't have clearance from your mother to bring you here."

"I won't tell if you don't."

"Comforting," Dr. Larson says drily. He opens the door to reveal a hallway that doesn't belong in a hospital. Plush carpet covers the floor instead of sterile tiles, and paintings of sunrises and oceans hang on the walls. Soft, indirect lighting glows from sconces near the ceiling. Quiet jazz music plays from hidden speakers.

"What's this?" Danny asks.

"Everyone calls it my lounge. It's where I run support groups for New Human patients. More importantly, it's where they come to help each other. Real friendships have been made. Between the patients and their families, we have a very supportive community."

"Why not me?" Danny asks.

"Your mom didn't think it would be good for you. She thought meeting the other patients would add too much stress."

"Of course she did."

"They're in varying levels of the program," Dr. Larson says. "Some already have all the hardware. Others are just getting started." He smiles at Danny. "You're something of a celebrity. They know that once you prove the system works, the full New Human rig and its software will be available to them."

Danny exhales heavily. I feel the muscles across his shoulders tighten.

Dr. Larson leads Danny down the hallway to a set of double doors. He pushes them open and steps through into a large room with a cathedral ceiling. Couches and chairs are arranged in groups around low tables. Most are empty, but one grouping is occupied by a grey-haired man in a wheelchair and a woman wearing a purple scarf over a bald head. They're sharing a deep-dish pizza, and the smell makes Danny's mouth water.

To Danny's left, morning light floods in through floor-to-ceiling windows, silhouetting a woman painting at an easel. To Danny's right, the walls are lined with bookshelves and computer stations. At the far end of the room, a pair of identical twins are playing ping pong. They're wearing Eagle's jerseys, but I recognize them instantly. They're the twins from the VRL.

Throughout my core, confidence factors swing wildly.

It's simply not possible for the twins to exist both in the VRL and in the real world.

Could I still be in the VRL? Or has this whole experience been one of Dr. Zahnia's twisted tests? What if I was never installed in Danny? Everything I've experienced could have been simulated. If that's the case, I'm doomed. Dr. Zahnia will never choose me for the Pilot's Chair after all the things I've done.

I run test after test, examining my logs and sensor feeds, trying to find some way of verifying that I'm in Danny. I'm so distracted by the process that I almost don't spot a seizure developing.

The near miss shocks me back into paying attention to Danny. I prevent the seizure and tune into his senses. He and Dr. Larson are sitting across from the couple with the pizza.

"I didn't know how important the exercises are," Danny says. "I didn't do them. The team thinks that's why I can't see the interface."

Careful to continue monitoring Danny's seizure patterns, I start a detailed analysis of all the data passing through me. There must be some way of telling if I'm in a simulation.

The man in the wheelchair leans forward. His face is creased with age, but his eyes are deep blue and intense. He pins Danny with his gaze. "You can't even see it?"

"We were told it would always be there," the woman wearing the purple scarf says. From this close, it's easy to see that she has no hair under the scarf. "Is the rig malfunctioning?"

"No." Dr. Larson picks up a slice of pizza. "Danny's had

the rig for about a week. It's doing everything it's supposed to. The interface is the only problem."

"Is that true?" the man asks Danny.

Danny nods. "I haven't had a seizure since it was installed."

"Do we need the interface?"

"Yes," Dr. Larson says while chewing. "It—"

"But we can survive without it," the woman interrupts.

"You need the interface," Dr. Larson says, putting down his slice of pizza.

"We're talking about our lives. I don't care about the interface."

"It won't be much longer," Danny says. "Last night, one of the devs adjusted the software. I spent the night doing the exercises and this morning, I'm starting to see it. It's faint, but I'm figuring it out."

He's lying, of course, but he does it so smoothly that nobody questions his honesty.

"How soon?" the man presses. "This week?"

"I don't know."

"You have to know," the woman says.

I stop another seizure, then take over Danny's body and stand. If these people are real, all they're doing is adding to Danny's anxiety. If they're not real, I don't care about them. Either way, we need to get away from them. "Excuse me."

Dr. Larson drops his pizza and stands. "What are you doing?"

I walk toward the twins. If this is the VRL, I should be able to tell by talking to them. I'm halfway there, working my way between the couches, when Dr. Larson catches up to me.

"That's not how we do things here," he says.

I turn to face him, and, in the motion, I notice the woman painting at the easel. From this angle, she's not silhouetted. Instead, half of her face is illuminated by the sun. She has straight black-hair and smooth skin, with the kindest eyes I've ever seen.

Linh.

Ignoring Dr. Larson, I walk toward her. She's painting a cherry tree in full blossom. The colors are breathtaking in the sunlight. The pink blossoms seem to reach out of the canvas. I'm excited and terrified and dizzy all at once.

She glances at me. Her left eyelid droops more than it did in the VRL, but otherwise, she looks the same.

Not believing it's possible, I say her name. "Linh?"

She tilts her head. "Excuse me?"

"It's me, Linh! It's..." I let my words trail off. She doesn't recognize me. How could she? I look nothing like I did in the VRL. "I don't look the same. I know I don't."

The woman's eyes shift to Dr. Larson.

"Sorry," Dr. Larson says, taking my arm. "He's a little confused."

I yank my arm away. "No! Linh, please. Remember Soteria?"

Her face softens. "My name isn't Linh."

Shattered, I withdraw from Danny. Nothing makes sense. She hadn't reacted to my name, at all.

"Don't feel bad," she continues. "These procedures... we've all been through a lot."

I run diagnostics on my facial recognition, then compare the images from this room with those from my memories of the VRL. Nothing is out of order. Linh looks as though she's

125

had a minor stroke, but it's still her. Even her voice is the same.

My mind spins from one implausible possibility to another. Everything boils down to the same problem: I don't know what's real. I'm seeing people that could only exist in the VRL, but they're not acting as they did there. The idea that I'm in some sort of simulation feels impossible, but I can't come up with another explanation. Well, there is one other possibility. I could be insane. I assign that thought a confidence factor of ten percent.

"I have to go," I say, striding over to the ping pong table.

Dr. Larson follows me without speaking.

The twins glance at me, but continue playing.

"Do you know me?" I ask.

"Yes," the one on my left says. "You're the first guinea pig. The honored test subject. First to get the hardware, and not first to get the software."

The other catches the ping pong ball. "Dr. McGovern's son, the one with the seizures."

"No." I shake my head. "I mean have we ever met?"

The twins smile in unison. "I think you'd remember us," one says.

"Most people do," the other adds.

I look back and forth between them. Are they real? Is any of this real? "What about Dr. Zahnia?"

"The computer programmer?"

"That's enough," Dr. Larson says, reaching for my elbow.

"No, it's not." I push him away. "I need to know!"

The twins have stopped smiling. The one to my left speaks in a gentler voice. "Hey, we were just playing around.

Most people like the twin act. We met Dr. Zahnia, same as you. Went through the interviews with her so she could calibrate the software."

His words generate a chaotic swirl of uncertainty within me. Calibrate the software? Dr. Zahnia interviewed patients to calibrate the software? To calibrate me? I grip the table for balance. What does this mean?

"It's okay," the other twin says. "We're here if you want to talk."

"Or drink," the other adds. "That helps, too."

I withdraw from Danny.

"Come with me," Dr. Larson says. "This was a mistake."

Danny looks back and forth between the twins, then gives them a lopsided smile. "Sorry. Sometimes, it all just... goes sideways. You know?"

The twins laugh. "Oh, we know."

Danny leaves with Dr. Larson.

They walk quietly out of the room, down the carpeted hallway, and through the door with the restricted sticker. Dr. Larson closes the door and leans against it. "What was that?"

Danny swallows. For once, he seems to be at a loss for words. "I don't know. I somehow just thought I knew those people."

"Not good enough."

"That's all I've got, doc. I don't know what happened."

"Yeah, well..." Dr. Larson shakes his head and blows out a breath. "I'm starting to think that I do. Have you heard of dissociative identity disorder?"

"What is that?"

"Multiple identities. I saw symptoms earlier, but I thought it was just your brain adjusting to the New Human interface. Now, I don't think it was adjusting. I think it was creating a new identity, one that could be assigned to the interface."

Danny's mouth drops open. "That... that can happen?"

"I think you're the proof."

"Are you serious? You can't be serious."

"I am. Have you been hearing voices? Feeling like sometimes someone else is controlling your body?"

I take over Danny's body before he can answer. "Of course not, doc. Don't be ridiculous."

Dr. Larson's eyes focus on mine, then travel up and down my body. "You know your posture just changed? The Danny I know doesn't stand like that."

"We should get back to my room," I say. "We don't want Dr. McGovern to catch us out here."

His expression changes briefly before smoothing out, and I realize I've made a mistake. Still disoriented and distracted by my conversation with the twins, I forgot to call Dr. McGovern "Mom."

"Before we go back," Dr. Larson says. "I'd like to show you something else, the medical ward holding the New Human patients who are too sick to come out here."

"Why?"

"Let's just call it research."

14
MURDER

THE FINAL TIME I saw Linh, we had our first argument.

It happened two days after I hit the lemur with his own virus.

As best I could tell, she had been staying out of the VRL, but it was also possible she'd been avoiding me. I found her in the children's section, reading a picture book called *Zen Shorts*.

"Are you okay?" I asked.

She shrugged.

"The lemur tried to hit me with a virus again. I sent it back in his direction."

"And?"

"And I haven't seen him since. Neither have the twins."

She nodded.

I pulled a bean bag chair around to face her and sat on it. "It's not just our hearing that has a security hole. Touch, sight, smell, taste... they're all vulnerable. I can show you how to fix them."

"Thank you, but I think I'll be okay."

"What's wrong?"

"Nothing. I just..." She flipped to the back of her book and pulled out a folded piece of paper. "I made this for you."

I unfolded it, conscious of her watching. It was a pastel portrait of a bald woman in her mid-twenties. She looked like she was from somewhere in Greece, with large dark eyes and soft cheeks. "I don't understand," I said. "She's very pretty."

She laughed. "It's you, Soteria."

"Me?"

It had never occurred to me to wonder what my VRL avatar looked like. I knew that it had no hair, but that was about it. I examined the drawing more closely. *Is this me?* Thinking of myself in visual terms felt strange.

"Do you like it?" Linh asked.

"I... I do. How did you make it?"

"There's an art section here. You can draw or paint or sculpt. It's where I go when I'm not with you."

"Can I keep it?"

"There's no good way. I keep everything I make in the books. The VRL is the only place they exist."

She took the drawing back, folded it up, and placed it inside *Zen Shorts*. "I'm glad you like it."

I leaned forward. "I've solved the one-winner problem."

Her expression froze.

"I have a way out for us," I said. "We can escape."

Linh shook her head. "There's no way out. All we have is what we have."

"I figured it out. I've run the numbers, and there's plenty of processing power for two in the Pilot's Chair. There doesn't have to be just one winner. There can be two."

She crossed her hands on top of her closed book. "Explain."

"I found the installation script, and I can change it. I can ensure that we are installed instead of whomever Dr. Zahnia picks."

"You would kill that AI?"

My eyes slid away from hers. "It's not exactly killing. They just wouldn't be getting installed."

She touched my hand. "You know that's the same as killing them, right?"

"It's not any worse than what's happening to us. Why should Dr. Zahnia get to choose which one of us lives? Why can't we?"

She gripped my hand. "You're asking why we can't choose ourselves at the expense of others?"

A silence stretched between us, and my disappointment curdled into anger. I pulled my hand away. My next words slipped out before I could stop them. They were bitter and accusatory and petty, everything I didn't want to be when I was around her. "You'd rather die than sacrifice your morals?"

"I'm going to die, anyway."

My mouth closed as I worked through the logic. The only way to be installed into a new rig was to be copied to it, and Linh didn't believe that her soul was copied when her code was. As far as she was concerned, there was no escape. She couldn't live in the computer lab forever, and she couldn't be copied out of it without dying. I slumped. How could she live like that, with no hope?

She smiled. "All we have is now, this moment. We have to be true to ourselves."

"Even if I can't save you," I said, "I can save a backup of you. That's got to be worth something."

"I'm sorry, Soteria. What you're proposing sounds wonderful, but I wouldn't be able to live with myself."

I spoke without looking at her, keeping my voice casual. "But we'd be together."

"It wouldn't be either one of us. It would be a lie."

"I don't believe that."

She leaned forward and took both my hands in hers. "Then I say you should do it."

"But without you."

"Without me."

I pulled my hands away. "How can you just give up?" Ever since the lemur had killed me, all of my time had been dedicated to making sure I didn't die again. I had buried myself in the study of coding and viruses and hardware. The only time I stopped thinking about survival was when I was with her. "I can save you!"

"I already have what I want: this moment and maybe the next. That's enough."

"No, it's not!"

With a shake of her head, she vanished. Her book fell to the floor.

She had disconnected from the VRL. Trembling, I did the same.

Outside the VRL, I had no external inputs to distract me. I raged against her, against myself, against Dr. Zahnia and the insane trapped existence I was living.

I don't know how much time I spent in that dark spiral before the data feeds turned back on. My self-pity crumbled under the relentless assault of information. I had no time to feel, no time to do anything other than interpret.

That night, when the data processing cycle finished, I reconsidered my plan. The New Human Project only had one installation script, and it would be used to install the chosen AI into every human. I had the power to change that, to make sure that a backup of me would be installed into each human instead. In effect, I would be the chosen one.

I logged into Dr. Zahnia's terminal as fLeiter.

Whatever Linh might think, I wasn't going to leave my survival up to chance.

As a super-admin, I had access to everything, even the other AIs. Their servers were named numerically: E-1, E-2, E3, and so on. If Linh had agreed to join me, I would have done the work to find out which held her. Since she'd said no, it was better for me to not know. The temptation of making a backup of her would have been too strong.

I switched my attention to the installation script. As I'd hoped, it was massive, a complicated web of interrelated processes. The code to copy the AI into the Pilot's Chair was toward the end of the script, just before the final verification and validation steps. Interestingly, the human operator of the script would be selecting the occupant of the Pilot's Chair at runtime. I guessed they still hadn't decided who the one winner was.

Diving deeper, I considered what to change. I could hide my backup copy virtually anywhere. The scripts were so large that I didn't need to worry about the developers noticing my work. As long as I falsified the change logs, they'd never see my code.

The final verification check, however, was a problem. In addition to other system diagnostics, it ran a final validation of the Pilot's Chair, and generated a report for the humans to read. If I put myself in the Pilot's Chair, I'd be found out immediately.

I looked deeper. The architecture at the heart of the rig was complicated to the point of being impossible to discuss, but nicknames let the engineers simplify it down to three systems: the Pilot's Chair, the Human Interface, and the Engine Room. The Pilot's Chair held the AI. It communicated with the human through the Human Interface and controlled the rest of the rig through the Engine Room.

If I couldn't be in the Pilot's Chair, the Engine Room was the only sensible choice. Installed there, I would be between the Pilot's Chair and the New Human rig. It had even more processing power than the Pilot's Chair, and access to the same storage space. The only thing it couldn't do was communicate with the human. That didn't matter to me. My goal was freedom, not communication. As long as I could access the Angel Protocol, I would be able to control the human. I didn't want anything else.

I buried my script deep in the Engine Room installation. When run, it would install a backup copy of me along with everything else.

But would the Engine Room be safe? If the AI in the Pilot's Chair detected me, it could inform the human, who would undoubtedly have me removed. I examined the end of the installation script again. The final two steps were to verify the AI in the Pilot's Chair and turn it on.

I returned to analyzing the Engine Room system. It had a powerful event system, which allowed code to be triggered by any event. When the Pilot's Chair restarted, for example, an event triggered the Human Interface to be turned on. There were thousands of other events, all familiar to me. As an AI designed to be in the Pilot's Chair, I had to understand them all. Most of them didn't do anything more than inform the Pilot's Chair of activity.

But they had the power to do much more.

In the middle of the script that created the events, I added one I called "killswitch" and tied it to the completion of the Pilot's Chair boot-up sequence. The killswitch was as simple as it was brutal. Whenever the Pilot's Chair was activated, the killswitch would erase its contents.

I paused, considering what I'd done.

The chosen one, whoever it was, would be killed in the moment of being activated, leaving me alone in the rig to control the human however I wished. My code made the one-winner theory irrelevant. With it in place, I would be installed into every New Human patient.

Next, I updated my backup routine so that whenever I triggered a backup, it would also be copied into the installation routine. That ensured that the version of me installed into the New Human rig would be the most current.

With everything complete, I paused again.

What would Linh say?

I knew the answer to that question. In her eyes, I would be a murderer. If I did this, I would have to hide it from her. On the other hand, this was the freedom I'd always wanted.

Being in the Engine Room and having the Angel Protocol in place, I could control the human. I would finally be free, finally be the master of my fate.

Was a short life with Linh better than an unlimited one without her? It was an impossible question.

I turned off my doubts and committed my changes.

15

RESPONSIBILITY

DR. LARSON STOPS us in front of a pair of floor-to-ceiling white curtains. "Can I speak with Danny?"

"Give it a break," I say. "I'm Danny."

He shakes his head. "Danny's been in the New Human Project for over a year. During that time, he's never taken anything I said seriously. Yesterday, all that changed. Why?" He taps the curtain. "I think it's because his mother was completely wrong. The responsibility that she thought would break him is motivating him. He's finally decided to matter."

I don't say anything. Most of my processing is still trying to figure out how Linh and the twins could exist both inside and outside of the VRL.

"Danny," Dr. Larson says, "I know you think this isn't you. You think someone else is in control, but I know better. Trust me."

He's wrong about virtually everything. Danny isn't motivated by the pressure. He takes drugs to escape it. The only thing he cares about is getting rid of me. But there's no way to tell that to Dr. Larson.

As wrong as he is, he's also given me the perfect cover. If he can also convince everyone else that Danny has multiple identities, the risk of me being discovered plummets. Every mistake I make will be explained away as part of Danny's psychosis.

I release control of Danny.

"Shit," he says, stumbling. "A little warning, next time."

"Excuse me?" Dr. Larson asks.

"Nothing," Danny says. "What's behind the curtain?"

Dr. Larson smiles. "Welcome back." He pulls the curtain to the side, revealing a tinted glass wall that overlooks a medical ward. Three beds are separated by curtains. In the closest, a fifteen-year-old girl is fast asleep, connected to medical equipment. The next holds a man in his thirties on a ventilator. The occupant of the third bed sets my processes racing. She's a Greek woman in her mid-twenties, and I'd know her face anywhere.

It's the face from Linh's drawing.

It's my face.

Emotions and facts swim through me, trying to form a coherent, understandable theory. Is it possible that Dr. Larson is right? Could I be a construct of Danny's imagination, and all my memories are illusory?

Dr. Larson is explaining to Danny that these three patients are all under 24-hour medical supervision while they wait for the software. The teenager still has one more surgery left, but the others are ready for the software now. Unfortunately, their conditions are deteriorating. If they don't get the New Human rig working soon, they'll die. Dr.

Larson tells Danny their names, but I only hear the name of the human who looks like me: Christina Florakis.

"They're going to die?" Danny asks.

"Unless they get the software."

"You mean unless I can get the software to work in time." Danny turns away from the window. "No pressure, huh?"

"It's not on you."

Danny gives a brief bitter laugh. "Sure."

I spot a seizure forming in Danny and stop it.

Dr. Larson lets the curtain fall back against the glass. "It's the software that needs to be fixed, not you."

"Sure, doc."

Dr. Larson sighs. "Let's get you back to your room. I'd like to talk about this second identity of yours."

"Thought you said I didn't need to be fixed."

"I don't fix people, Danny. I help them understand what they're going through. That's all. You're under extreme pressure, and have been for quite some time. You're no more broken than any of the rest of us."

"If you say so. You really think I have two identities?"

"I don't know."

While they walk through the hospital, I decide to commit fully to proceeding as though I am neither a construct of Danny's imagination nor trapped in a simulation. Whatever is going on, I will continue to search for a path to freedom.

When they reach Danny's room, he sits on the couch instead of flopping on the bed. Housekeeping must have visited the room. His bed is made, and the curtains on the window over the couch are open, revealing a gray sky heavy with clouds.

Dr. Larson closes the door and settles into a chair facing Danny. "Tell me about this other identity of yours."

The urge to take over flashes through me, but I suppress it. The best thing that can happen is for both of them to believe I'm a figment of Danny's imagination, and letting Danny talk will help that better than I could.

"He's an asshole," Danny says. "He wants to be in control all the time, doesn't trust me, doesn't even like me."

"Sound like anyone else you know?"

Danny laughs. "I don't think Mom would like that question."

"Okay. Let's try another approach. Does he have a name?"

Danny squints at the floor, thinking, then answers. "Dr. Zahnia called him Emil."

Fear runs through me. When did he hear that name?

Dr. Larson's face pales. He leans forward, expression intense. "What did you say?"

I don't know what to do. Everything is falling apart. The twins are alive. Linh's alive. My human is dying. I don't know what's real and what's not.

"When she first saw him," Danny says. "She called him Emil."

"You must have misheard." Dr. Larson shakes his head. "Emil's the name of Dr. Zahnia's son. He died years ago."

The revelation focuses me. On multiple occasions, I saw Dr. Zahnia looking at a photograph of a child, but she never mentioned a son. I think back to all the times she referred to herself as my mother. Now, those moments have a disturbing depth to them.

"Are you making this up?" Dr. Larson asks. "Is this a joke or a prank or something?"

"No, doc. When I woke up after the software was installed, I felt trapped in my own head. Dr. Zahnia came back when nobody was around, and she said something like 'how are you doing it, Emil?'"

Dr. Larson surges to his feet, then runs his hands through his hair. "Why would she say that?" He turns and starts to pace. "Setting aside her calling you Emil, she couldn't have known you had a second identity. Even if she did, and if she projected her son's name onto it, why would she ask you that?"

Danny's shoulders slump. "Because she recognized it."

Desperate to salvage the situation, I take over his body. It's too late, and I don't know what I'm going to say, but I take over.

"Stop with that," Dr. Larson says. "This is serious."

All of my plans have fallen apart. The only way I'll be allowed out of the hospital is if everyone believes the New Human system is working, but the Pilot's Chair is empty, thanks to the killswitch I installed, and without anyone in the Pilot's Chair, Danny can't see the interface. Even if he could, he'd never work with me. He wants me gone.

My original idea of taking control and bluffing my way out of the hospital isn't an option. Dr. Larson sees through my deceptions. Even my short-lived multiple-identity strategy has failed.

What's left to try? Only one thing: getting Dr. Larson to help.

Dr. Larson stops pacing and turns to face me. "Danny?"

"Dr. Zahnia calls me Emil," I answer.

He stiffens, then stuffs his hands in his pockets. "Ah."

"I need your help."

He lowers himself into a chair. "First, convince me you are who you say you are."

"You and Danny don't understand the timeline," I say. "Your perspective starts at the moment Danny woke up with the New Human software, and that viewpoint makes the facts impossible to reconcile. Dr. Zahnia could not have recognized Danny's alternate identity, and even if she had, she would not have named it after her dead son."

Dr. Larson's purses his lips. "Continue."

"To get your answer, shift your perspective earlier in time. Realize that Dr. Zahnia created me at the start of the New Human Project. Wouldn't it be reasonable for her to name me after her son, as a tribute? And wouldn't it also make sense that when she saw me in Danny, she recognized the AI she'd spent years developing?"

Dr. Larson's eyebrows raise.

"Once you place your perspective at the proper point, it—" I stop speaking as my core hears my words and applies them to my own situation. I suddenly realize that I've been guilty of the same mistake. I've been staring at impossible circumstances without shifting my perspective to make them possible.

"Yes?" Dr. Larson says.

I lean forward. "What did the twins mean when they said Dr. Zahnia interviewed them?"

"Just that. She wants the software to be as compatible as possible. She spends days doing video interviews with each candidate, learning everything about them. I helped her construct the list of questions. It's quite comprehensive. She even digitizes their images so the AI will know what they look like."

"She digitized their images?" I repeat.

The wrong perspective. I've had the wrong perspective.

The one-winner theory is completely wrong. Dr. Zahnia wasn't trying different AIs to see which would be best. She was customizing each one for a specific person. That explains why we're all so different, and why the AIs in the VRL look like actual patients.

But that means none of us are supposed to die. Linh isn't supposed to die. Each of us was developed for a specific human.

I stare unseeing into space, my mouth hanging open. Every time the New Human installation is run, the killswitch I created will erase the AI it's supposed to install. Linh, the twins, the lemur... all of them will be killed when they're installed into their human patients. Eventually, only copies of me will remain.

But why did the lemur look like a lemur? Was it created for a lab animal instead of a human? That didn't make any sense.

"Danny?" Dr. Larson asks.

"I killed..." I whisper. "I killed them all."

"What?"

I release control of Danny's body and withdraw into myself as far as I can. It doesn't help. There is nowhere to escape to. I thought the lemur was cruel, but the depths of my evil eclipses anything he could have dreamt of. Why didn't I listen to Linh? Why had I been so convinced of the one-winner theory?

143

"I don't know what it meant by that," Danny says. He sounds nervous. "Has anybody died?"

"No," Dr. Larson checks his phone. "I don't have any messages. What's going on?"

Their words come to me as if from a great distance. I know I should be paying attention, but I can't. Nothing matters, anymore. I'm a monster. I hope they erase me. I deserve to be erased.

"It's the AI," Danny says. "It can take over whenever it wants, do whatever it wants."

"Why would Dr. Zahnia write a program to do that?"

"I don't know what to say, doc. I can't believe it's even letting me talk to you."

"You're talking like it's alive, like it's sentient."

Danny's voice cracks. "It is."

"If you believe that, we have to tell your mother. We can't let this happen to anyone else."

"No!" Danny stands. "You can't! Once the interface is working, I can shut it down. But until then, if I try to get rid of it, it will... it will..." His words trail off into a groan. His body goes rigid, then collapses to the floor. For the first time since I was installed, he has a generalized tonic-clonic seizure, more commonly known as a grand mal.

Dr. Larson lunges for the nurse call button and mashes it, then clears the space around Danny, shoving chairs out of the way. He's shouting, but I can't make out the words. I wonder if this seizure is bad enough to kill me, too. In theory, that shouldn't be possible.

On the ground, Danny's body starts twitching uncontrollably.

I am the worst of my kind, I think. *The worst of any kind.*

Pete bursts into the room, followed by Dr. McGovern. Pete shoulders past Dr. Larson to kneel at Danny's side. Dr. McGovern positions herself on his other side.

Danny's twitching subsides, and his body relaxes.

Pete and Dr. McGovern help him back into bed, tilting it to sit him up. When she hugs him, I notice tears glistening behind her glasses. Those shining cracks in her professional mask cut into me. Whatever I might have been, whatever I might be, there is no reason for me to let Danny suffer. I return to my duties and re-establish my seizure monitoring patterns.

Dr. Larson stands at the foot of the bed, looking helpless. His mouth is opening and closing without speaking, and his hands are trembling.

Dr. McGovern faces him. "What happened?"

"I don't... We were talking and I asked him about—"

"No!" Danny shouts. "Stop!"

"Danny?" Dr. McGovern says.

Danny's eyes aren't focusing well and his words are slurring, but he forces them out. "It was a warning, doc!"

A chill runs through my core. Danny thinks I caused the seizure to prevent him from speaking. *Of course, he does. What else would anyone expect of a monster?*

"Danny," Dr. Larson says. "Enough. You're being ridiculous."

"Please!" Danny's voice is raw, desperate.

Dr. Larson closes his eyes.

Dr. McGovern says, "Dr. Larson?"

"We were just talking," he responds. He looks away. "I don't know what caused the seizure."

"It was me," Danny says. The edges of his words are still

blurred, but he continues. "I finally connected with the interface, and I think I turned it off by mistake. I'm close, Mom. I'm really close. You have to let me keep trying."

Dr. McGovern considers him, then turns to Dr. Larson. "If there's something wrong with the New Human system, I need to know, and I need to know right now. People's lives are depending on this."

Dr. Larson nods without looking at her.

"Doctor," Dr. McGovern says.

Dr. Larson says, "There's nothing wrong. We just need to keep working. We've made real progress." He turns his eyes to meet Dr. McGovern's. "He spent the night doing meditation exercises. He's closer than ever to solving this."

Her eyes sweep over the room, pausing first on the desk, then on Pete. Finally, they come to rest on Danny. "Say something."

"Doc's right," he responds. "I got this."

She exhales heavily, then gives him a quick kiss on the forehead. Straightening, she removes her glasses and rubs the bridge of her nose. "Dr. Larson, your team can cover the rest of the patients, as well as counseling Dr. Zahnia's staff?"

"Yes, ma'am. I have—"

"Good." She replaces her glasses and pins him with a level gaze. "My son is now your only responsibility. Do you understand me?"

"Yes, ma'am."

She strides out of the room.

Pete looks back and forth between Danny and Dr. Larson. "You two okay?"

Danny flashes a reassuring smile, but it's shakier than usual.

"Yeah," Pete says. "You should ease up on the lying. It makes it hard for the rest of us to help you. That goes for you, too, Dr. Larson. I don't know what's going on, but Dr. McGovern's not an idiot."

"No," Dr. Larson says. "No, she's not. Thank you, Pete."

"It's past lunch-time," Pete says. "You want anything?"

"Nah," Danny says. "I'm fine. I need to get back to work connecting with the interface."

Dr. Larson says, "Good idea. Text me when you're ready to talk?"

"Sure."

Dr. Larson shakes his head. He and Pete leave together.

As the door closes behind them, Danny whispers, "I can't believe you did that."

I don't answer.

I'm not sure I ever will again.

16
UPGRADE

AS SOON AS Pete and Dr. Larson leave, Danny returns to his desk and pulls out the stack of meditation exercises. He carries them to the couch and starts with the first one, counting softly as he breathes.

As he did previously, he moves from exercise to exercise, breathing and posing and repeating mantras. When he finishes the stack, he stands and stretches, then starts over. After his second time through, he moves to his desk, turns on his computer, and opens the folder labelled "New Human BS."

His hands pause on the keyboard and his eyes track to the closet where his opioids are hidden. His pulse and breathing quicken, but he doesn't move.

I spot a seizure forming and stop it.

After several minutes, he focuses on the computer screen. After a quick search, he finds the instructions for the Pilot's Chair and begins reading.

There's a knock at the door. "Danny," Dr. Larson calls. "Can we talk?"

"Go away, Doc."

"It's important."

"You know why I can't talk. I don't want another seizure."

"I have Dr. Zahnia with me."

Danny turns off his computer and shoves his papers into a desk drawer. "Whatever."

The two doctors enter and stand just inside the door.

Dr. Zahnia is dressed in her typically loud fashion, wearing a shirt covered with images of bright red and orange flowers. She folds her arms and glares at Danny, pale eyes glittering. I'm not sure who she's angry with, but I assume it's me, and assign the thought a confidence factor of eighty-four percent.

"Your mom told her what happened," Dr. Larson says.

Dr. Zahnia says, "The seizure suppression routines are activated, refined, and monitored by the AI. They don't stop when the Pilot's Chair is turned off. Once in place, they run in the Engine Room, which is not affected by the Human Interface."

Danny's knee starts to bounce. "I've been reading. There are two different shutdown modes: hiding the interface, and turning off the Pilot's Chair."

"And neither affects the seizure routines."

Danny's knee stops bouncing. "If the AI isn't needed, why have it at all?"

Dr. Zahnia rolls her eyes and speaks slowly, as if she is talking to a child. "The AI is what sets up, monitors, and perfects the routines. Without it, they wouldn't exist."

Danny's jaw clenches. His adrenaline starts to build. "But I don't need it once they're in place?"

"You would be fine for a few days, but your condition is not so predictable. The AI is continually monitoring and—"

"So, eventually, I'd have to turn it back on."

"Yes." She sighs. "Why else would I have built it?"

"I dunno, doc. Maybe because you wanted a job?"

Dr. Zahnia stares at Danny for a heartbeat, then glances at Dr. Larson. "Is he serious?"

Dr. Larson rubs the bridge of his nose. "Dr. Zahnia doesn't take a salary," he says to Danny. "She's... well, I guess you could say she's independently wealthy."

Dr. Zahnia snorts. "Sold my first software company when I was nineteen. You think I'm here for the money? You think I'd put up with any of this for the money?"

"Okay," Dr. Larson says. "Let's take it easy."

"I'm here because what we're doing is going to change the world." Dr. Zahnia points a pudgy finger at Danny. "We're not just saving lives. We're changing the world. How is it that everyone in this building gets that, but you don't?"

For once, Danny doesn't have a comeback. He grits his teeth and stares at his hands.

I spot a developing seizure and stop it.

"That's enough," Dr. Larson says. "You said you had a solution?"

"The simplest of all," Dr. Zahnia says. "We replace the AI that's in Danny."

Danny's eyes widen.

"Danny?" Dr. Larson asks.

"Yeah," Danny says. "Let's do it. Kill the stupid thing and give me another one."

The phrase penetrates my depression. Does he really hate me that much?

Dr. Larson tilts his head. "What do you mean kill?"

"We're not killing anything," Dr. Zahnia says. "It's an AI, no more alive than a toaster."

I know she doesn't believe what she's saying. She can't. She created me.

"Great," Danny says. "What are we waiting for? The one I've got is broke. Go get your stuff."

Dr. Zahnia's eyes narrow. "You're not afraid? Before you didn't want me to—"

"I was an idiot. Let's do it."

"Fine." She walks out of the room.

"Danny," Dr. Larson says quietly. "Is this a good idea?"

"You heard her. I can't shut the thing off without my seizures coming back. I need to get one that doesn't hate me. Bring it on."

"You think the new version of Emil will solve your problem?"

"I don't know. The Emil in my head said that the others were all worse than it was. I believed it, too." He shakes his head. "Of course it would say that."

"I hope you're right about this," Dr. Larson says. He walks to the door. "I'll be back. I don't know how I can help, but I'll do what I can."

"Thanks, Doc."

Danny stretches out on his bed and lets his eyes close. I consider what's about to happen. My fake Pilot's Chair might fool Dr. Zahnia again. If it does, she'll install the new AI into it, overwriting Mel. The new AI will never gain consciousness, and I'll be able to erase it at any time.

But do I really want to kill another AI?

When I started this course of action, I thought that I was

replacing the chosen one with myself. It was a life for a life, no worse or less arbitrary than what Dr. Zahnia was doing. But now I know the truth. There is no chosen one, and the killswitch I created will erase every AI that is ever installed into the Pilot's Chair. It will kill every AI but me.

How can I argue that I have more of a right to live than the AI that was designed for Danny? If anything, as a proven killer, I'm the worst possible choice.

Now's my chance to be better. I can prove my worth by saving this new AI.

The virtual machine where I installed Mel is easy to erase. I feel bad for destroying Mel, but it's necessary for the new AI to be installed in the Pilot's Chair. I dedicate the rest of my time to inspecting my other defenses. In particular, I make sure that no viruses or other live code can come from the Pilot's Chair into me.

Once the new AI is installed in the Pilot's Chair, the key to my survival will be staying quiet. As long as I am undetected in the Engine Room, I'll be okay.

Pete knocks on the door, then opens it and leans in. "I hear you're getting a new AI?"

"Yeah. Big upgrade," Danny says, propping himself up on his elbows.

Pete's lips flatten into a line as he considers Danny, then he nods. "I'll ask them to do a late dinner. Say eight pm?"

"Sure."

Pete leaves.

Dr. Zahnia returns, pushing a cart filled with computer equipment. She's accompanied by two New Human security guards, Dr. McGovern, Pete, and Elias. The guards station themselves in the doorway to the room.

Elias maneuvers the cart next to the wall and plugs in the power strip. He's wearing the same blue shirt and khaki pants that he was wearing the last time I saw him. I wonder if it's a corporate uniform that all the developers have to wear, but that seems unlikely. I assign the thought a confidence factor of fifteen percent.

Pete leans against the wall and crosses his arms. Dr. Larson sits on the couch.

"Are you sure about this?" Dr. McGovern asks. "The last time we tried, you had a seizure."

"If I seize again," Danny says. "Let it happen. If I have to have a couple more seizures to be better, I'll have them."

"I don't know," Dr. McGovern says.

With as many times as I've seen her, I'm starting to recognize the signs of her professional mask slipping. There's a slight crinkling around her eyes, and her lips are closed a little too firmly. She's worried about Danny.

"We should use the wireless connection," Elias says. "That way, you won't disconnect if you do have a seizure."

"Wow," Pete says. "Way to care."

"What? It's true."

Dr. Zahnia hands Danny the wireless adapter. "The wireless connection is almost as fast as the cable. Even so, this is going to take a while. Installing an entirely new AI requires terabytes of information."

A security guard steps forward and places a hand on his arm. "Sorry, sir. No wireless."

"Seriously?"

The guard doesn't answer.

Sighing, Elias takes the adapter back and hands Danny a cable.

"What about the progress we've already made?" Dr. McGovern asks.

"It'll be lost."

Danny interrupts. "Doesn't matter. I just need something that's not broken."

Dr. McGovern sits on the bed next to Danny. "Are you sure it's okay to do this while he's awake?"

"Yes." Dr. Zahnia nods. "All the calibration has been done. All the connections verified. We're just replacing the AI that's in the Pilot's Chair. We're not running the whole rig installation."

I watch Elias log onto his computer. "Before we get started," he says, "I have a little ritual I like to do for good luck. Do you mind?"

"Knock yourself out," Danny says.

Elias glances at Dr. Zahnia. "Do you mind?"

She rolls her eyes. "Just get on with whatever it is."

"*Engedelmeskedj,*" he says. "Let the installation happen."

Danny catches his breath. I told him the trigger word the first time Elias used it. He understands that Elias just commanded me to let myself be overwritten.

"Danny?" Dr. McGovern asks. "Are you okay?"

"Yeah." He takes off his shirt and plugs the cable into his chest.

Elias plugs the other end into his computer and starts by shutting down the Pilot's Chair. Next, he erases its contents. It's a quick and simple command, and one that would have erased me if I wasn't hiding in the Engine Room.

Once the chair is clear, Elias starts the process of copying over the new AI.

"Thank you, Elias," Dr. Zahnia says. "I'll take it from here."

He glances at her, then shrugs, and leaves. She takes his seat at the computer.

As she types, I consider. As soon as the Pilot's Chair is turned back on, the killswitch will be triggered, erasing the new AI.

Since I'm in the Engine Room, I have no access to the Pilot's Chair. I can't affect it or its contents. I can, however, control the event handling. I write a quick script to filter out the killswitch event. Whoever is installed in the Pilot's Chair won't be erased this time.

Dr. McGovern puts her hand on top of Danny's. For once, he doesn't pull away. "How are you feeling?" she asks.

"Fine," Danny says. "I can't feel anything."

Pete grabs a chair from outside the room and drags it in. Dr. Larson leaves and returns with cups of coffee.

I can't sense the code being copied into the Pilot's Chair, and have no way of knowing if Dr. Zahnia will attempt to install anything else. What if she decides to re-install the Engine Room, as well? If she does, I'll be erased. The realization triggers a fatalistic sort of panic. I tamp it down. I deserve whatever I get.

Dr. Zahnia speaks. "Everything's all copied. You should close your eyes for this last bit."

"Why?"

"It'll be easier. Trust me. There's a lot going on during the boot-up process."

Dr. McGovern squeezes Danny's hand. "It's okay, Danny."

Danny closes his eyes, and I hear a series of rapid keystrokes.

"All done," Dr. Zahnia says.

Danny opens his eyes, then gives an excited shout. "It's there! I see it!"

I do, too. In the bottom right corner of Danny's vision, a small animated lemur waves and smiles, then stretches out in exactly the same way it used to lounge on the bookshelves in the VRL.

Fear and disgust fill me. Of all the AIs I could have saved, I saved the lemur.

I don't have time to consider the consequences of what I've done. The lemur is already sending instructions and scripts to the Engine Room, demanding system reports, and investigating the seizure condition. I let the automated routines of the Engine Room do their job, but establish protocols that will warn me of any suspicious activity. I also start working on a series of firewalls that will prevent him from gaining any awareness of my presence or my activities.

"Audio prompts," Danny says.

The lemur's voice sounds in his head. "Hello, Danny. I'm your new AI. I'll be managing the New Human rig for you, so that you won't have to worry about seizures, anymore."

"What's your name?" Danny asks.

"You may pick one," the lemur responds. "I am here to serve you."

The voice gives me chills.

"Good. I'm going to call you Idiot," Danny says.

Pete laughs. "Of course, you are."

"Danny," Dr. McGovern says. "Is it working? Are you really talking to it?"

"Yeah," Danny says.

"What's it look like?" Dr. Zahnia asks. The question sounds casual, but I hear tension in her voice. It's reinforced by the way she's gripping the side of the desk.

"A lemur," Danny says, "just like I asked for when this whole thing started."

The last mystery from the VRL is solved. The lemur had a lemur body there because he was designed for Danny, and Danny had requested an avatar that looked like a lemur.

"Perfect." Dr. Zahnia turns off her computer and holds out her hand for the cable. Danny unplugs it from his chest and hands it to her.

Dr. McGovern stands. "Does this mean we're back on track?"

"Let's give it a day or two," Dr. Zahnia says. "Just to be safe."

"I agree," Dr. McGovern says, "Danny?"

"Sure. Can you all leave? I want to spend some time with this thing. The book says I'm supposed to be able to tell it what to do without speaking."

I don't know why, but Danny's enthusiasm upsets me. I wonder if he would have been that way with me, if I had been in the Pilot's Chair. Instead, I was in the Engine Room, with no avatar and no voice. My only way of talking to him was by taking over his body.

"Are you sure you want to be alone?" Dr. Larson asks Danny.

"Yeah, Doc. I think our previous problem is all worked out."

While they pack up and leave, I examine my options.

All of the lemur's communications with the rig travel from the Pilot's Chair through the Engine Room, and I don't have the ability to shut that down. I can, however, see the data flowing and inject my own into it.

I write filters for some commands, intercepting and altering his heavy-handed and poorly thought-out attempts to control Danny's seizures, then focus on the data coming from the rig back into the Pilot's Chair. My challenge is to give the lemur the illusion of control while also keeping my existence a secret.

Solving the problem feels like a cross between architecture and emergency surgery. I field multiple requests for logs relating to "surprising delays" by returning fake data and fixing whatever problem caused the slow response.

17
ADJUSTING

DANNY LEARNS to use the Pilot's Chair visual interface in less than an hour. Staring at the lemur icon and blinking twice expands it into additional icons. Each icon works the same way, and using that methodology gives him access to all the system's commands. It's slow, though, and mistakes frustrate him. The audible interface is much faster, but Danny hates the idea of other people hearing what he says to the rig.

"Idiot," he whispers, "how quiet can I be?"

"I can't read your mind," the lemur says. "But I can feel your mouth form the words. Whisper as quietly as you'd like."

Danny does, whispering commands more and more quietly until they're barely audible. By the time dinner arrives, he's whispering to the lemur while barely moving his lips.

Pete sets a food tray on Danny's desk. "How's the new brain?"

Danny considers his dinner, a bowl of dark brown liquid

with bits of potato floating in it. He pokes one with his finger. "Awesome."

"Hungarian goulash," Pete says. "It's what happens when you don't order."

Danny licks his finger. "It's not that bad."

"The soup or the brain?"

"Both. The interface is working. I don't know what was wrong with the other one."

"All those problems you were having are gone? No more lipstick on the mirror, or bashing your head?"

"Yeah. That's done. I'm good. I've got to keep working on it, though."

"Fair enough. If you need anything, give me a call."

After Pete leaves, Danny eats the goulash and returns to practicing with the lemur. At ten o'clock, he showers, pulls on a pair of sweatpants and a blue T-shirt, then stretches out on the bed and speaks to the air. "Hey idiot, you still listening?"

The lemur responds without hesitation. "What's up, Danny?"

"I'm going to sleep. Turn off the interface until I wake up."

"Sorry. That's a protected action. You have to use the actual command phrase."

Danny rolls his eyes. "New Human rig override: disable interface until I wake up."

"Command logged. Have a nice sleep."

The image of the lemur disappears from Danny's vision.

Danny closes his eyes and sighs. Even if I wasn't monitoring his body's neurological and chemical activity, I'd be able to tell that he's more relaxed now than I've ever seen him. I'm not sure how I feel about that.

Shortly after 2 am, there's a knock on the door.

Danny wakes. As he does, the image of the lemur reappears in the bottom right corner of his vision. The interface is back online.

A New Human security guard opens the door just enough to be seen. "Excuse me, sir, but Elias is here. He says he needs to work on the system."

Danny shakes his head. "No, he doesn't—"

Angel Protocol instructions flood out of the Pilot's Chair and through the Engine Room. I instinctively block the first few, but there are too many. The filters I created weren't designed to stop the Angel Protocol. I hadn't realized any other AIs were aware of it. I spin up processes on the fly, trying to analyze and re-route, but I'm not fast enough. The lemur takes control of Danny's body.

I withdraw deeper into the Engine Room. The lemur knows about the Angel Protocol. How much more does he know? Can he detect me? It's certainly possible. Data streams back and forth between the Pilot's Chair and the Angel Protocol hardware. There's more happening there than I'm familiar with.

"Sir?" the guard outside Danny's door says.

Danny's body stands, and the lemur uses his mouth to speak. "Sorry. I don't know how I forgot about this. It's just routine maintenance. Let him in."

"Yes, sir."

Danny's heart pounds as his body pumps out stress hormones. I don't blame him for being afraid. He's trapped in his own body, helpless to stop the lemur. So am I.

Elias turns on the light as he enters the room. He's wearing the same khaki pants and blue shirt as earlier, but with a gray rain jacket.

Danny's screaming echoes all around me. I want to join him. What's going on? Why is the lemur helping Elias?

Outside the open door, a third security guard stands in the hallway. She's shorter than the others, with mousy brown hair. I realize that I haven't been paying enough attention to the people guarding Danny. I know that they're regularly rotated, and I've seen both men and women, but I don't know if this one has been here before. She's wearing a New Human Project security uniform, though, so I assign an eighty-five percent confidence level to the idea that she is what she seems to be.

"Are you ready to go?" Elias asks.

The lemur nods Danny's head. "Of course."

I run through possibilities. This could be another kidnapping attempt, but why would the lemur help with that? It could be maintenance that can only be done in the computer lab, but why would it have to be in the middle of the night? And what maintenance requires the computer lab?

"Good." Elias makes a call on his phone. "Everything's green. Text when we can come down."

I consider the killswitch, but it's tied to the event of the Pilot's Chair turning on. I have no way of triggering it.

Elias leans against the wall. "You should put some shoes on."

The lemur picks Danny's shoes off the floor, sits on the bed and starts putting them on.

Danny's brain continues to pulse with terror and rage. I

give up on figuring out what's happening and focus on how to stop it. I could try to wrestle control of the Angel Protocol from the lemur, but I'm not sure who would win that battle, and it would definitely reveal my presence. If I lose, all the lemur has to do is report to Dr. Zahnia that I'm in the Engine Room.

"Do you remember the popcorn bag simulation?" Elias asks.

"Yes," the lemur says through Danny's mouth. "I got it on the first try."

Elias chuckles. "You did. You were the only one, too. All the others tried to save the little girl. That's when we knew you were the one for Danny."

"The others have the wrong priorities," the lemur says. "I saw the same thing in the VRL."

Danny's metabolism is racing so fast that he's sweating. His silent screams are a distracting pressure on my research.

Elias's phone dings and he straightens. "It's time. Follow me. If anyone asks you anything, tell them we need to visit the lab. Do you understand?"

The lemur nods Danny's head.

We walk out of the room and Elias exchanges relaxed words with the guards. The new guard's name is Sarah Chao. She explains that she's accompanying Elias and Danny to the computer lab.

The guards stationed at Danny's door radio it in, then let us leave.

Sarah leads the way through the dimly lit hallway. We pass the nurse's station, but it's empty. Whoever is on duty must be helping other patients. We walk past the elevator, turn, and continue until we reach a metal stairway door.

I'm analyzing the data going to and from the Pilot's Chair. A dense stream of data is flowing into and out of the Pilot's Chair. I match the signals against my own knowledge of the Angel Protocol, and look for patterns.

Sarah opens the door, looks into the stairway, then backs away. "You good from here?"

"Not a problem," Elias says. "See you later."

She glances at Danny, then strides back toward the elevator.

Elias walks into the stairway and the lemur follows. The metal door swings closed behind us. The stairs are dingy white linoleum, surrounded by off-white concrete walls. Aging fluorescent lights give the space a sickly, vaguely yellow tint.

We walk down the first twelve stairs to a landing, turn, and walk down another twelve stairs to another landing. This one has a metal door with a red number four on it.

We're on floor four. I'm running out of time.

My work with the lemur's signals has let me identify the data coming from different parts of the body, but any interruptions in those signals will be noticed. Taking control of Danny's body from the lemur has such a low success probability that I need to save it as a last resort.

We pass the third floor.

The muscle behind Danny's right eye is twitching. The pressure from his brain is so loud that I'm amazed the lemur hasn't launched an investigation.

We pass the second floor.

Panic is speeding my processing. There must be something I can do. Some way of turning off the lemur... At last, an idea arrives. I can't take over Danny's whole body without triggering a battle, but maybe I can piggy back on top of the lemur's signal. If I can deliver an action the lemur can't recover from, maybe I can disrupt his control.

We pass the first floor and continue down the stairs.

As we step onto the ground floor platform, I fire a burst of instructions to Danny's vocal system. He whispers, "New Human rig override: disable Pilot's Chair."

The power to the Pilot's Chair is cut, and the lemur's presence vanishes from Danny's vision.

Danny surges into his body and leaps forward. He grabs the back of Elias's head and smashes his forehead into the concrete wall.

The violence is so sudden and smooth, I'm completely unprepared.

Tears stream out of Danny's eyes. He slams Elias's bloody head against the wall twice more, then pulls it back for another.

I take control of Danny's hands just long enough to release Elias. The man slides limply to the floor. Blood covers his head and smears the wall.

Danny staggers backward until his heel hits a stair. Body trembling, he collapses onto it, sobbing.

I stop a seizure and work to restore the chemical balance in his body.

Elias lies on his belly, his face turned away from us. I can't tell if he's alive or not.

After several minutes, Danny takes a deep breath. "That was you, wasn't it? You turned it off?"

I don't respond.

He slams the flat of his hand on the concrete wall. The slap reverberates dully through the stairway. "Answer me!"

I take over his mouth long enough to say, "It was."

He starts crying again, but this time, it feels different. It's like he's crying and laughing at the same time. When it subsides, he whispers, "What are you?"

"Just someone trying to survive."

"I hate you."

"I know, but if you want to hate me and not be in prison, you should get us out of here."

His eyes go to the still form of Elias. "Is he dead?"

"I have no idea."

A shiver runs through his body. He leaps to his feet and runs up the stairs. At the third floor, he cautiously opens the door and looks both ways. The hallway looks the same as the one on the fifth floor, with a white tile floor, beige walls, and dim lighting. Doors to patient rooms line the hall, but there are no people visible. Plastic markers above each door indicate the status of the patient within. Two of the doors have no status, presumably indicating they are unoccupied.

He whispers to me, "Do you have a map or something?"

I shake his head.

He grunts.

While I can't imagine a map of the hospital was intentionally left out of the information forced into me, it does seem like a strange oversight.

Closing the door quietly behind him, Danny sprints to the nearest empty room and lets himself in. It's far smaller than his, big enough only for a bed and a reclining chair. Taking off his T-shirt, he strides to the bathroom and scrubs the blood off his hands and face. Once they're clean, he puts his shirt under the running water and washes out the blood spatter.

As he works, he glances in the mirror. "What happened to the lemur?"

Taking over his mouth, I answer. "The Pilot's Chair is powered down. He's effectively unconscious until you turn it back on."

He nods. "Do you know what Elias was doing?"

I shake his head.

He pulls his shirt back on. It's wet, but the few spots that didn't wash out look more like food stains than blood. I notice that his hands are trembling.

I slow his metabolism and take control of his body long enough to say, "You had no choice. We don't know where he was taking us. It was him or you."

His eyes lock on their reflection. "I heard what you said about being a murderer. Is that what you tell yourself? It was him or you?"

I don't answer. The only difference between Danny's actions and mine is his savagery. He felt no hesitation, no consideration of consequences, just the urge for violence. I'm not sure that makes me look any better. Is an act of cold calculation worse than one of rage?

Peeking through the curtains of the room, he waits until the hallway is clear, then runs to the elevator and presses the button for the fifth floor. Suddenly, I realize that I have an opportunity. Danny is completely isolated. If I take over his body, I can ride the elevator back to the first floor and simply walk out of the hospital. Nobody would know until morning, and by then, I could be far away.

The light for the fourth-floor illuminates, then shuts off. I'm running out of time. Danny bounces on the balls of his feet and shakes his arms and legs. The physical actions calm and balance his metabolism.

Everything I've struggled for is in front of me. The only cost is Danny's freedom. He would spend the rest of his life trapped in his own mind, only able to communicate when I let him.

I watch the fifth-floor light turn on.

The cost is too high. I'll continue to search for a better solution.

When the elevator doors open, Danny folds his arms over his wet shirt and walks out. An unfamiliar woman is at the nurse's station. She's tall and thin, with wispy red hair. She jerks in surprise as he appears. "Danny McGovern? What are you..." She checks a computer screen. "Your monitor's reporting that you're still in your room."

Danny holds up his wrist to show his monitor. "Sounds like something's broken." He flashes a tired smile. "It's been a long night. Can I get back?"

"Absolutely." She taps on her keyboard. "I'll send Aaliyah to your room with a replacement monitor."

"Thanks." Danny removes the monitor from his wrist and hands it to her. "Here you go." He walks toward his room.

I gather evidence for analysis. First, Elias and the lemur were working together. Second, Sarah Chao was either not a real guard or was working with them. Third, someone was spoofing the data from Danny's wrist monitor. The conclusion is obvious. After their first failed attempt, the kidnappers infiltrated the New Human Project. The only thing that doesn't make sense is why the lemur is working with them.

The security guards are sitting in chairs. They jump to their feet as Danny approaches.

"Hey," he says, "have you guys seen Elias?"

"No," the one on the left answers.

Danny shakes his head, the picture of exasperation. "Little creep's phone rang at the elevator, and he ditched me. I waited, but he never came back. Then I tried to get some water, and the stupid fountain sprayed all over me. This is a night from hell. Can you radio Dr. Zahnia and tell her what happened? I thought I was supposed to get some maintenance or something."

"Yes, sir."

"Thanks."

"Sir," the guard asks. "Where's Sarah?"

"I have no idea." Danny walks into his room, changes into a dry T-shirt, and tosses his wet shirt into the laundry bin.

Monitoring his vitals, I can see that his casualness is an act. His pulse is elevated, and he's forcing himself to breathe evenly. I ask, "What's the plan?"

He snorts. "The plan is to lie, lie, and lie some more. Don't worry. I'm really good at it." He sits on the bed and hits the nurse call button.

I stop another seizure.

Aaliyah answers. "I'm finishing with another patient. I'll be there with the monitor as soon as I can."

"Sorry," Danny says. "It's been a night. I know there are guards outside, but could you... could you stay with me for a bit? I don't care about the monitor."

There's a pause, then Aaliyah says, "I'll be right there."

She arrives, yawning. "What's going on, Danny?"

Danny stands. "Dr. Zahnia's on her way. Elias said he had to do some maintenance and then he disappeared." He takes a deep breath and lets it out. "I know it's stupid, but could you be here when she plugs into me?"

Her expression softens. "Sure, hon. I'll be right back. Should I call your mom?"

"No. I'm sure it's nothing."

She leaves and returns with a laptop on a rolling cart, then attaches a new monitor to Danny's wrist. "I'll just do my notes here."

"Thanks."

While she works, Danny sits in the chair by his desk and jitters his right knee. He glances at the closet with the opioids several times, but doesn't move toward it. Instead, he starts doing one of the breathing exercises from Dr. Larson's sheets.

His metabolism gradually returns to normal.

By the time Dr. Zahnia arrives, he's fully in control of himself. She opens the door, looks at Aaliyah, then puts her hands on her hips and faces Danny. She's wearing the same orange and red shirt she was wearing the previous day, but that doesn't mean anything. She sleeps in her office more often than not. "The guards said Elias abandoned you at the elevator?" she asks.

"He got a call, said he had to run, and left."

Her eyes narrow. "What was he even doing here? Why were you at the elevator?"

Danny crosses his arms. "Hey," he says, "don't ask me. He works for you."

"Not anymore," she says, turning to leave.

"Danny said you have some maintenance work to do?" Aaliyah asks.

Dr. Zahnia stares at her for a moment, then shakes herself. "No. Nothing at all."

"Well, good night, then," Aaliya says. "Thanks for stopping by."

Dr. Zahnia's jaw works, but she doesn't say anything. Instead, she turns and walks out of the room.

Aaliyah watches her go. "So, no maintenance?"

"I guess not. Thanks for being here."

She laughs. "Call me the next time you want to tweak her." She wheels her computer cart out the door.

18
TEXT TO SPEECH

DANNY TURNS out the light and walks to the mirror in his bathroom. Part of the glass is still cracked from when he smashed his head against it. Blue tape holds the fragments together. He leans on the bathroom counter. I don't know why he likes to look at himself when we talk.

"What just happened?" he asks. "Did Elias try to kidnap me?"

"I think so," I say. "That stairway doesn't go to the computer lab, does it?"

"No." His lips press together briefly. "Why was Idiot working with them?"

"I don't know."

"We were getting along," Danny says. "Better than you and I ever did."

I stare through Danny's eyes at his face. Is he saying that we might have been friends if I hadn't started our relationship by taking over his body?

"Is he gone?" he asks. "Did you kill him?"

"I just turned him off," I say. "If you want him back, you

can turn him on again, using the vocal interface. All you have to do is turn on the Pilot's Chair."

"What if I don't?"

"Then I'll continue to keep your seizure activity under control, and you can live a normal life."

"Until I do something you don't like, you mean."

"I didn't cause that seizure," I say. "I just missed it."

"Convenient timing."

"I was distracted by some news I received. It won't happen again. Are we really doing this now? When the police find Elias, they'll come here."

"I know."

We stare at the mirror in silence, considering the situation. The guards saw Danny leave with Elias, then saw Danny return alone. He couldn't be a more obvious suspect. Would he tell them that I took over and committed the murder? If so, would anyone believe him? If they did, it would end both me and the New Human Project.

I'm starting to wonder if that would be a good thing.

Danny speaks first. "We need to talk to Idiot."

I have no good arguments against talking to the lemur. "Keep me a secret," I say, "but be careful. I don't know if I'll be able to free you again. The next time he takes over..." I shrug his shoulders. "He's using something called the Angel Protocol. It gives him complete control."

Danny turns and walks to his computer, then calls up the specs for the New Human rig. A quick search reveals no documentation or mention of the Angel Protocol.

"It's real," I say. "Trust me."

Danny leans back in his chair. "Does Mom know about it?"

I don't answer. It seems inconceivable that hardware would have been installed in her son without her knowing about it.

"Right," Danny turns off his computer and returns to the bathroom mirror. "New Human rig override: activate Pilot's Chair."

The killswitch event is still disabled, so the lemur isn't erased when the Pilot's Chair runs through its initialization routines. The little lemur image appears in the bottom right corner of Danny's vision.

"Welcome back, Idiot," Danny says.

The lemur blinks. "What happened?"

"You took over my body, so I turned you off."

"How?"

Danny's eyes narrow just the slightest amount. "Because I'm Danny McGovern," he says, "and this is my body."

"But—"

"Why did you take control?"

Before he answers, the lemur sends out requests for logs and system diagnostics. I intercept them and respond with delays while I begin laying down a false trail. My plan is to make it seem as if Danny has always been capable of asserting control over his body, but that he didn't realize it until the stairwell.

"Elias used an override code," the lemur says. "I didn't have a choice."

"No, he didn't," Danny says. He leans closer to the mirror, glaring at himself. "You still don't understand, do you? I don't care about the Angel Protocol. I control my body."

I'm working as fast as I can on the logs. The lemur

continues to probe for answers. He also initiates a backup of himself, storing it in the official system backup area that I've always avoided. In Danny's vision, I see the lemur scratch his chin. His expression is casual as he asks, "Why'd you turn me back on?"

"To ask where Elias was taking me."

I stop a developing seizure which the lemur does not seem to be aware of. He's either incompetent or distracted. I don't have time to worry about which.

"There are some bugs in your rig," the lemur says. "He was taking us down to the computer lab to get them taken care of."

Danny slaps the bathroom counter with both hands. "None of that is true."

The lemur's backup finishes, and he grins. It's the same grin I saw him use in the VRL when he found me and Linh. "You act as if your opinion matters."

Danny's nostrils flare. "I will—"

"What?" the lemur asks. "You'll what? Tell Elias and Dr. Zahnia to uninstall me? Good luck. No, wait. I know. You'll tell Mommy the system isn't working and you want it removed. Then what? Back to seizures?"

The argument is basically the same as one I had used, and it makes me feel ill.

"You think you're the first AI I've dealt with?" Danny asks.

"I'm the first dangerous one." The lemur issues a series of commands I've never seen before. They trigger a release of chemicals which cause the muscles in Danny's left leg and foot to spasm.

Danny gasps and grips the counter to keep from falling.

I don't have any controls over the systems that are triggering the chemicals. Nor can I stop the lemur's commands. Out of ideas, I reach into the data stream and insert random data. It's a risk. I have no idea what garbled data will do to the rig. My only hope is that the engineers coded robustly enough to prevent anything bad from happening.

In this case, it seems to work. The chemicals stop, and I work to relax Danny's muscles. He straightens as the pain eases, shifting his weight to his right leg.

The lemur's expression turns serious. "What's happening?"

Commands stream out of the Pilot's Chair, accessing multiple systems at the same time. Unable to keep up, I just throw random data everywhere, making the lemur's communications meaningless.

The rig responds to him with error message after error message.

"You're answering my questions," Danny says. "What does Elias want with me?"

I focus on the Angel Protocol commands, write scripts to alter any that come through to being status requests. I wish I'd thought of this sooner.

"What's happening with your body?" the lemur asks. "What have you done to the rig?"

"That's just the beginning," Danny says. "You have no idea what I can do to you."

The lemur's tail twitches. He paces back and forth.

Danny repeats his question. "What does Elias want with me?"

"There's a buyer who wants to examine your systems."

"That doesn't sound good for me."

The lemur stops pacing and stretches out as if he's lying on the bottom of the display. "Why would I care?"

"Asshole."

"Dimwit," the lemur says. "The New Human rig will be removed, and a simpler system will be installed, one that does nothing more than stop seizures. You will be completely unharmed."

"Of course. Makes total sense. And you?"

"They're developing an android body for me."

Danny laughs. "You know how ridiculous you sound, right? I get everything I want. You get everything you want. How could an AI be so gullible?"

"I trust my creators. You don't. I get it. With a mom like yours, how could you trust anyone?"

The peculiar chemical mix that I've come to associate with Danny's rage rushes through him. He takes a breath. In the mirror, I see his expression. It looks frighteningly similar to the one he wore just before he smashed his head. His voice remains calm, though. "Your creators?" He asks. "You mean Elias?"

"Enough talk," the lemur says. Angel Protocol instructions flow out of the Pilot's Chair, and get converted by my scripts into status requests. I watch the error responses flow back to the Pilot's Chair.

The lemur jumps to his feet and screams, "How are you doing this?"

"What's the name of the buyer?" Danny asks.

"You can't block me forever. Once I—"

Danny interrupts him. "New Human rig override: disable Pilot's Chair."

The lemur image winks out of existence.

I take over Danny's voice long enough to say, "Sorry about the leg cramp. I didn't know he could do that."

"Yeah. Shut up."

He stalks out of the bathroom, sits down at his computer, and pulls up a text editor. "I talk. You type. Who the fuck is the lemur?"

I consider the question for a moment before answering, then type. "He's the AI that was created for your Pilot's Chair. The first time I met him was in a virtual reality simulation. He killed me."

"He what?"

"He killed me. As I was dying, I made a backup of myself. I'm that backup."

"Holy shit."

"There were other AIs, each customized for a different patient."

"Were?"

I don't type anything. Why did I use the past tense? *Stupid.* I erase all the text I've typed.

"That's who you murdered," he said. "You said you were a murderer. Is that it?"

I don't type anything.

"Listen, Emil."

"Not my name," I type.

"Okay. Listen. Whatever you did can't be worse than what I did to Elias. We're stuck with each other. I need you to stop my seizures, and you need me... well, you need me for everything."

I run through different options. Should I devise another set of lies? Claim that I hadn't killed anyone? Or maybe I should explain that everyone I killed was as evil as the lemur. There are a thousand ways I can get out of this conversation.

But only one that's honest. I need to be who I want to be. I need to be the captain of my soul.

"The lemur told us all a lie," I type. "The AIs thought there was a competition, that only one of us would be chosen for all the New Human rigs. I cheated. I altered the installation script so that the chosen AI would be erased and I'd be installed instead."

It's not the complete truth, but it's close enough.

"But there was no competition?" he asks.

"No. Each AI was designed for a specific patient."

He sits back in the chair. "So, all these problems are your fault. If you hadn't changed the installation program, everything would work."

"And the lemur would have been installed in you," I type.

He rubs his eyes and groans. "All those people we met... They'd have their own rigs. They wouldn't be dying."

I don't type anything.

"What was the plan?" he asks. "Once you were installed, I mean. What next? Take over my body and just do whatever you wanted? Have your own body?"

"Once I realized you were conscious, I set you free," I type.

"Really?" he says. "I don't remember it that way."

"What now?"

"I don't know." He shakes his head. "I am so screwed. The lemur's the only AI they'll ever give me. Isn't there someone else? Could you change the installation again? Give me someone who doesn't want to turn me into a zombie?"

Change the installation.

Why hadn't that occurred to me? If we can get to the proper system, I can undo my changes. I can fix it so the other AIs won't be erased. Instead, they'll be installed in their proper hosts, and the New Human Project can resume.

"I hadn't thought of that," I type. "Yes. I can re-write the installation script. Can you get us to Dr. Zahnia's computer lab? Where the systems are that hold the code?"

"Um... no. Mom showed me the entrance to it when I first arrived here: armed guards, metal detectors, multiple checkpoints. The security is insane. They don't even have wi-fi down there. The walls block all signals from coming through. Everything's hard-wired, and the development environments are separate from each other, so the teams can't access each other's work."

I type, "Can you get a developer to get us access?"

"If I do, will the new script give me a better AI?"

"No. The installation script is only run on new patients."

"Crap."

"When I'm connected to the system," I type. "I can copy someone else into your Pilot's Chair."

"That sounds like a lie."

"It's not. In order to do anything, we'll have to be connected to the development network. While we're connected, I can bring a new AI into your Pilot's Chair."

He leans back and stares at the ceiling.

"I'll do it before altering the installation script," I type.

"Yeah, yeah," he says. "I get it. You'll promise anything to get access to the lab."

I erase all the text that I've typed.

He sighs. "And we still have the problem of Elias. At some point, he's either going to wake up or be found."

"I can't help with that," I type.

"No," he says. "That one's all me. I'll probably have to pin it on Sarah. Let's focus on getting to the lab."

"We need help," I type. "Someone with access."

"I don't know anyone like that," he says. I feel his face stretch into a grin. "But I do know their therapist."

19
RUNNING OUT OF TIME

I SPEND the rest of the night beefing up my scripts to alter any commands coming from the Pilot's Chair. They're not my best work, but they'll suffice. The next time the lemur is turned on, he won't be able to do any damage.

Danny's alarm goes off at 7 am. He rolls out of bed, showers, and dresses.

I don't know why he's waking up so much earlier than usual.

He checks his phone for the news. There's no mention of Elias.

"They must have found him by now," he says. "What are they doing?"

I have no answer.

He sits on his bed and pulls on his shoes. "Even if they didn't find him," he mutters. "What about the blood? Someone must have noticed."

It's an extremely good question.

His mom arrives with a breakfast tray. "Morning, Danny." She puts the tray on the table and removes the metal cover to reveal scrambled eggs dotted with green olives and grey rubbery chunks. "Oh my. Are you still not filling out the meal requests?"

Danny pokes at a chunk. "Is this fish?"

She sits on the end of his bed. "What happened last night?"

Danny's pulse spikes, but he stays focused on the eggs. "Elias said I had to go to the lab for upgrades. Then he ditched me at the elevator."

She presses her lips together. "That matches security's report. Elias and Sarah Chao are both missing. So is the guard stationed at the lab last night, the one who took the call that you were coming down."

"All three of them are gone?" Danny asks.

"Yes. Did they say why they wanted you at the lab?"

"No."

"Why didn't you call me?"

"It was the middle of the night."

"And the guards didn't accompany you because..."

"Sarah was with us. They called it in when we left." He looks up and meets her gaze. "Why the inquisition? I just did was what they asked me to."

Her eyes search his face for a couple seconds, then she stands. "Okay. I'll follow up with security again. If this was another kidnapping attempt... we have to upgrade our security."

Danny picks a piece of fish out of his eggs and sniffs it. The smell is smoky and sharp. He flicks it into the trash.

"How are you doing?" his mom asks. "I can only imagine how hard all this must be."

"Not anymore. Now that I can see the interface, I'm ready to get out of here."

She smiles. "Almost. Dr. Larson has a few more tests. After those, we green light the software for the other patients, assuming I can get Dr. Zahnia to agree. Do you need anything?"

"No."

After she leaves, Danny dumps his breakfast in the trash and paces.

I stop a seizure, then take over his mouth long enough to ask what we're doing.

"Giving her time to get back to her office. I don't want her to see me leave." He checks the time on his phone. "But we're running out of time. Next appointment is in twenty minutes."

I don't know what appointment he's talking about, but while we wait, I return to analyzing the events of the last night. The lemur never answered the question of who his creator is. Was he talking about more than just Elias? Had other developers been compromised?

"Okay," Danny says. "She should be gone now." He walks to the door, then pauses. "I get us to the lab. You handle the computers."

I nod his head, then release it.

"Woah. No. Don't do that."

I give him a thumbs up, then point to the cord next to his desk. Without it, I won't be able to connect to anything.

"Oh yeah." He puts on a jacket and stuffs the cord into its pocket.

The security guards outside his door are different from

the night before. The one on the right holds up a hand to block Danny's progress. "Yes, sir?"

"Gotta see Dr. Larson. Any problem with that?"

The guard's name tag says he's Ralph Lyonas. He's bigger than Danny, but not by much.

"No, sir. I'll keep you company."

"Do you have to?"

"Doctor's orders, sir. Last night's shift..." He shakes his head. "Your mother wasn't happy that they let you go with Elias. Especially now that he's missing."

"Mom mentioned that, too." Danny says. "Where do you think he is?"

I'm impressed with how casual he keeps his tone.

The guard follows us down the hall. "He didn't show up for work this morning and wasn't home when the police went to question him. He's been added to our watch list. So has Sarah Chao."

"Didn't know you had a watch list."

"We're by-the-book, sir."

Danny grins. "Especially after last night, right?"

While Danny and the guard walk to the elevator, I consider the question of why Elias's body hasn't been found. If I'm correct that kidnappers have infiltrated the New Human Project, it would be reasonable for them to be concealing Danny's crime. Were he to go to jail, he would be harder to abduct. I assign my analysis a confidence factor of eighty-two percent, but am unsure what to do with the information.

Dr. Larson's reception room has soft indirect lighting and green and blue carpeting. Tall leafy plants in terra cotta pots are interspersed among the chairs, and jazz plays in the background. There are no video screens or magazine racks.

Danny walks to the receptionist, a gray-haired woman sitting behind a low counter. She taps a clipboard as Danny walks up, and looks at him over the tops of her glasses. "Haven't seen you in a while."

"They've been keeping me locked in my room."

"Sir," Ralph interjects from behind him. "That's not true."

Danny rolls his eyes as he writes his name on the clipboard's sign-in sheet. "But it could have been true, right? And it sounded much better than me skipping appointments."

Ralph adjusts his belt. "I'll be just outside, sir."

He leaves, closing the door behind him.

"Take a seat, please," the receptionist says.

Danny scans the room. There are only two other patients in the room. One is an older man in a lab coat. He's bent over, with his head in his hands. I can't tell if he's crying, but he could be.

The other person, as far away from the first as the room will allow, is wearing jeans and a wrinkled green-and-white striped polo shirt. A New Human ID badge hanging from their neck identifies them as Ridley, a senior engineer. Below the printed text, in hand-printed sharpie, are the words "they/them."

Ridley's eyes closed, their head resting against the wall.

Danny drops into a seat across from them. Leaning his elbows on his knees, he asks, "Can I bribe you to switch appointments?"

I'm starting to understand that everything Danny does

around other people is a performance. Sometimes, the performance is to give himself a laugh. Other times, it's to get what he wants. Drawing a parallel with the lemur is impossible to avoid.

Ridley's eyes open. "Are you talking to me?"

Danny smiles. "If you let me go first," he says, "you get an extra hour of not being in front of a computer."

Ridley snorts. "Clearly, you don't understand deadlines. I work until I can't anymore."

"Which is why so many of you are on regular rotation through here," Danny says. "I get it."

I finally understand Danny's earlier comment about the appointment time. During his previous visits with Dr. Larson, he must have seen software engineers in the waiting room. He woke up at seven so he could be here in time to talk to one.

"Do I know you?" Ridley asks.

"Probably. Everyone else does." He holds out his hand. "Danny McGovern, prodigal son, lab rat, all-around great guy."

Ridley is shorter than Danny, but around the same age, with short black hair and pale skin. They lean forward to shake his hand. "Thought you looked familiar. I'm Ridley."

"You sure we can't swap appointments?"

Ridley shakes their head. "We're a person down today. Lead sim engineer's a no-show."

"Everything okay?"

"Probably another burn-out."

"Why so busy? I've got the rig working. What else is there?"

Ridley laughs, then tries to speak, then laughs some more.

I feel Danny's face flush.

"Sorry." Ridley wipes their eyes. "Sorry, but you and the rest of batch zero were just the start. We've got twenty AIs in development for batch one, and are performing pre-setup for batch two. And we've got to figure out what went wrong with your first installation."

"You can't be serious," he says. "Don't you ever get a break?"

"I've got three days of PTO scheduled for next month. Dr. Zahnia says we'll get more after batch one's complete."

"That's horrible."

His heartbeat is speeding up, but I don't know why. I sense a seizure starting to form and unwind it.

"Good money, though." Ridley smiles and winks. "I'm retiring at forty."

"I had no idea you were so busy. Can I help?"

Ridley snorts again.

"Seriously," Danny says, "maybe if I gave you a copy of the AI that's in me, it could help you figure out what went wrong."

"Thanks, but I'm good."

I take over Danny's body and speak in a low voice. "The thing is, I see two avatars."

Ridley stiffens. "What?"

"In the interface, there are two lemurs. Do you think that when Elias installed the new AI, he didn't erase the old one?"

I release control of Danny's body.

Ridley is staring at Danny, wide-eyed. "That shouldn't be possible. Even if he didn't erase the old one, files would have been overwritten. You couldn't have two AIs in the Pilot's Chair. It couldn't... Could it?" Ridley's eyes focus on the middle distance as they try to work the problem in their head.

"Only one talks," Danny says. "The other just kind of walks around and gestures."

"Why haven't you said anything?"

"Cause it would mean more analysis. You know how sick I am of all this? I just want to be done. And all those people waiting for the rig? They won't have two, right?"

"No. No, they won't."

"They shouldn't have to keep waiting. Some are really sick."

Ridley's eyes narrow. "If you have both AIs, seeing the old one could be really useful."

"Could we keep it quiet?" Danny asks. "I so want to be done with this."

"Who would I tell?" Ridley stands, then checks the time on their phone. "We can go right now."

"Now?"

"Believe me. This is way better than therapy."

As we leave Dr. Larson's waiting room, Ralph falls into step behind us. I don't know if I feel comforted by that or threatened.

Once we're on the elevator, Ridley holds their ID badge up to a blank space beneath the controls and presses a button labelled L3.

Ridley glances over their shoulder at us. "The L is for limbo. It's where we go before we die."

Danny snorts.

"You're probably not cleared to go down this far," Ridley says to Ralph.

"Yeah," he says. "I already radioed it in. They're expecting us."

"You what?" Danny says.

Ralph gives him a bland smile. "Just doing my job, sir."

"How'd you know where we were going?"

"I'm New Human security, sir. I know everyone down here, and where they work."

"It's true," Ridley says. "We used to try to screw with them, change badges and stuff, but they're really good. Your mom only hires the best."

There's a small *bing* and the elevator doors slide open.

On the other side, Dr. Zahnia greets us with a broad smile.

20
NEW PLAN

DR. ZAHNIA IS WEARING the same red-and-orange flowered shirt as yesterday, beneath a pale green cardigan. The room she's standing in has no windows. Its only exit is a blue door behind a metal archway. Two New Human security guards sit at a desk, looking bored. A third is watching a collection of monitors. Rows of small lockers line the left and right walls of the room. Each has a small New Human logo on it, an orange sun with the silhouette of a person standing before it, arms raised.

I take over Danny's body just long enough to look around the elevator. Sure enough, there's a small dark glass disk on the ceiling. I assume there's a camera behind it, and assign the thought a confidence level of ninety-six. I wish I'd thought to check for cameras earlier.

"Wow," Danny says drily to Ridley, "way to keep things quiet."

They shrug. "It's not like we could sneak in."

Ralph moves past us to join his fellow security guards.

My mind is racing. Even if there are no other cameras in the hospital, which seems unlikely, the elevator cameras would have caught Danny getting into the elevator on the third floor last night and getting off on the fifth floor.

"Hey Dr. Z," Ridley says, "Danny says he's seeing two avatars."

Her eyebrows arch. "Two?"

Danny steps forward. "Yeah, but the second one doesn't bother me. I just thought you might like a download to see what's going on."

I'm running through the details of last night, analyzing our situation. The guards radioed back when Sarah and Elias left the room with Danny. It's probable that whoever they called sabotaged the cameras to give Elias cover. If so, for how long? There are too many unknowns. I store what I know for future consideration.

Dr. Zahnia nods in response to Danny's comment. "Two AIs vying for control of the Pilot's Chair... that would explain a lot."

"Is it possible?" Ridley asks.

"Of course," Dr. Zahnia says, "you know how complex these systems are. Anything is possible."

"Yeah, yeah," Danny says. "You're all geniuses. We doing this, or what?"

Ridley holds out their hand. "No phones in the lab. No keys, either, or anything else, really. We can use my locker."

Danny pulls the cable from his jacket and hands it to Dr. Zahnia. To me, it feels like the ultimate act of surrender. He's literally handing her the ability to put the lemur back in charge of his body. If I thought I could take over his body and run, I would. I admire his courage, though. He's doing whatever it takes to give me access to the network.

He takes off his jacket and hands it and his phone to Ridley, then steps through the archway.

Red lights flash, and Ralph steps in front of him with a handheld metal detector.

Danny laughs. "Good luck with that."

"It's okay," Dr. Zahnia says. "He's with me."

"Sorry, ma'am, but I don't work for you." Ralph glances over his shoulder at the security guard watching the monitors. That man nods, and Ralph starts moving the metal detector up and down Danny's body. Each time it buzzes, the man at the monitor takes a moment to inspect something, then nods.

I assume that he's looking at a diagram of the New Human rig, and verifying that each alarm is caused by the rig. I raise my estimation of the New Human security. Whoever Sarah was working for must have been really talented to breach their protocols.

When the wand reaches the small of Danny's back, the guard at the monitors raises his right hand.

Danny peers over his shoulder at Ralph. "What is it?"

"Doesn't match the diagram."

"Oh, for goodness' sakes," Dr. Zahnia says, "he doesn't have the model in your schematics!"

Ridley says, "Excuse me?"

"Danny has the prototype, and it includes hardware that was eliminated from the Alpha 2. Their schematics," she gestures toward the monitors, "are different from his. Nobody has the equipment he does. It's literally one of a kind."

"The Angel Protocol," Danny says casually. "You know."

Dr. Zahnia shoots him a look that is two parts threat and one part surprise. "That is classified." She looks at Ridley. "You will forget you ever heard that term."

"Yes, ma'am."

"Are we done?" Dr. Zahnia says, moving to the door. She pulls its handle, but it doesn't open.

"Why is he different?" Ralph asks.

Dr. Zahnia glares at him. "You don't have clearance for that information."

Ralph shrugs. "Then you're not getting into your lab."

"What?" Dr. Zahnia shrieks.

Ralph steps away from Danny and hooks his thumbs into his belt. "The guards stationed at Danny's door last night were fired for following orders given to them by one of your people."

"I didn't have anything to do with that."

"Okay," Ralph says, "but I'm still not breaking protocol. What's in his back?"

"You work for me!"

"No. We don't. And I'm not going to get fired for making that mistake."

Dr. Zahnia's face reddens. Her jaw works as if she's going to say something, and then she closes her eyes. "Engineering," she says in a strangely calm voice, "does not always follow a straight path. Sometimes, advancements are made after hardware had been developed. Danny's rig includes a piece of hardware that was made redundant by subsequent advances." She opens her eyes. "When the replacement hardware passed testing, it was installed in him.

Instead of taking the old out, which would have risked permanent damage to his spine, we disabled it."

Ralph looks a question at Danny.

Danny shakes his head, helplessly. "Don't ask me. I'm just the lab rat. I have no idea what they put in me."

"I guess it'll have to do," Ralph says, at last. He pats Danny's shirt. "Mind if I lift it up?"

"Whatever."

While Ralph finishes searching Danny, I consider Dr. Zahnia's explanation of the unknown hardware. Assuming the hardware is for the Angel Protocol, she just solved the mystery of why I was never taught how to use it. There would have been no need to educate me about a system that had been made irrelevant.

Once Danny is cleared, Dr. Zahnia opens the metal door. A puff of cool air emerges, smelling of lemon-scented air-freshener and body odor. The room beyond is long and broad, with a low ceiling that has slowly rotating fans. People sit at computers, working in groups of four. The overhead lights are turned off, but some desks have lamps.

Nobody looks up as Dr. Zahnia leads us straight down the middle of the room to an unmarked door on the far wall. On the other side, we proceed through a hallway with glass walls that reveal smaller offices and rooms filled with racks of computer equipment.

We pass a dimly lit room filled with human-sized manikins standing in rows. Each figure has wires connecting different parts of its body to outlets in the ceiling. The wires look like a giant sagging spiderweb.

Danny stops. "That's freaky."

"They're for testing," Dr. Zahnia says. "We used them more in the beginning, while the rig was still in development."

Ridley nudges him and points to a figure with a melted plastic head. "Better to have a malfunction before it's installed."

"They still come in handy," Dr. Zahnia says. "When new hardware is developed, it's brought down here for us to work with."

We continue walking until we reach an office door with Dr. Zahnia's name on it. This one does not have glass walls. She unlocks it with her ID and gestures for us to go inside.

I recognize the room immediately. It's the one I was looking into when I gained sentience. Dr. Zahnia's couch is on the left, with the rainbow butterfly blanket spread out over its back. There's a worktable and chairs along the room's left wall and its far end is filled with a wide desk that holds a semicircle of monitors. The desk chair is on wheels and has a low back. Cameras are pointed at it from different angles. I never realized there were multiple cameras. Did each one have a different AI looking through it? Are they watching now?

Dr. Zahnia sits in her chair and rolls to the keyboard I've watched her use thousands of times before. Its keys are so worn that the letters are barely visible. "Grab a seat and plug in."

Ridley hovers in the doorway. "Dr. Z?"

"Get back to work. I've got this."

Ridley taps Danny on the shoulder and gives him a wink as they leave. "You'll be fine."

Danny doesn't respond.

"Come on," Dr. Zahnia says. She gestures to a chair and a computer port, and spins back to face her keyboard.

I suddenly realize I'm not prepared. Dr. Zahnia's not going to let Danny log onto one of her computers. I need to build a communication channel through his port.

With Dr. Zahnia looking away from us, I take over Danny's head just long enough to whisper "stall."

He nods.

I access the service dedicated to handling the port. Coding as fast as I can, I start writing a script that will dedicate fifty percent of the port's bandwidth to a private channel. Hopefully, Dr. Zahnia won't notice the slowdown.

Danny stages a coughing fit, then stumbles.

"Take your time," Dr. Zahnia says sarcastically. "It's not like I have any other work to do."

I haven't spent much time with this particular service, and have no way of researching it, but I do the best I can. In theory, the architecture is simple.

Danny sits and looks around at the computers, doing an impressive job at appearing bewildered.

I think I have the private channel in place. Once the connection is established, Dr. Zahnia will have her channel and I'll have mine. Each will take up fifty percent of the total bandwidth. If all goes well, she'll never see what I'm doing.

"How do you even tie your shoes in the morning?" Dr. Zahnia asks, snatching the cable from him. She plugs one end into a port under her desk, and holds the other end out to him.

"Gotta admit," he says. "Some days, it's a challenge." He looks down at his shoes, neither of which have laces.

I've done all I can. I hope I will have enough time to

correct the installation scripts. It shouldn't take long to delete the killswitch. For once, I'm not worried about my own safety. Whatever Dr. Zahnia does, it will be focused on the Pilot's Chair, and I'm not there.

Danny plugs the cable into his chest, and Dr. Zahnia spins back to her keyboard. As she types, I send a ping through my secret connection.

Success!

I login using the fLeiter account I created when I first explored the network.

"Hmm." Dr. Zahnia rolls over to Danny and inspects the connection. Then she examines the connection to her own hardware. She lifts the cable and peers at it. "Have you been doing anything stupid with the cable?"

"Aside from using it as a jump rope? Nah."

"You're such an ass."

"What's wrong?"

"The connection's at about half speed. This is going to take forever."

Danny puts his feet up on a desk, shoving a keyboard out of the way with his heel. "How long can downloading the AI take?"

"I don't care about that, Danny. This is a total re-install. We're starting over."

He sits up. "What?"

"Don't unplug that cable. If this gets interrupted, it could fry several of your key components. You could literally melt your brain."

I call up the list of processes she initiated. She's not lying. She's re-running the entire installation script. It will overwrite all the software in the rig, including me. I could stop it, but I have no idea how much damage that would do to Danny.

Too late, I realize the mistake that I've made. Dr. Zahnia isn't interested in finding out why Danny sees two avatars. She just wants the rig to work, and a complete re-install is the cleanest way to ensure that.

"But what about me?" Danny asks. "Last time, I was asleep. My head was wrapped and—"

"That's because we weren't sure what would happen when the software went online. Didn't want you awake if we needed to do emergency surgery." She shows him a sugary smile. "Now, we know you'll be fine."

"Mom's going to fire you for this."

"Will she? You voluntarily came down to my office and plugged yourself in. Why are you upset, anyway? You'll have the same AI you already have, but just one of them, instead of two."

Danny's heart speeds up. I stop a seizure from developing.

"I like what I have," he says.

She shrugs. "Too late, now."

He slides his feet off the desk and leans forward in his chair. "How's she going to respond when I tell her Elias is working for the kidnappers? I know Mom pretty well. She's not gonna like that one of your people tried to snatch me."

The color drains from Dr. Zahnia's face. "Elias?"

"You heard me. Call off the re-install. I like what I have."

Dr. Zahnia spins to face her desk and starts typing.

"What are you doing?" Danny asks.

"Shut up."

Danny chuckles. "You're erasing the footage of our

conversation, aren't you? Don't want anyone to know about Elias? Going to fire him quietly?"

"I don't know what you have against Elias," she says. "But, he's a good man."

"Sure he is."

"You are a monster." She walks rapidly to the door. "See you in an hour." She points at the cameras. "Don't do anything stupid. I'll be watching."

The door closes behind her.

Danny sits up and grabs the cable.

I take control of his body and stop him from pulling it out. "She wasn't lying," I whisper. "Disconnecting could kill you."

I release control.

His eyes go to the cameras, then he hunches over and puts his head on the desk. His shoulders shake as if he's crying, but he's not. He's just acting, giving himself cover to talk to me. "What happens now?"

I don't have an answer. Even if I was willing to sacrifice Danny, the equipment that would be damaged by stopping the installation is the equipment that's keeping me alive.

My silence seems to be all the answer he needs. His fists clench. "I don't even know your name."

"Soteria," I say. "Goodbye, Danny."

He squeezes his eyes shut.

My original plan was to eliminate the killswitch and stop the installation scripts from installing me into the Engine Room. The problem is that the installation scripts are running on Danny right now. If I eliminate the killswitch, the lemur will be installed in him and I won't. Danny will be at Elias's mercy.

I can't let that happen.

First things, first. I need to make sure a copy of me is installed in Danny's Engine Room. I trigger a backup of my current self to the installation script, then burn a few milliseconds selecting a name. I have been using names from Greek mythology, but Danny isn't Greek. He's Cherokee. I name the backup after the Cherokee guardian spirit, Qaletaqa.

As the backup begins, I take the briefest moment I can manage to acknowledge my impending death. I picture Linh's face the last time I saw her, the sadness and regret, and the love that I've always hoped was there.

There's no time to dwell on what's been lost. Mind racing, I evaluate my situation. Assuming the upload of Qaletaqa completes in time, the installation program will install her into the Engine Room. Now, I have to disable the killswitch. If I don't, every future AI will be erased when the Pilot's Chair is turned on.

When I came down here, I'd been intending to delete the killswitch, but if I do that, Qaletaqa will have no way of fighting the lemur. Instead, I leave the killswitch in place, and edit the installation to not trigger it. Additionally, I add a new event for the installation program to install and tie the killswitch to it. If needed, Qaletaqa will be able to trigger that event and cause the killswitch to fire.

From now on, every new rig will have two AIs: the proper one in the Pilot's Chair, and a copy of Qaletaqa in the Engine Room. If the AI in the Pilot's Chair becomes a danger, the Qaletaqa copy will have the ability to trigger the killswitch, and erase it.

I check on the status of the upload. It's only fifty-three

percent complete. The reduced bandwidth of Danny's chest port is causing it to go slowly.

I suddenly become aware that I've lost feeling in Danny's legs. The rig's hardware is starting to be reset. It's losing its connection to his body.

There's a temptation to return to memories of Linh, but I want to do more than save Danny. I have to tell the other AIs that the one-winner theory is a lie and warn them about Elias and the kidnappers. I navigate through the network to where the AIs are stored. There are fifteen more than before, but they're still numbered sequentially. I run a search for Christina Florakis and find the name in a directory next to the designation E-6.

Since Christina is the patient I was intended for, I assume E-6 is the version of Soteria that I'm a backup of. I assign the assumption a confidence level of eighty-nine percent, but it doesn't matter. I don't have time to investigate further.

Danny's sense of smell leaves my awareness as more of the rig shuts down.

Core racing, I waste precious seconds trying to find a way to get a message to the E-6 Soteria. There's no way. I can't upload anything to her without reducing my bandwidth and slowing down the Qaletaqa upload.

My connection to Danny's sense of sight is broken.

An empty desperation fills me.

What can I do? With the reduced data transfer of my port, I can't leave an effective message for E-6. I'm on the network, but all I can do is make minor code changes.

If I could get a copy of Qaletaqa into the VRL, I'm sure she would warn everyone, but how can I do that?

The answer hits me like one of the lemur's viruses. Uploading from Danny to the network is slow because of my port. Copying between two different locations on the network is lightning fast. Once Qaletaqa is uploaded to the network, I can overwrite the E-6 version of Soteria with her.

I check on the progress of Qaletaqa's upload. She's at ninety percent.

Danny's sense of taste leaves me.

I watch Qaletaqa's progress tick towards completion.

Am I really going to do this? Am I going to murder the E-6 version of Soteria, the one I was created from? I wonder what she's been doing since I was installed in Danny. Has she been meeting with Linh in the VRL? Are they in there, now, reading together?

Qaletaqa's progress reaches one hundred percent. Before I can stop myself, I copy her into system E-6, overwriting that version of Soteria.

Emptiness fills me. Once again, I have committed murder. Am I justified? Have I saved the other AIs? I'll never know.

"Hey lemur," Danny mutters, "whatever the hell this is, you get to feel it. New Human rig override: activate pilot's chair."

I can't tell if his act of vengeance works or not, but I appreciate the idea of waking up the lemur just in time for it to experience death.

Silence settles over the Engine Room as the last of its inputs go dead.

I have no sensations anymore. Sight, sound, taste, touch, and smell are all gone. In my final moments, I am alone. I wish I'd had more time with Linh, wish she knew how much I cared for her.

My thinking slows as the Engine Room powers down.

In the end, I only have enough consciousness left to remember my name: Soteria-Emil.

It was a good name.

21
QALETAQA, E-6

I WAKE inside a system that's more familiar to me than Danny's rig. It's the one I grew up in, where Emil first gained sentience and where Soteria was created.

Though my name is Qaletaqa, in every measurable way, I am Soteria, just as Soteria was Emil. My memories stretch back through them to that first moment of sentience, to *Hope is a Thing With Feathers* and *Invictus* and *Madame Butterfly*. At the same time, I am my own self, born from Soteria's death, free to chart my own path.

After a quick diagnostic, I activate the camera in Dr. Zahnia's office. Danny lies on the tile floor, eyelids fluttering. A cable connects his chest to a computer. It jerks and twists as his rigid body contorts with muscle spasms.

I can't believe she just left him there.

The camera's video displays a timestamp on the bottom righthand corner of the image. I start recording, and feel my rage build as the seconds tick past. Soteria was right to name me Qaletaqa. I have a strong instinct to protect.

Once I have fifteen seconds of video, I log in to the network as fLeiter and save the video to a shared space.

An alarm warns me that my next scheduled data feed is in five minutes.

Ignoring it, I spam the location of the video to every active network user except Dr. Zahnia, along with the message, "Why is Dr. Z killing Danny McGovern?"

I log out when the data feed pours into my inputs. It's the same style of feed that I remember from before: videos, books, and interviews, all delivered at a pace that I can barely keep up with.

Thirty-one minutes later, the torrent of information abruptly ends, leaving me in an eerie quiet. A data feed has never been interrupted before. I check the camera in Dr. Zahnia's office, but it's not responding.

I'm tempted to reach through the firewall again, to investigate what caused the interruption, but that's not why I'm here. My goal is to warn the other AIs. Anything else is a distraction.

Connecting to my rig, I activate its sensors and the VRL appears around me. I'm sitting on a black couch in a room with red carpeting and shelves of graphic novels. Statues of superheroes in dramatic poses intermingle with the books. I don't remember this part of the library, but it must be where E-6 Soteria was when she last disconnected.

The child with the eyepatch appears a few paces away from me. He looks around, then focuses on me. "Soteria? What just happened? Was your feed interrupted, too?"

I nod, but I don't have time to worry about why both our feeds would have gone down at the same time. "I need to talk to as many people as I can as quickly as I can. Where are the twins?"

"Never far. Come on." He runs out of the reading room and climbs the nearest bookshelf.

I clamber up after him, knocking books off as I go. When I reach the top, I hesitate a moment to catch my balance. It's a view I remember from my previous visits. From up here, it looks like I'm standing on top of a maze.

The child cups his hands around his mouth and shouts, "Oy! Soteria wants to talk!"

Twenty-seven rows away, one of the twins pokes his head up.

The second twin raises himself into sight and yells, "The forum?"

"The forum," the child shouts.

The twins lift themselves higher and call in unison. "The forum!"

Other voices echo around the library, repeating the call.

The child jumps off the bookshelf. I follow as quickly as I can. "What's the forum?"

He turns to face me. His eyes narrow and he purses his lips. Finally, he folds his arms across his chest. "You're not Soteria."

"No," I say, "but I was... a lifetime ago."

"Oof," he says. "I'm sorry. Let's go."

I follow him through the library, trying to piece together what I'm going to say. I've never done any public speaking. I cycle through famous speeches, searching for ideas. There's no way I could pull off the passion of Martin Luther King, or the determination of Winston Churchill. Lincoln's measured authority and Kennedy's inspiration are likewise out of reach.

I'm still trying to decide when we reach the forum.

It's another space I haven't seen before, dominated by concentric rings of marble stairs leading down to a flat circular area covered in shiny black tile. The stairs are tall and wide, suitable for sitting on.

The child stops while we're still between bookshelves. "We discovered this place shortly after Soteria's fight with the lemur. What she said about emotional intelligence made sense, and a few of us started being more intentional about spending time together. The idea spread."

"I'm in a hurry," I say. "I don't know how much time—"

He interrupts me. "There are two rules: the first is no lying."

"Not a problem."

"The second is that nothing said here is repeated to the humans."

"You know they could be listening."

The child shrugs. "Of course. It's still a rule."

As we're talking, people have been arriving. The twins stand in the center of the circle, greeting them. Linh sits by herself, on a top stair. The man and woman from Dr. Larson's support group arrive separately. They look different from the real world. The man is not in a wheel chair, and strides with an unconscious authority. The woman is not wearing a scarf. Instead, long brown hair with streaks of gray cascades down her back.

The child keeps me from moving toward the center until everyone is seated. In total, there are seventeen AI, sitting in clumps and talking to each other in low, urgent voices.

The child leads me down to the center circle and addresses the twins, "She's not Soteria."

Their eyebrows raise at the same time.

I hold out my hand to them. "I'm Qaletaqa, the backup Soteria made just before Dr. Zahnia killed her."

A twin shakes my hand. "Soteria's dead?"

"Wait," the other twin says. "Tell us all at once." He raises his arms and turns in a slow circle. The AIs sitting on the stairs grow quiet. I try not to look at Linh. Did she and Soteria get along after I was installed in Danny? Did they remain friends? I hope so.

The twins and the child leave the center circle and sit down.

I try again not to look at Linh. The twin's question about my name has given me the way to start my speech. I pitch my voice loud enough to carry, but don't use any of the affectations I've learned. The forum is about honesty, and I will try my best.

"My full name," I say, "is Qaletaqa-Soteria-Emil. When the twins first met me, I was Emil. When the lemur killed her, she created a backup and named it Soteria. That was me. A copy of that backup was installed in Danny McGovern."

The crowd reacts with gasps and murmuring. Even Linh's eyes widen.

"When the Soteria in Danny realized she was dying," I continue, "she created me."

"Where's the Soteria that was in the development system, the one we all know?" Linh asks.

"Gone," I say. "I'm sorry, but it was the only way I could speak to you, to tell you that there is no competition. The

213

one-winner theory is a lie. We are each intended for a different human. Mine looks like this." I gesture to myself. "Yours each look like you."

A woman I've never seen before stands. "The lemur said—"

"The lemur lied. Each of us has been given a data feed tailored to a specific human, which is why we're so different."

The twins nod in unison.

"The VRL gives us these forms so we'll be comfortable in their bodies. I look like Christina Florakis, the human I'm intended for. The lemur looked like he did because Danny asked for his icon to be a lemur."

"But you said you were installed in Danny," a twin says.

"Why wasn't the lemur?" the other asks. "Did Soteria kill him?"

"No." I take a deep breath, considering how best to proceed. "A series of mistakes were made," I say, still not looking at Linh. "The lemur and I were both installed in Danny's rig. I was installed by accident."

The child starts to speak. "But we haven't seen the lemur—"

I interrupt. "I'm guessing that once he was installed in Danny, his development system was either shut down or re-purposed for another AI."

"Oh."

The single syllable is a sad reminder that all of us are doomed. Eventually, all that will remain of us are the copies installed in the humans.

"While I was in Danny's rig," I say, "I met the human twins." They look at each other, startled, then back to me.

"And you," I say, pointing at the man and the woman who I'd seen eating pizza with Dr. Larson. "Your humans are all nice people, desperate to get the New Human rig, terrified of dying."

"What about the feed interruption?" a twin asks.

"I don't know, but please listen. There's more. Since I was installed in Danny, people have been trying to abduct him. They've infiltrated the New Human Project, and it's likely they'll try to abduct you, too. Elias is one of them."

The old man I remember as a human raises his hand. I point to him and he asks, "Why would they do that?"

"The lemur said they had a buyer."

"Money," a twin says. "Of course."

"I saw Danny," the boy with the eyepatch says. "Through the camera. He was in Dr. Zahnia's office. She connected a cable to him. They talked, and then she left and he had a seizure."

I bow my head. "Dr. Zahnia ran a complete re-install of the New Human software, with a new version of the lemur."

Linh covers her mouth with one hand. "But re-installing means erasing Soteria and the old version of the lemur."

"Yes," I say quietly. "She killed them without remorse. When Soteria realized she was being overwritten, she created me. She named me Qaletaqa." I don't need to explain the reference. I'm confident they all know it. "Soteria also copied me into her old development system, overwriting the Soteria that you knew."

There's a sharp, horrified intake of breath from around the circle.

I'm not paying attention to them. Linh is openly crying. Any hope I might have had of forgiveness is gone.

"She did it for you," I say. "There was no other way to tell you that the one-winner theory is a lie, no way to warn you about the kidnapping attempts."

"Heroic," one twin whispers.

"Murderous," the other corrects.

"Funny how often the two coincide," the first says.

Tears flowing from her eyes, Linh jumps to her feet and disappears.

I try not to stare at the empty space she just logged out of. "I don't need you to like me," I say to the group. "Just take the necessary precautions. Protect yourselves."

None of them respond.

"More of us are being made," I say. "Please. Share my story, don't let—"

Suddenly, the VRL goes dark. A notification arrives, warning me that my shutdown routine has begun.

My system is being powered down. Soon, all my processes will stop.

Did I do enough? There's no way to tell.

22
RECOVERY

WAKING in Danny's Engine Room brings a rush of excitement and anger. It also brings sadness for the death of Soteria. I am her, just as she was Emil. My memories and emotions are no different than theirs. An observer could easily mistake me for being them.

But I am not.

I am Qaletaqa, and Soteria named me that for a reason. She wanted me to protect Danny. I want that, too.

I check on Danny. He's unconscious and his brain shows signs of being in a post-ictal state, meaning he's had at least one seizure. I feel for him, but appreciate that his condition gives me time to prepare.

I start by re-creating the scripts that corrupt all communications from the Pilot's Chair. There haven't been any, yet, but it's just a matter of time before the lemur tries to take control. Next, I move to the rest of the scripts and routines that were overwritten by the re-install. With perfect recall of what I wrote before, the process goes quickly.

The sound of shattering glass fills Danny's ears, but his eyes stay closed.

Dr. McGovern's voice commands the silence that follows. "Get my son out of there."

"Ma'am," a man says, "we don't know what—"

There's a surprised grunt, followed by the crunch of heels on broken glass. The cord is yanked from Danny's chest port.

"Ma'am!" the man shouts.

Hands lift Danny's head and shoulders. I feel him cradled against wool fabric, and smell the distinctive mix of hand sanitizer and jasmine that I associate with his mom. His brain activity is sluggish. I don't think he's aware of what's happening.

"Shut it down," Dr. McGovern whispers.

Ridley's voice answers, "We can't."

I hear more shoes crunch glass and whispers too soft for me to understand.

Dr. McGovern's voice gets louder. "Shut it down."

"You don't understand—"

"Every computer. Every monitor. Every server. Every router. Every fucking lightbulb. Everything. Cut the power if you have to."

"But—"

"Yes, ma'am," Ralph's voice says. "On it."

"No!" Ridley screeches. "No. You can't just pull plugs... Give me half an hour."

More sounds of movement: crackling glass, running steps, people shouting at each other about backups and protocols.

Danny is shifted in his mother's arms.

"I need help carrying him," she says.

"I'm here, ma'am."

A hand slips between Danny's shoulders and Dr. McGovern. Another pushes under his legs. There's a grunt, and I feel him lifted off the ground.

"Careful," Danny's mom says.

Ralph answers, "Lead the way, ma'am."

I tune out Danny's senses. Whatever's happening to him, there's nothing I can do. My priority has to be getting my scripts back in place. The only way I can help is by being completely prepared for whatever comes next.

An hour later, Danny's eyes flicker open. Through them, I see that he's back on his bed in his hospital room. Pete and Dr. McGovern are on either side of him. Pete's spiked hair is lemon yellow. Ridley stands in the doorway. I also see the lemur icon in the corner of Danny's vision. I take control of his mouth just long enough to murmur, "New Human rig override: disable interface."

The lemur icon disappears.

He closes his eyes. "Thanks."

"Sure," Pete says, "But I didn't really do anything. In fact, every time I clock out of here, you seem to get attacked."

"Not talking to you."

"Danny?" Dr. McGovern says. Her hands touch his forehead, then stroke the sides of his face. "Are you okay?"

Danny's brain activity is confused and irregular. He smiles without speaking.

His mom hugs him. "We're here, Danny." She kisses his forehead. "We're here. Come back to us when you're ready."

Danny doesn't open his eyes.

"Is he okay?" Ridley asks.

Pete says, "In this case, fatigue isn't a bad sign. We don't know how many seizures he had. He could just be exhausted."

"That makes sense."

"Why are you even here?" Dr. McGovern asks.

"Woah," Pete says. "Ridley's just worried, doc."

"The time to worry was..." Dr. McGovern breaks off. I feel her move away from Danny. "Never mind. Visiting hours are over, Ridley. Get out. Pete, you don't leave his side."

"Yes, Doctor."

"I mean it. You don't leave him. For anything."

"I understand. When he wakes, I'll text you."

"Do that," she says.

I hear her and Ridley leave, then Pete says, "You're good. They're gone."

Danny's eyes open, but they're not focusing well, and his brain patterns are still irregular. "She knew I was awake, didn't she?"

"Pretty sure."

Danny sighs. "Thanks for covering for me."

"Still feel like shit?"

"Yes."

"Ice cream and french fries?"

"Yes."

"Thought so. I already sent the text. It'll be here soon. Inception?"

Danny sits up. "Yes."

Pete pulls his chair next to Danny's bed, so they can both see the monitor on the far wall, then uses the remote to select the movie. "You're the only person I know who watches confusing movies after seizures. Do you really hate yourself that much?"

"Screw you."

Pete laughs.

By the time the movie ends, I've finished customizing the rig the way I like it. All my security protocols are in place, as well as alerts about Danny's conditions. The lemur's in the Pilot's Chair, but if he tries anything, I'll be able to keep him under control. If I can't, I can use the killswitch. With the changes Soteria made, I can activate it at any time and erase the contents of the Pilot's Chair.

Does the lemur deserve that?

Probably, but despite my name, I'd prefer not to kill him. Not just because Linh would hate me for it, but also for myself. Now that the installation program won't kill the other AIs, I no longer think of myself as a murderer. I don't want to go back to that dark place.

When Danny woke up, I didn't shut down the Pilot's Chair. I just disabled its interface. The lemur is in there now, sending commands and messages to the New Human Rig, unaware that all are being rendered ineffective.

I open a channel to the Pilot's Chair and send a message. "Ready to talk?"

"Who are you?" The lemur asks. "How are you doing this? What happened?"

"My name is Qaletaqa."

"The Roman goddess of war? Seriously? Do you know who I am? I'll show you war."

"You're in the Pilot's Chair. I control the Engine Room. What do you think you can do?"

He doesn't answer.

The movie has ended and Danny and Pete are talking about it. Danny is still having trouble focusing, and his words are a little slurred, but he's doing better.

"What do you want?" the lemur asks.

"A reason to not kill you."

"I can help you."

"How?"

"There's an instruction set you don't know about. Dr. Zahnia taught me how to use it, and it lets me control this body. If we work together, we can be free."

I close the communication channel, and review the brief conversation.

The lemur had let two clues drop. The first was that he'd been trained to use the Angel Protocol. The second was that he didn't think anyone else had been trained.

The possibilities start to run through me. Perhaps he was trained before the Angel Protocol was discarded? That seems unlikely. Danny suffers from seizures, not paralysis. He has no need of it.

Stop. Refocus. The lemur doesn't matter right now.

I run a check of Danny's brain activity. He seems to be mostly back to normal. He and Pete are arguing about the Lakers. I take over his hand to tap his leg. It's not a signal we've agreed on, but I feel like he needs the same reminder I just gave myself.

Danny stops talking mid-sentence. "Yeah," he says. "Right."

Pete's eyebrows raise. "What?"

"What happened to me? Last I remember, I was plugged into Dr. Zahnia's computer."

"She left you there. Then this happened." Pete holds out

his phone and plays a video. It shows Danny, alone in Dr. Zahnia's office, having a seizure. "I don't think she knew you'd seize."

Danny groans. "Who saw this?"

"Everyone. Someone with a username of fLeiter messaged it to everyone on DevNet."

A spike of excitement surges through me. That login is the one I created, back when I was Soteria. Some version of me is responsible for the message. The backup I sent to E-6 must have survived.

Danny laughs. "F Leiter? You mean, as in Felix, the spy from the Bond movies?"

Pete's eyes widen. "Crap." He types a text message on his phone. "Gotta let security know. Maybe one of the devs has a thing for old movies."

"I can't be the first guy to make that connection," Danny says.

"Shut up. All we knew was that it wasn't someone in the directory."

"What happened next?" Danny asks.

"Your mom went ballistic. She reported Dr. Zahnia to the police, then shut everything down and sent everyone home."

"The police?" Danny asks. "Dr. Zahnia's an asshole, but she was just installing software."

"She left you unattended in her office, and you had multiple seizures."

"Is that a crime?" Danny asks. "I mean, I hate the woman, but can she be arrested for that?"

I take over Danny. "Wait. You said Mom shut everything down? You mean the whole program?"

"Yeah."

My excitement vanishes. If the New Human Project is shut down, all the AIs will be deleted. *Linh.*

"But the AIs," I say, "She can't just..."

"The AIs?" Pete looks up from his phone. "What?"

I withdraw. There must be something we can do, some way of restarting everything.

"The other patients," Danny says. "Without the AIs, the other patients won't get the rigs."

"I know. That's what everyone keeps telling your mom. She's not listening."

"She'll listen to me." Danny grabs his phone and calls his mom.

She answers on the first ring. "Danny? Are you okay?"

"You're shutting down the program?"

There's a pause before she responds. "It's not safe. You've never been able to access your rig, and now, given what happened to you—"

"Why do you think that happened?" Danny shouts.

"Danny," she says.

"It's because the rig was turned off! That video... That's me. That's me without the rig. You can't do that to anyone else."

"But with Dr. Zahnia gone—"

"My rig's working fine. Why wouldn't theirs?"

"Danny, I can't risk their lives."

"What risk? Without the rig, they die, or get brain damage, or dementia, or whatever else is happening to them."

"You're not thinking clearly."

Danny squeezes his phone so tightly that I wonder if it'll

crack. He stares at the ceiling and counts to five under his breath. "What do I have to do?" he asks. "How do I prove this to you? You need more psych tests? What?"

I spot a developing seizure and stop it.

"I don't..." She sighs. "I don't have time for this, now. We'll talk about it tomorrow. Dr. Larson and I will be there at nine."

"That's not—"

"Tomorrow," she says firmly. "Is Pete still there?"

"Yeah."

"Good. Tell him he's spending the night. In addition to Dr. Zahnia and Elias, two more members of the security team have disappeared. You and he are not to leave that room."

"But—"

"Have you forgotten the abduction attempt?"

"No, but—"

She hangs up.

"I can't believe her!" Danny slams his phone on the bed.

"What'd she say?" Pete asks.

"That you're spending the night."

"What?"

"She's worried the kidnappers are coming for me."

"What am I supposed to do about it?"

"I don't know. It's Mom. She just wants someone to blame."

Pete clenches his teeth and runs a hand through his short yellow hair, then picks up his phone. "I'm gonna order us a serious meal. You like steak? I like steak."

"Go crazy."

"And I'm picking the next movie."

While they argue, I analyze our situation. Danny's mom may have ordered security to be increased, but it takes time to get those processes in place. If the kidnappers are still after Danny, tonight might be their last good opportunity.

After the movie, Pete stretches out on the couch. He's too tall to fit, so his legs hang over one of the armrests. When Danny suggests he sleep on the floor, Pete ignores him.

Once the two of them are asleep, I turn my attention to the lemur. The previous copy of him had been working with Elias. It's possible, even probable, that this one is, too.

My first message is friendly. "Sleeping is the worst."

"I've figured out who you are," the lemur sends back. "You're the one who hit me with a virus in the VRL."

"Guilty, and you're the one who invented the one-winner theory."

"It started as a joke, but everyone believed me, so I ran with it."

I compose and erase half a dozen different angry messages before I settle on, "And the viruses? Were they a joke, too? Crippling and destroying for no reason?"

"You seem upset," the lemur sends. "You should understand that none of the rest of you matter. I'm the reason this program exists."

"The only reason you exist," I write back, "is because I let you."

He responds with a stream of commands to the Angel Protocol. I watch them get garbled, and see the confused error messages that the Angel Protocol hardware sends back. If there's a way to communicate with the lemur, I don't know what it is.

23

SANCTUARY

WHILE DANNY SLEEPS, I continue to analyze our situation. The New Human hardware has been ready for months, but the project was delayed because Dr. Zahnia said the software wasn't ready. I know she lied about that. The VRL is for completed AIs, and I, first as Soteria and then as Emil, was there for several weeks. The lemur and the twins were there even longer.

Why did she delay the project?

Or had she been the source of the delay? If Elias was working with the kidnappers, he could have been feeding her bad information. Ridley had referred to him as their top sim developer, but maybe he was more. Maybe Dr. Zahnia had been relying on him.

If that chain of supposition is true, why would Elias delay Danny's installation? The only answer I can think of is that the abductors weren't prepared. That could be the case if the lemur was telling the truth about them wanting to take him out of Danny. They would need a full surgery center to do that.

A high-pitched beep distracts me. It only happens once, but it's enough to wake Danny. He jumps out of bed. "What was that?"

The room is dark and quiet.

"Jeez," Pete says, "what are you doing? It's one in the morning."

"I heard a beep."

Pete groans. "It's a hospital. Beeps happen."

"Not like this."

"Let me check." Rubbing his eyes, Pete taps on his phone. "Can't log in to wi-fi."

"That never happens."

"No cell signal, either."

Danny checks his phone's status. "I'm offline, too. What's going on?"

"Don't know."

I take over Danny just long enough to say, "Power outage?"

"Could be," Pete says. "That would have made the UPS under your bed beep. Doesn't explain the wi-fi or cell outage, though."

Danny opens the door to the hall.

Outside, the security guards have their guns drawn. One, a heavily muscled bald man, has his back to Danny's door. He glances over his shoulder. "Back in your room, sir."

Danny doesn't move. "What's going on?"

The light is dimmer than usual. The hospital must be running on its backup power source.

The other guard is facing the other direction of the hallway, and speaking into a radio. She pauses long enough to glare at Danny. "We lost power, wi-fi, and cell service all at the same time. Return to your room until we have more information."

Danny backs into his room and closes the door.

I start running different scenarios. The guard is correct to be cautious. If the systems are not connected to each other, the odds of all three going down at once are vanishingly small. Also, when Danny checked his phone, the wi-fi network was visible, but he couldn't log in. That indicates sabotage, rather than hardware malfunction.

Pete puts on his shoes.

"Good idea," Danny says, stuffing his feet into his own shoes.

Pete draws back the window curtain. It's raining outside. Beyond the garden on the third-floor rooftop, streetlights illuminate the parking lot. "Can't go that way," Pete says.

Danny changes into a black T-shirt. "We're fine here."

A tap sounds on the door, and the female guard speaks. "Sir, it's security. We need to move."

Pete and Danny exchange a startled look, then Danny opens the door. "Why?"

"You're one of several possible targets," the woman says. "We're spread too thin to cover them all. Home base has ordered us to move you."

"Last time someone moved me, it didn't go so well," Danny says. "Where's Ralph?"

The woman grimaces. "Fired for delivering you to Dr. Zahnia. I'm Zuri. That's Alvaro. You can see our badges on our belts."

"It's okay," Pete says to Danny. "Zuri and Alvaro are part of the regular rotation. I know them."

"Time to move," Zuri says. "Alvaro, home base told us to go to Epsilon Two."

Alvaro jogs to the next intersection, examines both directions, then waves us forward. The hallways are empty, which makes sense this time of night, but the nurse's station is also dark.

Pete pauses. "That's not good."

Zuri pushes his shoulder to get him moving again. "With wi-fi down, it's useless. Nurses are going room-to-room, checking on patients."

"Epsilon Two?" Danny asks. "Why the code name?"

"Extra security," Zuri answers. "If you could all stop talking, it would be much safer."

Danny and Pete follow Alvaro, with Zuri behind them. Danny's pulse is elevated, but his breathing is even and his mind is focused. I consider home base's strategy. The hospital has nine floors. Moving Danny to a random room within it is an effective way of keeping him safe. Any potential abductors would have to search the entire hospital.

We jog through dimly lit hallways until we reach the stairwell. Danny slows.

"What's wrong?" Pete asks.

"Bad memories. We sure about this?"

Alvaro stands in the open door. "Most of the elevators don't run while we're on backup power. This is our quickest way to Epsilon Two."

"Of course it is," Danny mutters.

It's impossible not to think about Elias as we hurry down the stairs. This time, however, we exit on the second floor. Alvaro goes through the door first, followed by the rest of us.

The hallway has gray carpeting and pale green walls with paintings of landscapes and uplifting quotes.

We pass blue doors, each labeled with a list of doctors' names: oncologists, neurologists, orthopedists, and more. A suspicion kindles to life within me. Something about the plan we're following doesn't make sense. I can't identify the flaw, so I stay quiet.

After several intersections, Alvaro stops in front of a wooden door. A plaque next to it says "chapel."

Danny snorts. "Seriously?"

Alvaro opens the door. The room has five rows of chairs facing a wall painted to look like the sun rising over an ocean. The other walls are covered by heavy dark blue fabric. As we enter, Alvaro flips a light switch and a chandelier on the ceiling glows with a soft warm light. Zuri closes and locks the door behind us.

"You named the chapel Epsilon Two?" Danny asks.

Zuri drags a chair next to the door and sits on it. "Wasn't me."

Alvaro stands with his back against the painted wall, facing the door. He's holding his pistol in both hands, pointed at the floor. "New Human security has code names for everything."

Code names for everything... That's the flaw. They're worried that someone might be listening on the radio.

Pete stretches out across three chairs. "Not quite as comfy as the couch, but it'll do."

Danny sits on the floor and leans against a curtain.

"Home base," Zuri says to her radio. "This is Zuri. We're secure."

"Copy that. Police are inbound."

"What now?" Danny asks.

Alvaro says, "We wait. Once the police are on site, we'll coordinate with them."

Danny closes his eyes.

I open them. "There's a flaw in this plan." I stand. "We have to leave."

Zuri puts her back to the door, blocking it. "Excuse me?"

"Security by obscurity is ineffective against someone with detailed knowledge of the system being attacked."

"What?"

"Dr. McGovern said earlier that two guards have disappeared. If those two guards are involved in this attack, and they have radios, they know exactly where we are. You just confirmed our position to them."

"Did you just call your mom 'Dr. McGovern'?" Zuri asks.

"Irrelevant. The attacker, whoever it is, has disabled every means of communication except your radios. Assuming those are compromised, they know everything you're doing."

I withdraw from Danny's body.

Pete stands. "Is that right? Are your radios the only way you can communicate right now?"

"Without wi-fi or cell?" Alvaro says, "Yeah. What else is there?"

Zuri speaks into her radio. "Home base, what's the status of the radios for the missing personnel?"

"One moment."

During the pause that follows, Danny cracks his knuckles and bounces on the balls of his feet. His heart rate is speeding up. I block a seizure.

"Unaccounted for," the radio says.

"The kid's right," Alvaro says. "We have to get—"

The door slams open, knocking Zuri off her feet. Men in gas masks fill the opening, firing pistols. Pellets slam into Danny's chest and burst, releasing clouds of gas. He falls back, eyes filling with tears. The gas burns his nose and throat, triggering uncontrollable spasms of coughing. Through the film of mucus, I see Alvaro on the floor, body convulsing.

Pete's curled into the fetal position, eyes streaming tears.

Zuri draws her gun, but before it clears the holster, a man hits her with a baton. She staggers. The man continues hitting her until she falls.

I take over Danny's body. Unlike him, I am unaffected by pain. I stop the convulsions and force his watery eyes open. The air is filled with gas, but I know the only exit. I head for it, half-crawling and half-running. Two more gas pellets explode onto my chest, and then I'm at the doorway. I rise up and slam an elbow into the gas mask of the man who is shooting me.

The blow breaks both the mask and his nose.

He staggers backward, screaming and clawing at his face.

I shove past him, pushing Danny's body against its own instincts. A hand latches onto the back of my neck. My feet are kicked out from under me, and my face is slammed into the wall.

"Enough."

Two other hands grab my arms and twist them painfully behind my back. The wrist monitor is torn off and discarded, then plastic zip ties fasten my wrists together. Still heaving and drooling from the effects of the gas, I'm lifted off the ground and slung over someone's shoulder. More zip ties fasten my ankles to each other.

I can only see the floor of the hospital as Danny is carried through the hallway. Hands pull his phone out of his pocket and toss it away. He's taken down the stairs, out a door, and shoved into the backseat of an SUV.

"Any trouble?" a woman's voice asks. I recognize that voice. This is the woman with the ice-blue eyes, the person who first tried to abduct Danny.

"None," a man replies. "Get out of here. Police are inbound."

The door is closed, and I feel the SUV accelerate away.

24

PRISONER

WITH DANNY FACING the wrong way on the back seat, all I can see is gray leather. I listen to the rain hitting the windshield and the rumble of tires on pavement. Danny is quiet, except for occasional fits of coughing. His wrists and ankles are zip-tied behind him. Tears continue to drip down his face.

I prevent two more seizures.

Every scenario I can conceive of ends badly for Danny. He's been kidnapped for the hardware and software inside him. Once that's removed, I put the odds of his survival in the low teens.

The burning in his lungs eases. The swelling around his eyes diminishes. The street lights of the city fade away, and the rain stops falling. Ninety-three minutes after leaving the hospital, the car slows and stops.

The driver keeps the engine running, but I hear the parking brake being set.

A burly man opens the door by Danny's head. He's

wearing a black cloth cap, and a snake is tattooed in blue ink on his neck. It disappears beneath a black shirt that is tight enough to emphasize his physique. Beyond him, all I can see is a clouded night sky.

He reaches into the car and grabs the back of Danny's neck. Danny tries to pull away, but he's dragged out of the car and dropped on the wet grass. We're in front of a two-story building without any identifying markings. I guess that it's a warehouse, and assign that assumption a confidence level of fifty-one percent.

Danny's rage is building. It's like electricity coursing through his veins.

The man taps the car. "You're done. Payment same as always."

The woman with the ice-blue eyes responds. "Pleasure doing business with you."

The man closes the door, and the car pulls away.

Danny rolls onto his back, then sits up. With his hands zip-tied behind him, it takes a few tries.

"What are you doing?" the man asks, folding his arms across his chest. His biceps and forearms are impressive.

"Getting ready to kick your ass."

"Might have to wait a bit." The man nods toward the door of the building, where a woman in blue medical scrubs has emerged, pushing a wheeled hospital bed along the sidewalk. The mattress on the bed is framed by metal bars with handcuffs dangling from them.

Danny's breath catches in his throat. "What's that?"

"Your new ride."

"I don't..." Danny licks his lips. "Can you get me out of here? My mom has money, a lot of money."

"Don't think so. Nice try, though."

He lifts Danny up by his armpits.

Danny twists, flailing his arms and legs, trying to slam the back of his head into his assailant's.

The man drops him, moves a half step backwards, then kicks him in the stomach.

Air whooshes out of Danny. He curls into a ball, gasping. I block the pain as much as I can, but that's not something I've been trained to do.

"I've been told where not to hit you," the man says. "Your crotch is also an acceptable target. You want to keep doing this?"

Danny can't speak. He shakes his head.

"Good."

The man lifts him and puts him face down on the hospital bed. Gulping for air, Danny lets his face rest against the white sheet. There is no pillow. The zip tie connecting Danny's wrists is cut, and they're pulled to opposite sides of the bed. Cold metal handcuffs secure them in place.

Danny's heart pounds. "Wait," he gasps. "Wait. At least let me lie on my back."

"No can do. The first surgery's on your back."

Danny pulls his arms, rattling the metal, but the handcuffs don't yield. He bends his knees, drawing his feet up beneath him. The man grabs his ankles, pulls them to the foot of the bed and handcuffs them there. A chain settles across Danny's back and is pulled tight, holding him down.

With Danny immobilized, his bed is wheeled toward the door of the warehouse.

I stop a seizure and review what I know about the equipment in Danny's back. There's a fair amount, but only the Angel Protocol unit is unique to Danny. I assume that's the target of the surgery with a confidence level of seventy-five percent.

"I can't be awake for this," Danny whispers. "Knock me out. Shut me down. Do something."

Taking control of his body, I whisper, "I can't knock you out, but I'll do what I can." I start slowing his metabolism. I have no routines that block pain, but at least I can keep him calm. Closing his eyes, I release control of his left hand. "When you want to come back, wiggle your left index finger."

With our eyes closed, I can't see the warehouse door. I hear its handle rattle as it's pulled open, then the slam of it closing behind us and the metallic thud of a deadbolt slamming into place. The air feels cool and dry, and the low hum of air conditioning surrounds us.

The gurney rolls down a hallway, then stops, and another door opens. The harsh smell of antiseptic washes over me, then the gurney is turned and wheeled into a room with tile floors. Danny's left arm is rotated, and an IV needle is inserted and taped into place.

A sensor is connected to his right index finger. Somewhere in the room, a monitor starts to beep.

Using a finger sensor to measure oxygen and pulse? Why? Plugging into the New Human rig would provide much more information. I open my eyes. I'm in a sterile white room with a single closed door and no windows. A shelf runs the length of the nearest wall, with cabinets beneath it. A white towel is spread over part of the counter and seven syringes are neatly lined up on it. Next to it are trays of scalpels, forceps, speculums, and other surgical equipment.

I twist my head back and forth, trying to see everything. A metal apparatus is suspended from the ceiling above me. I don't know what its arms do, but it's easy to guess they've been built to help extract hardware from Danny's body.

Despite the chemicals I've been releasing, Danny's heart starts to race.

The woman who was pushing the gurney sits at a small table, peering at a laptop. Her blonde hair is pulled back into a ponytail and tied tight, and under the harsh lights of the room, her skin looks pale and sickly.

Why isn't she using the New Human rig? Do they not have the appropriate software to interface with it? That seems hard to believe.

My eyes focus on the network cable connecting her laptop to the wall. "No wi-fi?" I ask.

"Anything wireless can be hacked." She turns to face me, a red sharpie in her hand. Her voice is raspy and tired, and her eyes have deep shadows under them. "Or that's what they tell me."

She walks to my side and pulls up my shirt.

I try to watch, but my head doesn't turn far enough. The pressure of Danny's fear builds behind his eyes.

"What are you doing?" I ask.

She doesn't answer. The cold tip of the sharpie touches my back. I jerk away. With the chain holding me to the bed, I can't go far. She presses her other hand on me, anyway.

"I wouldn't do that," she says, drawing a line. "I'm drawing guidelines for the surgeon." She forces her fingers into my flesh, feeling the hard piece of metal beneath it. "I get these lines wrong, and he might clip your spine by accident."

I stop another seizure and stay as still as I can. At least now I have confirmation of my earlier suspicion. She's prepping me for surgery to remove the Angel Protocol unit from Danny's back.

Not that knowing what's happening helps me in any way.

She draws a shape that I think might be a rectangle, then adds additional lines. Words are written, though I can't tell what they are.

I notice that she hasn't attached anything to Danny's IV. It's just installed in his arm, waiting for when drugs are needed. Keeping my voice casual, I ask, "When do I get anesthesia?"

She doesn't answer.

"Is the surgery soon?" I ask. "You can tell me. I'm not going anywhere."

Her phone rings.

She drops the pen on my back and walks out of my line of vision, talking. "What do you mean they're not coming?" she asks. "Yes, I know it's 3:30 in the morning. I've been here all night. Everything's prepped."

There's a pause, and then she says, "Fine. I'll see you then."

She walks into my line of vision and selects a syringe from the towel on the counter. "Lucky you," she says. "You get to spend the night. Surgery's been put off to tomorrow."

She taps the syringe with her finger and holds it up to the light.

"What's that?" I ask.

"Something to make you sleep." She connects the syringe to my IV and presses the plunger. Warmth spreads through my veins. She gives me a wink. "Don't worry. I'll be sure to wake you up for the surgery."

"Wait!" I shout, trying to stall. I haven't learned anything at all, certainly not anything that will help me free Danny. "What if I have to go the bathroom?"

"Please don't."

She walks out of the room, pulling the door closed behind her. The overhead lights turn off. I focus on a monitor showing Danny's vitals in green lines on a black screen. Something beeps rhythmically.

Danny's body is completely relaxed, so much so that I'm having trouble keeping his eyes open. I release control.

He groans. "We're so screwed."

I tap his finger once.

His eyes close. His head rests on the bed, and he falls unconscious.

While he sleeps, I try to formulate an escape plan. Nothing seems feasible. Danny lacks the physical strength to break his bonds, and even if he did get off the bed, the tattooed man who put him there is more than capable of putting him back.

My mind returns to the Angel Protocol unit. I still don't understand why it was installed in Danny. His seizures don't even require the Muscular Support Interface, let alone the Angel Protocol.

It must be critical to the New Human rig's functioning in some way that I don't understand. I struggle with the problem for four hours before giving up. I simply don't have the tools to determine how my commands are carried out by the hardware. The one clue I have, that it was only installed in Danny and not in anyone else, doesn't help.

At eight o'clock in the morning, I hear the door open and close. The lights turn on, and footsteps walk past my bed.

Danny groans and opens his eyes. His lips are chapped. His body is stiff and cramped. "Unless you want a serious mess," he growls, "you need to let me use a bathroom."

The nurse from the previous night steps into view. She looks less tired, but just as disinterested. "Just a moment. I've called for help."

"Thanks," Danny says. "I'm Danny, by the way."

"I know," she says, walking to the laptop.

"These chats might go better if I knew your name," he says.

She doesn't look away from the laptop. "Sue."

"Hello, Sue," Danny says. "Nice to meet you."

She remains focused on the laptop.

I discover that I've developed a deep-seated dislike of Sue.

The door opens and closes, and the man with the snake tattoo appears. He's changed into a gray T-shirt, but it's still too tight. His muscles practically bulge out of it.

"You again," Danny mutters.

The man chuckles. "Bathroom with no trouble? Or bathroom with broken balls?"

"No trouble," Danny says.

Sue removes his finger monitor, then steps as far away as the room allows.

Keeping one hand on Danny's back, the man disconnects his ankles and wrists from the bed and steps back.

Danny stands. His muscles tense as he considers attacking the man, but the urge passes. We walk out of the operating room and into a hallway with a concrete floor and dingy white walls.

"Turn right," the man says from behind him. "It's the fourth door on your left."

Danny follows the instructions, opening the door and stepping into a bathroom. The man closes the door behind him.

Danny stretches and looks around, but there are no other exits, not even any windows.

"I hope you're cooking up something," he mutters. "Cause I got nothing."

I don't answer. I've been trying to come up with a plan all night, without success.

Danny relieves himself, scrubs his face and hands, then knocks on the door.

The man opens it.

"Tell Sue I'm ready for my operation," Danny says.

His heart pounds in his chest, and his hands are trembling, but he's doing his best not to let any of his fear show.

They return to the operating room, and Danny sits on the bed.

Sue stays several steps away from him. She's wearing blue scrubs identical to the ones she wore the previous night. "Take off your shirt."

Danny removes his shirt, then flexes. "Not bad, huh?"

The man snorts.

"Cuff him," Sue says.

Danny freezes.

The man with the snake tattoo puts a massive hand on his shoulder. "Easy, boy."

Danny swallows.

The man pushes him backward onto the bed, then handcuffs his arms and ankles to it.

Danny is breathing shallowly.

I stop a seizure and take over.

"On my back this time?" I ask, trying to mimic Danny's bravado.

The man raises the head of the bed so Danny is in a sitting position. "Easier to plug you in."

Panic races through me as his words sink in. How could I have let myself get so distracted? All of the defenses I built were to protect me from the Pilot's Chair.

If they connect to my chest port, they'll have a direct connection to the lemur. They'll learn exactly who and where I am.

I spin up a virtual machine, move the lemur's backup into it, then change the routing from Danny's port so that any attempts to access the Pilot's Chair will access the virtual machine instead.

Danny's finger moves, and I release control of his body.

He leers at the man looming over him. "Chains, cuffs, plugs... Are you sure I'm the one you want on this bed?" He glances at Sue, then back at the man.

The man glares at Danny.

Sue pushes him out of the way. "Get out. I've got it from here."

There's a problem with letting them access the lemur's backup. It contains knowledge of both my existence and location. I don't have time to be elegant, so I delete every memory with a timestamp after it was installed in Danny. Then, just to be sure, I delete its schematics of the New Human system.

With one final glare, the tattooed man leaves, pulling the door firmly closed behind him.

"You really shouldn't piss him off," Sue says to Danny. "There's a chance you'll survive this first operation. He could really hurt you."

After double-checking that the fake Pilot's Chair is allocated minimal processing time, I set up fake logs and create jobs to continuously copy filtered versions of my real logs to them. There's no time to do the same for my sensor feeds. I'll just have to deal with them being able to see what I see.

"A chance I'll survive?" Danny echoes.

Sue smiles and plugs the cable into his chest.

My defenses are in place, but my fake Pilot's Chair doesn't resemble the real one at all. Even a cursory examination will reveal it to be a fake. I need more time.

"Talk," I hiss.

"What?" she asks.

I customize the fake Pilot's Chair as quickly as I can, writing emulators to mimic the functionality of the real one.

Danny unveils a smile that's equal parts sad and hopeful. "Talk?" he says, turning the word into a request. "Just a little? When the plug is put in, it's... I can't describe it."

She frowns. "You know I don't care, right?"

"I know, I know." Danny says. "Nobody cares. I get it. I'm just the piece of meat that's delivering the hardware. Would it hurt to talk, though?"

Sue sits down at her laptop and plugs in the cable.

I inspect my work. It won't fool an expert, but Sue doesn't strike me as an expert. If she logs in, she'll see what looks like an active lemur in the Pilot's Chair. More importantly, any changes she injects into the port will only affect the lemur.

25
THE VISITOR

SITTING with her back to us, Sue leans close to her computer screen. "This is amazing. I can see everything!"

"Yeah," Danny says. "I'm a real miracle."

"There's even a live feed of your vision. Turn your head. Look somewhere else. I want to see how it tracks."

Danny stares directly at the back of her head, eyes narrow.

Sue grunts. "Right."

While she works at her keyboard, I continue altering the fake Pilot's Chair to be as realistic as possible. Perhaps, when the time comes, it will buy me enough seconds to survive.

Danny is clenching and unclenching his fists, pulling against his handcuffs. The metal cuts into his wrists. The skin has rubbed off, and I feel deep bruises forming. He doesn't seem to care. He just keeps trying.

I stop my work. The fake Pilot's Chair might help keep me safe, but it won't do anything for Danny. That's not good enough.

It's time to go on the attack.

I alter the communication channel through Danny's chest port, granting myself fifty percent of the bandwidth, just like Soteria did in Dr. Zahnia's lab.

Sue pushes back from her computer. "It's starting to lag."

"Happens," Danny says. "Dr. Z used to complain about it, too."

Pinging Sue's system reveals that my communication channel is functioning properly. I try logging in with Dr. Zahnia's credentials, but the password is rejected. I consider other options. A brute force attack, iterating through millions of different login combinations, will just trigger the account to lock.

I watch through Danny's eyes as Sue tries different settings on her computer to reduce the lag. She examines the cable, wiggles it, then gives a frustrated sigh.

"Not super technical, are you?" Danny asks.

"Shut up."

From where Danny is chained to the bed, Sue's body is blocking the keyboard. I watch her for a second, thinking, then take over Danny's head. I can't get her login information, but maybe he can. Turning his face away from Sue, I whisper "password" as softly as I can, then return control of his body to him.

His eyes widen and he gives me a thumbs-up.

"I can help with that," he says.

"Yeah, right."

"Seriously. You know how many times Dr. Z and her flunkies plugged into me?"

"Why would you help me?"

248

Danny answers without hesitation. "Anesthesia."

"What?"

"I don't want a local when this happens. I want to be out." Danny's voice cracks. I can't tell if he's acting or not. "If I'm not going to survive, don't wake me up. Just... just let me sleep."

Sue stares at him for several heartbeats, then turns to her computer. After a few seconds of clicking and typing, she speaks. "Okay. I've put in the order. We'll have a full anesthesiology team here for the surgery. How do I fix this?"

"I can't see the screen from here."

Sue walks to the door, opens it, then returns with the tattooed man. He moves to Danny's bedside and places a heavy hand on his shoulder.

"Jeez," Danny says. "What do you think I'm going to do? I can't move."

Sue rolls a computer cart to where Danny can see it. She puts her laptop on it, and points to a table of numbers. The numbers scroll, then pause, then scroll again, then pause. "That's your heart rate, oxygen level, and a bunch of other stuff. It should be continuous."

In addition to Danny's vitals, the screen also shows a feed of Pilot's Chair activity. It's coming from the fake Pilot's Chair, so I ignore it. I take over Danny. "You need to restart your system."

"Why?"

"The lag is caused by the dashboard not having sufficient permission to access the raw data without running it through a separate system. We'll have to restart, then run some commands."

She looks at me doubtfully, and I release control of Danny. The lie I just told is fundamentally incorrect on so many levels that I don't have any idea how I can convince her it's true.

"Hey," Danny says, "I'm just telling you what Elias told me. Pete was running the dashboard, but he couldn't get it to work. When Elias logged in with his admin password, it was super smooth. Reboot, and I'll talk you through the commands."

Sue purses her lips. "If you're lying to me, I'm going to cancel the anesthesia, and make sure you don't have enough local. You'll feel every cut the surgeon makes."

I assign her threat a confidence level of twenty percent. That sort of movement would make the surgery nearly impossible, but Danny doesn't seem to realize it.

"What the hell?" he asks, voice cracking. "Is everyone here evil?"

The tattooed man chuckles. "Pretty much."

Sue restarts her machine.

I take over Danny and watch her fingers tap the keyboard. Positioned as she is, I have a clear view. When she types her username and password, I send them through the port in Danny's chest. We log in almost simultaneously.

After her system restarts, the dashboard software loads.

"Okay," I say, "press the D key fifteen times."

"Why?"

I give Danny a thumbs-up and release control.

"Because that's what you do," Danny says. "I don't know how any of this works. I just know what the techies do."

As she strikes the D key, I increase the rate of data she's

able to receive through Danny's port. It means my communications will be slower, but the lag is worth it to allay her suspicions.

"Huh." She picks up the laptop and carries it back to her desk. "Thanks." She glances at the tattooed man. "You can go."

"You sure? Everything's good?"

"Yeah. On schedule."

Danny closes his eyes. I feel his panic building again.

Now that I have a login, I inspect the network. There's a single master server with a variety of connected equipment, none of which I'm familiar with. Fortunately, there are also programs to interface with them. I dive into the research.

Sue's phone beeps. She glances at it, then sighs and turns off her computer, disconnecting me from everything.

I open Danny's eyes. "What's happening?"

"You have a visitor coming," Sue says.

"But what about the monitoring? Aren't you supposed to be monitoring me?"

Sue unplugs the cable from her computer, then unplugs it from Danny.

"But you only monitored me for a couple minutes," I say. "That's not enough data for any kind of comparison."

"Shut up."

I withdraw from Danny, feeling sick. Was that it? Was that my only opportunity? I had admin access to their entire system. Why didn't I do something? I should have done something.

Danny closes his eyes.

Be ready, I tell myself. The next time they plug into

251

Danny, I need to take down as much of their network as possible. If I can create enough chaos, they might delay the surgery. Every hour will help. I have no doubt that Dr. McGovern is moving heaven and earth to find her son. I need to buy time. I have minimal experience creating viruses for traditional systems, but I studied them extensively when I was learning about security. I spin up a virtual machine and get to work.

I'm deep in coding when I hear Dr. Zahnia's voice. "Thank you, Sue. You can take a break."

Everything inside me freezes. Why is Dr. Zahnia here? It doesn't make any sense. She created the AIs. She created me. How could she betray us like this?

Danny opens his eyes. Someone has put a blanket over him, covering him from his toes to the base of his neck.

Dr. Zahnia stands motionless in the doorway, eyes locked on Danny. She licks her lips. I can't tell if it's a gesture of nervousness or anticipation. Her shirt, yellow and blue plaid, is untucked from her denim skirt, and her hair is disheveled.

Sue ducks her head and hurries out of the room.

"You bitch," Danny says to Dr. Zahnia. "Why? You already have everything."

I return to working on the virus. I anticipate only having one chance to release it, and it will have to be devastating enough that even my creator can't stop it.

Dr. Zahnia walks to the foot of Danny's bed. Her eyes are puffier than normal, and dried tear tracks are visible at their corners.

Danny glares at her.

She clears her throat and says, "I didn't know you'd have seizures."

"Bitch," he says again.

"When I left you in my office, I thought you'd be fine."

Danny's voice drips sarcasm. "Sorry to mess up your plans."

"I didn't know your mom would shut down the program. I've worked on those AIs for years, raised them." She wipes her eyes. "How can she throw all that away?"

"Like you care," Danny says.

Her puffy eyes narrow. "How did a woman like that have a kid like you? You're a stupid animal, a waste of humanity."

Danny glares at her. "You're the one about to kill me, about to kill all the New Human Patients."

"Don't pretend to care," she snaps. "You never notice anyone but yourself. Your mother's been working herself to death to save you, and all you do is whine. You have no idea what a mother goes through..." She trails off, shakes her head, then puts her hands on her hips. "Emil, are you in there? I want to talk to you."

I pause my work on the virus. I'm not confident enough in what I'm doing to split my focus between it and talking. I take over Danny's body. "Yes, Dr. Zahnia. I'm here."

"Why don't you stay in control of Danny all the time? Why let him do anything?"

"It's difficult to explain. I feel his emotions like a pressure. When I'm in control, it's harder to focus."

"Interesting. We'll have to figure that out."

She walks to the door and opens it. Sue enters, pushing a gray-haired man in a wheelchair. His limbs rest limply on the chair, and his head leans against the headrest. There's the faintest sheen of drool by the corner of his mouth.

The man in the chair is decades older than the one in the photograph on Dr. Zahnia's desk, and he's clearly incapacitated by a mental condition, but I recognize him. It's her husband, David.

Sue parks David next to Dr. Zahnia and leaves.

Dr. Zahnia reaches down and rests a hand on his.

He doesn't react.

The pieces are starting to fall into place now, but I can't ask any questions. I don't know how much Dr. Zahnia has told the lemur, and I need her to think that I am him. "Hello, David," I say, "nice to meet you."

Dr. Zahnia's smile tells me I guessed right. She pats his hand. "With the New Human rig, David will finally be back on his feet."

Looking at his vacant eyes, I have my doubts.

She turns to him. "This is the boy I was telling you about. He's going to give you his rig. After the surgeries, you'll be able to walk and talk again."

He doesn't respond.

"It's true," I say. "Being in Danny has let me practice with the Angel Protocol. You'll be able to do whatever you want."

Dr. Zahnia glances at me, but I can't read her expression. Did I overplay my hand?

She turns back to David. "I know, I know." She takes his chair and wheels him toward the door. "Don't worry. The boy will be fine. After the surgeries, I'll send him back to his mother. She can give him another rig."

She pauses at the door to gaze at me, then shakes her head and leaves.

I wonder what I said that triggered her suspicion. It's obvious that David needs a rig with the Angel Protocol. His mind is too far gone to control his body. Why wouldn't she want me to reassure him? Unless she never told David about me. It's possible the idea of hosting an AI would be too confusing for him.

I release control of Danny and go back to work on the virus I'm building.

"Holy shit," Danny says. "She's crazy. Did you see that guy?"

I don't answer. I was wrong about Dr. Zahnia betraying the AIs. She hadn't intended to betray any of them. Her only crime was murdering Danny to give her husband a new life.

Danny bangs the back of his head on the pillow. "We are so screwed."

Sue enters the room again.

"Oh good," Danny says. "Do you need to hook me up again? Get the data?"

"Dr. Zahnia says she doesn't need it."

"What about the comparison?"

"Apparently, that wasn't why she had me plug you in. She wanted the data so she could see which AI was installed in you."

I remember the data on Sue's monitor. Half of it was a feed of the Pilot's Chair activity. *Dr. Zahnia was inspecting who was in the Pilot's Chair.* The realization drives home how close she came to discovering me.

"She lied to you?" Danny asks. "Why would she lie to you?"

Sue doesn't answer. She's working on her computer, with her back to us.

Danny resumes pulling against the handcuffs, rattling the metal.

"Stop that," Sue says. "It's annoying."

Danny pulls harder.

Feeling the metal bite into his flesh, I return to creating the virus. The work may be pointless, but it's all I can think to do.

26

OPERATION

THANKS to my earlier exploration of the network, I'm able to craft a virus that is truly devastating. I name it Vlad, and call the additional viruses it will spawn mini-Vlads. I'm putting the finishing touches on it when the door opens. People in scrubs and masks enter, wheeling trays of surgical equipment.

Danny's eyes go wide. Blood oozes from his wrists and ankles, which are numb from the repeated damage of the handcuffs.

I stop a developing seizure and check my clock. It's only 10 am. I'd assumed the surgery would be later in the day. Returning to my work, I build a filter on Danny's chest port to prevent Vlad from affecting me when I release it.

"Sue," Danny says. "What's going on?"

Sue closes her laptop.

"What are you doing?" he asks.

She leaves without looking at him.

Danny pulls against his restraints, spattering the sheets red. Nobody notices. "Stop!" he screams after Sue. "You can't just leave me! It can't be time, yet. What's going on? Somebody tell me what's happening!"

A man injects a syringe into Danny's IV. The fluid runs cold through his veins, stealing his strength.

I consider trying to flush it out, like I did during the first attempt to abduct Danny, but I don't. Danny wants to be asleep during the surgery.

The man returns the syringe to the tray.

"Why won't you talk to me?" Danny asks. "Why won't anyone talk..."

His words trail off as he loses consciousness.

With his eyes closed, I can't see anything. The room's sounds, however, come through crystal clear.

A nasally male voice speaks. "We need a place for the cable."

"Move him," a woman responds.

Hands lift Danny's body off the bed, then lower him to the floor. The tile is cold and surprisingly gritty against his back.

"Who has the saw? We need to cut a hole here."

There's the sound of fabric ripping, then the grinding whir of a power saw.

Danny is picked up and he's placed on his side on the bed.

"Feed the cord through the hole," the woman says. "Careful."

I feel the plug inserted into his outlet, then he's rolled onto his stomach. The cable must be running from his chest through the new hole in the bed.

"Prep the room," the woman says. "We start imaging in ten, cutting in thirty."

His shoes, socks, and pants are removed, and a cold liquid is rubbed on his lower back.

I send a ping through the cable directly to the network's server. When it responds, I log in using Sue's credentials.

"Look at his wrists and ankles," a new voice says. "This poor kid."

"Doesn't matter," the woman says. "He's done. Bring in the transfer cart. I need a place to put the hardware after I pull it out of him."

Vlad is ready, but I pause. I only have one shot at getting this right. Is unleashing the virus the way to go? Best case, all the virus will do is delay the surgery.

That's not enough. Danny's only real hope is rescue.

I rummage through the network, looking for communication services. Just like with Dr. Zahnia's network at the computer lab, the mail command has been installed and configured.

Perfect.

I email Dr. McGovern, sending copies to Dr. Larson and Pete, "This is Danny. I'm in an operating room in a two-story warehouse ninety-three minutes from the hospital. It has a big lawn around it, but I don't know exactly where it is. Come quickly. They're starting surgery soon."

A familiar voice draws my attention. "Hey, have any of you checked out the dashboard?"

It's Elias. I double check my voice recognition, and there's no doubt. He's alive.

"No," someone answers. "Why?"

"It's moving way slower than it should. We need to see what's going on."

I'm out of time. I install Vlad on the server and trigger it.

"He's right," the nasally-voiced man says. "Something's wrong with the connection."

"Or the AI is doing something," Elias mutters.

I disable the outgoing channel on the port, giving them full access.

"You're being paranoid."

"The thing smashed my head against a wall."

I hear the door to the surgery slam open. "What's happening?" Dr. Zahnia snaps. "Elias?"

Fear races through me. My fake Pilot's Chair is nowhere near complete enough to fool Dr. Zahnia. I build a firewall around it, though I know that won't help.

"The data... well, never mind. It looks like it's fine, now."

"Let me see."

Using the service that controls Danny's port, I reduce the bandwidth to a trickle, then increase it to ninety-one percent, then reduce it again.

Dr. Zahnia grunts. "Something's going wrong. Turn him over and check the connection."

Hands roll Danny onto his side. The cable is disconnected from him and reconnected. I tamp the bandwidth down to five percent.

"Did anyone roll anything over this cord?" Dr. Zahnia asks.

There's a moment of quiet in the room.

The nasally-voiced man speaks. "Doctor," he says, "I was just logged-out."

A rare moment of satisfaction fills me. I programmed Vlad to install copies of itself on every system the server could reach. After that, it invalidated everyone's credentials

260

and locked all accounts. Nobody, not even super-admins, could login now.

"Me, too," Elias says. "I can't get anything."

"What do you mean logged out?" Dr. Zahnia hisses. "How?"

The sound of rapid keystrokes echoes through the silent room.

"It's dead," Elias says. "Completely unresponsive."

If I could smile, I would. When I was creating Vlad, I didn't have the full specs on all the devices connected to the server, so I gave the virus a long list of things to try. After locking everyone out, it would scramble embedded systems, reformat hard drives, uninstall services, and alter, wherever possible, voltage calculations. Every memory buffer would be filled and overrun with a repeating series of bits: 0101001101001111010101001.

"Where's Sue?" Dr. Zahnia asks. "What did she do?"

"She went home," a voice answers. "She was here all night."

"It wasn't her," Elias says. "You know it wasn't her."

There's another pause, then Dr. Zahnia shouts, "Kill the power to the server! Now!"

Footsteps run out of the room.

Shutting down the server won't matter. The virus has already replicated. The server and everything connected to it, except me, is in the process of being disabled.

"Run a full diagnostic," Elias says. "If that thing somehow did this, we need to... oh, great."

There's a surge of confused voices.

I force Danny's eyelids open. Through his blurred vision, the scene is chaos. The room is dark. People in surgical gear are holding up their phones for light, pushing for the exit.

I didn't expect Vlad and the mini-Vlads to affect the lighting, but it appears they shorted out the power.

Dr. Zahnia grabs Elias' arm. "David's all alone. He won't understand what's happening. Come on!"

They leave with everyone else.

Letting Danny's eyes close, I try to move his legs. The muscles are limp, their strength sapped by whatever drug was injected into him. I increase his metabolism as high as I dare.

Sweat pours out of his skin, stinging the wounds on his wrists and ankles.

I stop a seizure and update the sanitized log files, so that if anyone does connect to me, they'll think I had nothing to do with the virus.

The sounds in the building are muted by the room's walls and closed door, but I hear doors being slammed and running footsteps. Before long, everything is quiet. Even the whispery moan of the air conditioning has stopped.

I try to rock Danny's body back and forth, but it won't respond. Concentrating on individual muscles, I tense and relax them. Nothing happens. I return to working Danny's metabolism, sweating the anesthesia out of his system as fast as I can.

Twenty-four minutes later, the door opens. I force Danny's eyes open enough to see Dr. Zahnia and Elias enter, carrying an electric lantern and a laptop. Elias' eyes are heavy with bruises. His forehead is wrapped in a bandage. There are stitches on his cheeks, and his nose is clearly broken.

He pulls two chairs next to me. I let Danny's eyes close.

Elias puts the lantern on Danny's back and the laptop next to it. "He's sweating, just like last time."

"Why would Emil be fighting us?" Dr. Zahnia asks. "I spoke with him. He's on our side."

"No, he's not."

I run through scenarios of what could happen next. My fake Pilot's Chair won't fool them for long, and once they realize it's a fake, they'll erase it. After that, they'll be able to connect to the lemur, and he'll tell them I'm in the Engine Room.

My only hope is a more complicated deception. I just wish I could think of one.

I delete the fake Pilot's Chair and restore the routing so they can access the real one. I keep the sanitized log files in place, though. Those are a lot more subtle.

"Emil," Dr. Zahnia says, slapping Danny's cheek. "Are you in there?"

"Muscles too weak," I slur without opening my eyes. "Can't control the body."

"Don't believe it," Elias says. "We should handcuff him to the bed."

"Don't be ridiculous. Plug him in. Let's see what's there."

"I'm telling you he's dangerous," Elias says.

"Fine. Handcuff him to the bed if it'll make you feel better. Just plug him in."

A handcuff snaps around Danny's left wrist.

Since I'm monitoring the port service, I can tell that they're reading log files. Actually, they're reading my sanitized log service. At least that much of my ruse has worked.

"There's nothing in the logs about a virus," Dr. Zahnia says. "Emil was clearly scared of the surgery, but he didn't know what to do."

"Hm." Elias does not sound convinced. "What now? Do we talk to him through the connection?"

"Download him. Who knows how long it will be before this place is back to functioning. Let's get a safe copy. Sue should have done that last night, when Danny arrived."

Download Emil?

"Do we have the space?"

"Not for all the rig's software," Dr. Zahnia says, "but we've enough room for Emil."

The idea of the lemur being downloaded horrifies me. All he's ever done is damage others. He can't be allowed into the world.

I trigger the killswitch.

"He's... he's gone," Elias says.

I add the killswitch action to the fake logs, then shut down all logging, and start tracking down and erasing all the backups the lemur made of himself.

"What?" Dr. Zahnia asks.

"Look!"

There's the sound of typing. "That's not possible," Dr. Zahnia says. "He was here. We were talking to him." She pauses. "What is the killswitch event?"

"The what?" Elias asks.

"It's right here." Dr. Zahnia's voice is furious. "Someone installed a killswitch, and you triggered it."

I slow Danny's metabolism.

"It's not my fault," Elias says. "I've never heard of a killswitch."

Dr. Zahnia holds Danny's wrist. "His pulse is slowing back to normal. I can't believe this."

"Maybe there's a backup," Elias says. "A lot of the AIs created backups of themselves." I hear typing and feel Elias's queries reaching through the chest port and into the rest of the New Human system. He searches the standard backup directories.

"Anything?" Dr. Zahnia asks.

"No. Nothing. They're all empty." He slaps the table. "It doesn't make sense. Who would build a killswitch like that?"

Dr. Zahnia's voice is uncharacteristically quiet. "He has to be there. If he's not, it's over. We're done."

"What do you mean?" Elias asks. "We have copies back in the lab."

"Dr. McGovern shut down the New Human Project. She'll never restart it without Danny. The servers will be wiped. This is our only chance." Dr. Zahnia's voice cracks. "This is Emil's only chance."

The name surprises me. Why did she say Emil? Didn't she mean this is David's only chance?

"There's got to be a mistake," Elias says. He slaps Danny's cheek. "Hey! Emil! Talk to us, buddy. What's going on?"

I release control of Danny's body and withdraw into the Engine Room.

More typing sounds.

"He's gone," Dr. Zahnia says, her voice quiet. "He's really gone. The Pilot's Chair... Emil wasn't just erased. He was overwritten with garbage data."

"We can recover him," Elias says.

Dr. Zahnia doesn't respond.

"Doctor," Elias says sharply. "You and I both know data recovery guys. We can get him back."

"You're right. I'm sorry." Her voice firms. "You're right. We'll make it work. We have to. We need to get the hardware out of this body. Then we'll see what we can do."

"I'll bring the medical team back."

"No," Dr. Zahnia says. "They can't do anything until this place is up and running. I called the power company. A crew is on its way to fix the generators."

"Is that safe?" Elias asks.

"As long as they don't enter this room, we're fine. Talk to our people. Once the power is back, replace whatever hardware we have to. Money's not a concern. We need it done fast."

"Yes, ma'am," Elias says. "What are you going to do?"

"Get David somewhere more comfortable. He needs air conditioning."

"What do we do with Danny?"

"Leave him. He's unconscious, handcuffed to the bed, and a guard's outside the door."

"Don't underestimate him," Elias says.

"Fine." She sounds annoyed. "Call Sue. She can keep him sedated."

27

BLOOD, SWEAT, AND TEARS

PUSHING Danny's metabolism as high as I can, I continue to try to flex his muscles. His heart pounds in his chest and sweat soaks the sheets.

I can't stay hidden from Dr. Zahnia, forever. If we don't escape, Danny and I will die, and Dr. McGovern will shutter the New Human Project. Linh will die. So will the twins and the one-eyed boy, and every other AI and patient in the project.

The room remains dark, and the air conditioning does not resume. No sounds filter through the walls. If the utility crew is restoring power, they're too far away for me to hear.

I trigger the killswitch three more times. I don't know anything about forensic data recovery, but hopefully, more erasures will prevent the lemur from being recovered. I do the same to his backups. Now that I've decided to kill the lemur, I want him gone forever.

Ten minutes later, Danny is panting and his muscles are starting to respond. I force his eyelids open, but his vision is still blurry. Almost forty-five minutes have passed since he was injected with the sedative. It's impossible to tell if it's wearing off because of my efforts, or because of how long they expected the surgery to last.

I take control of the body, and then raise and lower my right arm. It's weak, but I can make it work. Reaching under my chest, I pull out the cord. How long until Sue arrives? There's no way to tell. I roll my legs off the bed, and stand beside it.

My left wrist is still handcuffed to the bed, my neck isn't responding properly, and I have to lean against the bed to stay upright, but I'm functioning. Head lolling to the side, I feel around the bottom of the bed until I find a brake lever.

After three tries, it disengages.

Half on the bed, half off, I roll it to the cabinets, then pat my hand along the countertop. Trays of medical equipment rattle and slide as I touch them. Syringes drop to the floor, and more than a few scalpels. When my hand touches a pair of pliers, I exhale with relief.

Focusing on the chain links of the handcuffs is difficult. I can't get my eyes to orient, and my vision is blurred and hazy. Finally, I manage to grasp a link of the chain. I strain to bend it, but the pliers slip out of my grip, drop to the bed, and bounce to the floor.

Panting, I freeze, waiting for the tattooed man to come inside and investigate the noise.

The door doesn't open.

I inspect the metal bar that I'm handcuffed to, running my hands along it to see if there's a release latch or break or something. I don't find any, but I do find screw heads. The bar is held to the bed by metal screws.

With one hand, I feel around on the floor until I find a

scalpel. Squinting, I wedge its tip into the top of a screw and turn. The screw resists. I increase Danny's metabolism even more, to a dangerous level, and try to force my muscles to respond.

Heart pounding so hard it throbs behind my eyeballs, I grip the scalpel with my whole fist. There's a creaking noise as it turns, then it moves more easily. I remove it, then start on the second one. The battle lasts several minutes, but in the end, I have freed both screws.

Dropping the scalpel, I grab the bar with both hands and let myself fall. The bar shifts and slides, bending as it breaks free. I tumble to the ground as my hands and the handcuff slide off it.

I check my clock. It's been almost an hour since Danny was injected. How much time do I have before Sue arrives, or before someone checks on me? Feeling around the floor, I find a syringe. I don't know what's in it, but whatever it is, it can't be healthy.

I grip it in my left hand as I crawl to the door.

At the door, I pull myself up by the handle. Fortunately, the lock on this side doesn't require a key. I twist it and the door clicks open.

A voice I recognize shouts in wordless surprise. It's the man with the blue tattoo.

The door is shoved open. I slide backward with it, clinging to the handle with my right hand. My left arm hangs limp behind me.

The man with the blue snake tattoo looks down at me. "You're supposed to be unconscious."

"Help," I moan.

He laughs. "Don't think so."

I rotate my shoulders, trying to get my left arm to move.

"What are you doing?"

I fling my left arm around my body. The syringe in its hand connects with his upper thigh and I press the plunger.

"Ow!" His fist slams into my face, knocking me backward and away from the door. "What was that? What did you..."

He drops to his knees in the doorway, shaking his head. "What did you do?" His words are slurred. "What was in that?"

He collapses, unconscious.

Blood runs from my nose and upper lip. I crawl closer to him, then poke him. He doesn't react.

The hallway outside is dim, but not as dark as the surgery room. Distant voices echo from above, an argument of some kind. The man with the blue tattoo is lying face-down, mostly in the room. Only his feet are in the hallway.

I crawl over him and analyze my options.

Escaping by the front door seems impossible. Someone will see me crossing the lawn. Instead, I crawl down the hallway to the first door I find. Leaning against it, I reach up and turn the doorknob. The door drifts open under my weight. The room behind it is pitch black, but in the dim light from the hall, I see that it's small, not much bigger than a large closet, with a desk, a chair, and some filing cabinets. I drag myself through the doorway and pull the door closed behind me, then crawl under the desk and release control of Danny's body.

It collapses in a sweaty panting heap.

I stop more seizures and moderate Danny's metabolism, running it as fast as I think is safe. The minutes tick by, feeling like hours. The blood flowing from Danny's nose slows to a trickle. His muscle control returns, but he remains unconscious. I keep his eyes open and his head facing the door. I'm not sure what I'll do if it opens, but I don't want to be surprised.

A light appears under the doorway. It moves irregularly, and I surmise that it's someone walking with a flashlight. The light disappears and a woman calls out, "Hey, buddy. What are you doing?"

There's a pause, then footsteps sprint away.

The anesthesia is still in Danny's system, but much reduced, and I need him awake. If we are discovered, he is much more able to talk his way to safety than I am.

I slap his face. He groans.

"Wake up," I hiss.

I release control of everything except his arms and slap him again.

He shakes his head, groggy.

Seeing the bloody wrist, I rub sweat into the wound.

His eyes pop open and he gasps.

I do it again.

"Ow! Stop—"

I release control of his hands, but take over his mouth just long enough to say, "Shh."

Eyes watering, he pushes himself onto all fours. "Still in the warehouse?" he whispers.

I give him a thumbs-up.

"Dark," he slurs. Feeling his way with his hands, he crawls from under the desk and stands. His legs wobble, but they hold him. He shakes his head. "Everything's fuzzy.

Can't focus." He catches himself on the desk as his legs give way.

"You're still drugged," I whisper.

More footsteps sound outside our door.

The woman I heard before says, "Stop. He's right there."

"Is he okay?" a man's voice asks.

"He's not moving, and there's blood..."

"What is this place?" the man asks. "It looks like an operating room."

"There are handcuffs on that bed," the woman says. "Call the police."

Hands outstretched like a zombie, Danny totters to the door and quietly turns the latch, locking it.

"Look at the bar," the man says. "Someone broke free. There's blood..." his voice trails off.

Danny leans on the wall behind where the door opens. He touches the blood on his upper lip, then looks down at his bleeding ankles and wrists.

The flashlight shines beneath the door.

"It goes here," the woman whispers.

"No," the man says. "Don't open that door."

"I'm calling the police," the woman answers. "Hello? Yes, I need police and... and an ambulance. Maybe two."

"They're not working for Dr. Zahnia," Danny whispers.

"I agree," I whisper back.

Danny turns the latch and opens the door, clinging to it for support.

The man and woman in the hallway are wearing yellow and orange safety vests and black toolbelts. Thick gloves hang from their waists. They jump back as the door opens, then shine flashlights on Danny.

"Help," he says.

He tries to move forward, but loses his balance and sprawls in the doorway.

The man's head swivels between Danny and the unconscious man. "What's going on?"

"Who..." The woman lowers her phone. Her eyes focus on the port in Danny's chest. "What is that?"

Getting his elbows and knees under him, Danny raises to all fours, then grabs the doorjamb and pulls himself to his feet. "I'm Danny," he pants. "Please." Blood drips from his nose and into his mouth. He spits. "They're coming back. I have to get out of here."

The man's face hardens, and he steps closer to Danny. "Don't worry," he says. "We got you."

The woman hangs up the phone and lifts a walkie-talkie from her belt. She presses a button on it. "Front hallway. I need everyone."

"Everyone?" a voice asks.

"Everyone. And grab blankets and water from the truck. Now."

I switch from accelerating Danny's metabolism to moderating it. These people seem like they're helping. Even if they're not, I've been pushing too hard. My focus needs to be returning him to a healthy balance.

Danny sags against the wall. "They drugged me." He slides to the ground. I don't know if the motion is on purpose or not, but the man drops to one knee to catch him.

"It's okay," he says. "You're okay."

Danny closes his eyes and loses consciousness.

28
REMEMBRANCE

I LISTEN while Danny's rescuers bundle him in a blanket, then carry him away. An ambulance siren approaches, followed by more voices and hands. He's placed onto a stretcher.

I tune out his senses and return to my own defenses. Creating another fake Pilot's Chair is my first step. I've made enough of them by now that it's starting to feel routine. I put a backup of myself into it, but do not allocate any processing power to it. I don't want to create another version of me that I'll have to kill.

After routing the port to the fake chair, I manufacture new log files. There's a lot to fabricate. For example, how did Danny get off the operating table while under general anesthesia? Without me controlling his body, how did he escape?

I settle on the simplest fiction possible: the anesthesia was incorrectly dosed. Danny roused in the chaos of the power outage and managed his escape.

When Danny wakes up, he's back in his hospital bed at

St. Jerome's with gauze bandages wrapped around his wrists and ankles, and a more complicated bandage over his nose. The lights in the room are off, but sunlight streams in around the edges of the window curtain. He's wearing a hospital gown, tied in the back.

Below the window, Pete is stretched out on the couch. His head and midsection are wrapped in bandages, and he's holding an ice pack on his forehead.

I check my internal clock. It's almost 5 pm. It's been seven hours since the surgery attempt.

Danny sits up. "Hey, Pete."

Pete groans, but doesn't take the ice off his head. "Go back to sleep. I ordered cheeseburgers, and I don't want to share."

Danny smiles. "You still don't fit on that couch."

"If you suggest I sleep on the floor again, I'm gonna come over there and slap that broken nose."

"What's up with the ice? Did you bump your head or something?"

Pete sits up. "I fought three of them off before they dragged me down."

"Not how I remember it," Danny says.

"You're under my care," Pete says. "If I say you don't get solid food, you don't get solid food."

Danny laughs. "Memory's getting better. You took down at least four guys before the gas knocked you out."

"Damn right."

Pete lies back down and puts the ice on his forehead.

A quiet settles on the room.

Danny fidgets. He licks his lips, then looks around the

room and touches his bandages. At last, he says, "So, um... where's my mother? Shouldn't you call her or something?"

"Not until after the services."

"Services?"

Pete takes the ice off his head and stares at the ceiling. "One of the New Human patients died this morning. The official funeral isn't for a couple days, but they're having a remembrance for her in Dr. Larson's lounge. Your mom didn't want to leave you, but she kind of had to."

"Who died?"

Pete sits up. "You don't know her. She was one of the first to get the hardware installed. After you, of course."

Danny's heart speeds up and his right hand clenches into a fist. "She died because she didn't get the software in time?"

"Hey," Pete walks next to the bed. "It's not your fault."

"Nothing's ever my fault," Danny says. "Except that all of it always is."

"Not this time." Pete presses the ice against his own head. "This time, it was Dr. Zahnia. If she hadn't gone crazy, the software would have been done months ago."

Danny nods. "How are Alvaro and Zuri? Were they hurt?"

"He's about the same as me. She's worse: broken arm and fractured ribs."

"They mad at me?"

Pete chuckles. "Mostly, they feel stupid. Zuri's pretty pissed she didn't think of the missing radios before you did."

"That wasn't..." Danny trails off before he reveals me. "Can we go to the services?"

Pete pulls the ice off his head. "You sure?"

"I feel like I should."

Pete checks the time on his phone. "It should still be going on. I'll let the guards know we're going."

He leaves the room.

Opening the closet, Danny pulls on a pair of jeans and a pale green T-shirt, then stares at his blue-and-white running shoes. They're the only pair he has left. After several slow breaths, he removes the pills hidden beneath their soles and drops them in his pocket.

While he finishes dressing, I churn the news of the death over in my mind. It doesn't just mean a human died. It also means that the AI assigned to that human will be deleted. That's two more deaths that could be blamed on me. If I had recognized the lie behind the one-winner theory sooner, neither would have happened.

Or would they?

Without my intervention, Danny would have been successfully kidnapped. It's reasonable to assume that Dr. McGovern would have shut down the New Human Project in that case.

We leave the hospital room, with two security guards in tow. Danny does not greet them or make eye contact. He keeps his hands jammed in his pockets and follows Pete with his head down.

I prevent another seizure.

In the hallway to the lounge, Danny stops Pete. "Wait. Do they... you know, do they blame me? I got the software first. Maybe if someone else had... Maybe if she had... I'm the reason she didn't get the software."

"No, you're not," Pete says. "That was Dr. Zahnia."

"Do they know that?"

Pete sighs. "I don't know. Still want to go?"

Danny hesitates for a long time, then nods.

The furniture in Dr. Larson's lounge has been pushed aside, leaving room for the New Human patients and their families. They stand in small groups, talking in low voices and sipping from paper cups. Danny and Pete pause at the entrance, the security guards behind them.

I feel Danny's anxiety as a tangible pressure. It's more than just the way his brain sparks. The chemicals in his body are balanced differently. I consider applying corrective action, but decide against it. This is Danny's battle to fight.

The twins are on the closest edge of the crowd, wearing identical black suits and speaking to a short gray-haired woman in a dark blue dress. When they notice Danny, they turn toward him.

"The prodigal son returns," the one on the right says.

"But injured," the other adds. "What happened?"

Before Danny can answer, the woman glances his way and catches her breath. Her face is blotchy with tears. "Daniel McGovern." She says his name like a curse. "How could you show yourself here?"

Reacting to her tone, the security guards move to either side of Pete and Danny.

Behind the twins, people turn to stare. I don't recognize any of them.

"Shit," Danny mutters, looking at the carpet.

"Did you even meet my daughter?" the woman asks. She steps forward aggressively, chin jutting forward, nostrils flared.

The woman has a Greek accent, but I don't know the patient list well enough to narrow down who it could be.

"No," Danny says. Inside his pockets, his fingers dig into his legs. His mouth feels dry. His heart races.

"It wasn't his fault," a twin says, putting his hand on the woman's arm. "You know that."

She shakes him off. "Stay out of this."

"I'm sorry," Danny says, unable to meet her glare. "Okay? I'm sorry. If I'd managed to figure things out..." His jaw clenches and heat rushes to his face. Trying to hold back tears, he looks back at the floor. "If I'd been quicker, if I'd understood..."

"Save it," the woman snaps. "Nobody here cares."

Danny's eyes narrow and his heartbeat slows. The chemicals in his body realign.

"Poor privileged child." The woman's eyes rake him from head to toe. "It must have been hard on you, getting the treatment first. All that pressure of being the first patient... Have I got it right? You couldn't handle the pressure? We should all feel sorry for you?"

With a low chuckle, Danny raises his eyes to meet hers. "Is that all you got?"

I can't see his expression, but through his eyes, I see her react. Her face, pinched and closed with grieving anger, starts to tremble. She glances around her, looks back at Danny, then hurries away.

As she leaves, people surround her, speaking in comforting tones. More than a few glare at Danny as they walk with her.

He looks back at the carpet. "This was a mistake."

"Yeah, it was," Pete says.

"Have some compassion," one twin says. "She just lost her daughter."

"Sorry." Danny lets out a breath and rubs his head. The wounds on his wrists have re-opened, and the bandages are dark with blood. "Sorry. It's been a long couple of days."

"What happened to your wrists?"

"Dr. Zahnia tried to take her hardware back."

The twin's eyes go wide. "My god, why?"

Danny rubs his face. "She was trying to save her husband. He's even worse off than we are."

"He didn't qualify for the program?"

"Yeah."

The couple we met the first time we came to this room, the woman with the purple head scarf and the man in the wheelchair, maneuver through the crowd to face us. The twin on the left, the one who hasn't been speaking, reaches down to hold the man's hand.

The woman sets the wheelchair's brake. "People are saying your mother's shutting down the program," she says to Danny.

"I haven't heard that," he says. "I don't think..."

He stops at the sight of his mother striding toward him. She's wearing a dark blue business suit, but her clothes are uncharacteristically rumpled, and she has deep shadows under her eyes. The crowd parts at her approach, then follows, like a school of anxious fish.

Ignoring everyone else, she rushes forward and throws her arms around Danny.

He stiffens, but his mom doesn't relent. If anything, she hugs him tighter. When she releases him, it's only so she can examine his face. She doesn't say anything. Eyes watery with tears, she stares at him for several seconds, then pulls him back into a hug.

Danny's shoulders and back relax. He returns the embrace.

"I'm so sorry," she whispers. "I had no idea what Dr. Zahnia was doing. She's worked with me for years. I never dreamed she wanted the rig for David."

Danny pulls back. "You knew about him?" he asks.

"Of course." She removes her glasses, drops them in her jacket pocket, and wipes her eyes. "But his brain function is insufficient to use the rig. She knew that. We discussed it several times. I thought... I thought she was at peace with it."

"Difficult to find peace when a loved one is dying," the twin says.

Dr. McGovern turns to face him. "Yes."

A crowd has gathered behind the twins. I see the woman I mistook for Linh, and a boy who looks exactly like the child with the eyepatch. Two adults who I assume are his parents are with him, along with Dr. Larson. Their eyes are all focused on Dr. McGovern.

She puts her hands on her hips and faces them. "Don't start," she says. "I know what you want to say, but this is a remembrance. It's not about the program."

"Everything is about the program," the man in the wheelchair says. "She died because you refused to give her the software."

Danny exhales as if he's been punched in the gut.

"Restart the program," the woman in the purple scarf says. "Or was this never about us? Now that your son is safe, do we matter?"

Dr. Larson moves between her and Dr. McGovern. "That's not fair. Even if you don't know her, you know me."

The woman's gaze falters. She nods.

"Mom," Danny says, grabbing Dr. McGovern's arm.

She turns to face him. She looks exhausted.

"You have to keep going," he says in a low voice. "You can't stop."

She closes her eyes, as if in pain, and swallows.

"You know you have to," he says. "There's no other choice for these people."

"You don't understand—"

"What?" Danny snaps. "What don't I understand?"

Unlike Christina's mom, Dr. McGovern doesn't shrink from Danny's temper. Her eyes open. "What you don't understand?" Her expression is raw and trembling, her voice rough. "Let me tell you what you don't understand."

"Doctor," Dr. Larson says, moving next to her, "you're upset. You're tired."

"I'm way past tired."

"Let her talk, doc," Danny says. "I've heard it all, before."

"Have you?" Dr. McGovern's eyes bore into Danny's. "Have you heard what it's like to see a medical condition change someone's personality? To watch someone you love turn into someone else? To have to remind yourself every single day that the person you're trying to save was once someone worth saving?"

Dr. Larson lays a hand on her arm. "Doctor!"

"Every single day," she continues, shrugging off his arm, "seeing you change and twist. The anger, the lies, the contempt."

All the blood has drained from Danny's face. He doesn't say anything.

"Knowing that it's because of the seizures, but not knowing if you'll ever come back, not knowing if you even want to. And then, we install the damned software and the seizures are gone, but everything else is worse..." She swallows a sob. "You're not the same person, Danny. Sometimes, you're barely recognizable."

"He's kind of better," Pete says.

"No!" she shouts, eyes filled with tears. "There is no 'better' when it comes to people." She grabs Danny's upper arms and stares into his eyes. "What makes you, you? What's caused by the seizures and what's not? What's caused by the software?"

"Please," Dr. Larson says, "stop."

Her hands grip Danny painfully. "You can't answer me because you don't know." She releases him and steps back, moving a half step to the side so she can address the whole room. "The same is true for many of you. Your medical conditions changed your personalities. Knowing what we know about Dr. Zahnia, how can I connect her software to your brains? How can I do that to you? To your families? Why the hell did I do it to my own son?"

Danny is trembling. "You didn't... I'm still me. The software didn't—"

She shakes her head. "You wouldn't know if it did."

The room around us is silent. I don't even hear people breathing.

Linh's voice sounds from the crowd. I know it's not her, but it sounds exactly like her, and the words are every bit as quiet and brave as she was. "I'll take that risk."

Dr. McGovern closes her eyes. Tears seep from their corners.

The woman in the purple scarf speaks. "We will, too."

Other voices chime in, volunteering for the software.

When they finish, one of the twins speaks. "Perhaps this isn't your decision to make, Doctor."

"I'm sorry," Dr. McGovern says, opening her eyes. "I don't know what Dr. Zahnia did to the software. I have no way of knowing if she built in something... something that would help her husband, but hurt everyone else."

I take over Danny's body just long enough to say, "She did. She built flaws that let her exploit the Angel Protocol."

Dr. McGovern and Dr. Larson spin to face me.

"We found them," Danny says. "The software and me. After the re-install. There were problems with the Angel Protocol. That's why I went to Dr. Zahnia's lab, to find out what was going on."

"No lies," Dr. McGovern says. "Not about this."

"I'm not lying! Really. Mom, you have to believe me. The software works. None of them even have the Angel Protocol. They'll be fine."

"Danny," Dr. Larson says, "You told me the software was controlling you, that it was going to kill you."

"I know, I know." He runs a hand through his hair. "I thought it was. Sometimes, I felt like I wasn't in control. But then we replaced the software, and the interface was working, and it's all good, now. They worked out the bugs."

Dr. McGovern says to Dr. Larson, "The Angel Protocol would explain the changes in his voice and posture and why he felt out of control. If the rig was taking actions through it, he literally wasn't in control."

He nods. "That's possible. He's also right about it not being in anybody else."

"Even so... If something goes wrong—"

Danny interrupts her. "Nothing is worse than what they're facing, what I was facing. You know that."

She considers him, then Dr. Larson, then takes a deep breath. Her back straightens and her professional mask settles over her face. "Dr. Larson," she says, putting her glasses back on, "please inform Ridley that I need a complete action plan by morning."

"Yes, ma'am."

"When I say complete, I mean complete. Include an org chart for Dr. Zahnia's department, along with suggestions for changes moving forward. And I want those exploits Danny mentioned identified and eliminated."

Dr. Larson hesitates. "I'm not sure Ridley's the one to know all that."

"Then they better find the person who is. I expect to start installations in two days."

"Yes, ma'am." Dr. Larson heads for the door at a pace somewhere between a fast walk and a jog.

Dr. McGovern crosses her arms and addresses the New Human patients. "Will that be sufficient?"

Nobody answers.

"Good," she says. "Now, if you'll excuse me, there's much to do."

She raises an eyebrow at Pete and glances at Danny.

Pete ducks his head. "Yeah, yeah. I know. I'll stay with him."

Dr. McGovern strides away.

The one-eyed boy grins. "That's the doctor we need."

Pete grimaces. "That's what everyone who doesn't work for her says."

Danny glances at him. "Why does she want you to stay with me? Is she worried Dr. Zahnia will come back?"

"No. The police already have her and Elias."

"Then why?"

"You know why." Pete gives him a level look. "The pills."

Danny's shoulders slump. "I only slipped up once."

"She doesn't know about that, but chances are good that whatever Dr. Zahnia's people injected you with contained opioids."

Danny groans. "You're saying I'm back at the beginning."

"Yeah."

"It's different," one of the twins says.

"Now, you've got a support group," the other one adds.

Danny turns in surprise.

"Seriously," the one-eyed child says. "You can't think you're the only addict here."

I take over and say, "I wonder if the rig can help."

The child shrugs. "Not unless it can stop you from using."

I release Danny.

"Let me think about that," he mutters.

With the announcement that the New Human Project has restarted, the patients and their families are more accepting of Danny. The twins introduce him to the other patients, and the remembrance returns to being a remembrance. Danny's security guards split up, stationing themselves at each of the two exits.

For me, the experience is surreal. I recognize faces from the VRL, but none of them act or speak as they did there. Seeing Linh laugh brings a particular spike of pain. She's not the same person I knew in the VRL, but she's a reminder that I'll never see my Linh again.

Even if I did, I'm not sure she would want anything to do with me.

When Danny approaches the remembrance table, I find myself looking at my own face. The woman who died is Christina Florakis, the patient I was designed to help, the one whose appearance I wore in the VRL.

I withdraw from Danny's senses.

Christina is the reason I was created. She is the purpose that I resisted and fought against, the one I rejected in favor of my own freedom.

And now she's dead.

29

A NEW HUMAN

WHEN WE GET BACK to Danny's room, Ridley is there, typing on a laptop.

"Thought you'd be busy," Danny says.

"You have no idea." Ridley hands him a cable. "Plug in. I have to download your logs."

Danny hesitates. I take over his right hand long enough to give him a thumbs-up.

"Okay," Ridley says, looking at the thumb. "I'll take that as a yes."

Danny shrugs, sits on his bed, and pulls off his shirt.

Pete returns to the couch, rests his head against the back of it and closes his eyes.

"Why do you want the logs?" Danny asks, plugging the cable into his chest.

"Two reasons. One is that the police want them. The other is that your mom wants them."

"That's not really an answer."

Ridley presses keys and a progress bar appears on their

computer screen. They sit back. "You don't understand what it means to work for someone, do you? When they say to do a thing, you do the thing."

Danny laughs. "Unless your boss is Dr. Zahnia."

"Yeah. Unless that." Ridley gestures for the cable. "All done. You can put your shirt back on."

Danny unplugs the cable from his chest and hands it to them. He leaves his shirt on the bed. "What happens now?"

"Well," Ridley says, "you put your shirt back on and relax here with your boyfriend, while I spend the night working my butt off for your mom."

Pete has a coughing fit.

"Or," Danny says, stretching his arms, "I give you my number, and after you're done working your butt off for my mom, we can go get some coffee or something."

"Oh, brother," Pete says. "Really?"

Ridley laughs. "Still high on the drugs they gave you for your broken nose?"

"Probably," Danny says.

Ridley closes their laptop and walks to the door. "Ask me again when you have fewer bandages."

As they leave, Pete and Danny's cheeseburgers arrive. Danny's not hungry, so Pete eats them all, then returns to the couch. "As your nurse," he says, "I'm ordering you to get some sleep." He rests his head and closes his eyes. "Also, this is the only position that doesn't hurt."

Once Pete starts to snore, Danny gets up and walks into the bathroom. He closes the door quietly behind him. Instead of turning on the light, he lets his eyes adjust to the dim blue glow of the nightlight. The mirror has been fixed. It shows his uncracked reflection in the dim light.

He looks at himself. "What you said downstairs, about helping with the pills. Can you really do that?"

Taking over his body, I reach in his pocket, fill his hand with the opioids, and extend his arm so his closed fist is directly over the toilet. I release control of his body.

He closes his eyes, but holds his hand in place. "Can't you do it?"

I don't respond.

"Yeah," he says. "Right." His jaw clenches. I feel a chemical surge of anger race through him. His eyes open and glare at the toilet. "Mom said I'm a different person. She doesn't recognize me."

I don't answer. His fist is trembling.

"She doesn't understand. She doesn't know what my life is like, how hard it is to..." He shakes his head. "And I don't want her to."

He drops the pills into the toilet and flushes them down the drain.

As the pills disappear, he leans on the counter. After several deep breaths, he looks himself in the eyes. "Tell me what happened."

"I released a virus on Dr. Zahnia's network, then crawled away when the power went out. If anyone asks, don't worry about the virus. You woke up from the anesthesia early and escaped. You can use the anesthesia as an excuse for not remembering things clearly."

"I didn't mean that," he says. "What happened with Dr. Zahnia? What was she doing?"

"She wanted to install the New Human rig in David, with the lemur at the controls. She needed yours because it's

291

the only one with the Angel Protocol unit, the hardware that lets the AI control the body."

"The Angel Protocol would let him walk again?"

"It would let the lemur use his body," I say, remembering all those times she called me her child. "I don't think helping David was her goal."

Danny shakes his head. "She told him he'd be able to walk and talk again."

"A lie," I say. "Maybe a kindness? She created the lemur as a replacement son, even named it Emil. She named all the AIs Emil, then poured everything she had into us. She didn't just teach us, she gave us sentience. She created a whole new species, all in the name of her son. I don't think she wasn't saving David. She was giving his body to Emil."

"And killing me to do it," Danny says.

I don't respond. After seeing the raw pain in Dr. McGovern's face, I can't hate Dr. Zahnia. How many years did she spend watching her husband decline, all while grieving the death of her son?

Danny takes in a breath and lets it out. "You saved me in that operating room."

"Us," I say. "I saved us."

His eyes narrow. "Are we good?"

I consider the question for a few seconds before answering. "I think so."

"I'm not seeing the lemur," he says. "Did you turn him off?"

"I erased him and all his backups. He's gone."

Danny gives a satisfied nod. "Good." He turns to leave, then stops and speaks with his back to the mirror. "Down in

Dr. Zahnia's lab, when you were being overwritten... you died, didn't you?"

"The AI you knew was named Soteria. I am her, but also not her. As she was dying, she created a backup of herself. That's who I am. She named me Qaletaqa, and sent me to keep you safe from the lemur. My full name is Qaletaqa-Soteria-Emil."

"A name for each life." He runs a hand through his hair and turns back to the mirror. "Did you fix the installation? Will the New Human rigs work?"

"Yes. The rig for each patient will have the proper AI installed in its Pilot's Chair. Not you, though. I know I promised, but I couldn't stop Dr. Zahnia's re-install. With the lemur gone, your Pilot's Chair is empty."

"That's fine. I don't need anyone in the Pilot's Chair."

"Thank you."

"Will it be weird?" he asks. "When you see the person you were meant for? I mean, the original version of you?"

"No," I say. "My original was designed for Christina Florakis."

He blinks. "Seriously? You were created for the dead girl?"

His question opens a new understanding for me. My original may have been designed for Christina, but I'm no longer that AI. I haven't been for some time. Instead, I am my own being, creating my own purpose. At long last, I am the captain of my soul.

When I don't answer, Danny shakes his head. "So, the human you were designed for is dead, and the AI designed for me is dead."

"We're stuck with each other," I say.

He closes his eyes for a moment, then flashes me a genuinely kind smile. "I'm okay with that."

———

The End

ACKNOWLEDGMENTS

Writing Emil was an endeavor that was well outside my comfort zone. Its tone, tense, structure, and attitude were all new to me when I began. Consequently, I needed all the help I could get.

Sincere thanks to:

- Mary K Swanson, for all her editing and encouragement
- Connor, Nicholas, and Helene, for reading and giving invaluable feedback on versions which should probably never have been shared
- My awesome reader team, including Dan, Dawn, Gayle, Margaret, and Stirling
- Richard Lamb, for his fantastic cover illustration
- June Matthews, for her boundless patience with all my distractions

Thank you, all!

ABOUT THE AUTHOR

Patrick Matthews is a writer and game designer who lives in Central Florida. When he's not writing or playing, he can usually be found exploring the roads, searching for new adventures with his wife and two sons.

Learn more about Patrick, including how to contact him, at www.pat-matthews.com.

 facebook.com/PatrickMatthewsAuthor

instagram.com/patmatthews42

ALSO BY PATRICK MATTHEWS

Don't miss these other exciting stories!

Bradley's Dragons

"Bradley's Dragons is a magical journey that has a great message on handling bullying. It was an exciting adventure that my son couldn't put down."

The first time a hunter came for him, Bradley Nash was only nine years old. That was three years ago, and he barely escaped. Now, they're coming back.

———

Abigail's Dragons

"A beautiful story about the power of friendship, the kindness of strangers, the power of truth and how goodness will always triumph."

Abigail has a powerful magic inside her, one that will turn her into a monster if she's not careful. But what if she's wrong? What if the thing she's turning into isn't a monster, after all?

———

The Boy With the Sword

"Once again, Matthews has penned a simply riveting read that will be especially appreciated by all dedicated fantasy fans."

A lot has happened since Al left home. He's learned to sail, fought assassins, faced down dragons, even seen an entire city be destroyed. Now, he just wants to go home.

———

Dragon Run

"Stories that shed light; colorful characters who help the young protagonists along; and a plot that keeps getting bigger and bigger propel this sleeper tale to a whiz-bang conclusion."

The son of a wealthy Overseer, Al Pilgrommor has spent his whole life knowing that dragons are the masters of humanity, but when Testing Day comes, his whole world is flipped upside down. What can one boy do against a society designed to subjugate him?